BIBLIOTHECA NEERLANDICA

A Library of Classics of Dutch and Flemish Literature

MARRIAGE

ORDEAL

GERARD WALSCHAP

MARRIAGE

ORDEAL

SYTHOFF LEYDEN / HEINEMANN LONDON
LONDON HOUSE NEW YORK
1963

The short novels in this book were originally published in Flemish under
the titles *Trouwen* and *Celibaat*
and were translated into English by A. Brotherton

Published with the aid of the Prince Bernhard Fund

Library of Congress Catalog Card Number: 63-22463

© *A. W. Sijthoff's Uitgeversmaatschappij, N.V. 1963*

Printed in the Netherlands by A. W. Sythoff, Printing Division, Leyden

MARRIAGE

1

The Steenackerses had a maid with them for years and years;
Karlien she was called. She had been brought up in an orphanage
from the age of five. The day she turned seventeen she went to see
the Mother Superior and the Mother Superior wrote to the
convent where she had been a novice herself long ago that it was
the dearest wish of our foster-daughter Caroline to enter the Order
and devote her life to serving our heavenly Bridegroom. But the
life of a novice in that convent fell far short of what Karlien had
expected and just two weeks before she was to take her first vows,
this time without saying a word to anyone, she slipped out and
away as quiet as a mouse. That was how she came to be maid to
Madame Steenackers, the brewer's wife, who knew her because
she used to come and collect bundles of mijnheer's old clothes for
the convent gardener, and there she stayed for twenty years. For
twenty years she bought all the spices and everything else she
needed for the kitchen from the shop with the signboard 'The
Coffee Bean', opposite the brewer's house. Every year, for four
days, she used to see Toon there.

Toon was the youngest brother of the grocer's wife. Before he
turned eighteen Toon had gone along to the abbey with a
Carmelite Father, who preached the virtue of constant devotion,
to become a brother. The first thing he didn't like was that the
brothers wore grey, which wasn't so distinguished as the white
robes of the friars. One thing after the other disappointed him;
maybe he was something of a disappointment too. In any case,
whatever it was, Toon ended up as a handyman around the
monastery instead of becoming a brother. Toon wasn't without
ambition. In three years he was already assistant gatekeeper, and
then the gatekeeper was kind enough to take advantage of the
only chance that came his way in his profession to have an accident.
He was up on a plank supported on two stepladders, giving the
impression of dusting a painting, when the ropes of one of the

7

ladders snapped and the ladder collapsed. Anyone young enough could have jumped off in time, an older man might have had his wrists broken, but this gatekeeper must have thought of Toon. As the one ladder fell he toppled forward, and the other ladder caught him behind the knees toppling him backwards, so that he smashed his head on a marble flagstone. The monastery was very good to him. In the hospital in Diest he was put in a private room, and Toon took over as gatekeeper.

A gatekeeper at the monastery can, if he is wide-awake and conscientious and polite, always get on. All sorts of important dignitaries, deacons, canons, vicars, even bishops, come visiting, and that's how you get noticed. They see you're young and neatly dressed, quick but never flurried, friendly but always respectful. If there's ever a vacant place in the Bishop's palace then they remember you, and so it happened that His Eminence the Bishop of Malines remembered Toon. Watched with envy and admiration by all the brothers and the servants in the monastery, he departed for the Bishop's palace.

He never got a holiday but every year he came and spent four days at his sister's, sitting around in her shop. In those four days of each year he used to see Karlien there. He wore a white-and-red striped vest, and fine, soft slippers lined with rabbit fur. He would fold his hands over his stomach and relate to Karlien and other customers that a new church was to be built in such and such a place and somewhere else they were going to appoint a new priest and how His Eminence never went out without asking him first: 'Antoine, what will the weather be like today?'

'Ah, Toon, so the Bishop calls you Antoine?' 'Yes, His Eminence always calls me Antoine, and the vicars and the deacons as well.'

His sister and her husband decided to sell the shop. The grocer had been a painter and decorator's helper as a lad and after he was married he took on odd jobs just to make a little extra money, then as time went by he got more and more work. The village was too small for two house-painters. So the master found himself losing customers to a competitor who had once been his apprentice, and it went so badly with him that he had to put his well-stocked workshop up for sale. The former apprentice bought it and the painter and his family moved to the city, the last refuge from misfortune and disgrace.

Once, when the shop was full, Toon's sister announced that she had asked Antoine whether he was thinking of staying with the Bishop for the rest of his life. Karlien blushed. It was all very well, a place in the Bishop's palace, but all the same he wasn't any more than a servant. He was well over forty but a man can always get married even if he is getting on, and Karlien blushed a deeper red. With this shop Toon could be his own master and he could put enough by to be comfortable in his old age. He couldn't do better.

Toon jumped at the chance, and he must have known which way the wind was blowing for he had no sooner settled in than he was off across the road to the Steenackerses'. In one evening everything was settled and none of that walking-out together for years and years—three months later he and Karlien were married. That was the twenty-second of March and, just as you could expect, on New Year's Eve Karlien was lying in the bed upstairs with little Rik by her side. 'Hey, Toon,' they said in the shop, 'you were in a hurry, weren't you? Like you were fishing after the season had finished.' Toon nodded, very serious, and said yes. After all, they couldn't have expected that the Lord would give them this joy, Karlien wasn't so young, you know. Generous in his happiness he put little packets of sweets with the half-pounds of coffee or vermicelli.

A good Catholic beginning—a mother who had been brought up by the sisters in the orphanage and a father who had been servant to the Archbishop of Malines, Primate of Belgium. But that Rik was a terror; there was nothing you could do with him.

Toon used to serve in the shop because he got on well with everyone; he liked a joke or a bit of gossip, and, besides, Karlien could earn a little extra by helping with the cleaning and washing at the Steenackerses'. She used to take the child with her because she didn't trust Toon to look after him. Madame, mijnheer and his sisters, the two old spinsters, all helped Karlien to spoil him, running to soothe him at the slightest cry and giving him so many things that he tired of any toy after a few minutes. When Karlien had to go off home to prepare supper they said just leave the little chap with us, we'll bring him over later. Toon used to get him to say prayers and cross himself; a good smack on the bottom now and then would have been better. But Toon never dared try it a second time. That once Karlien had flown at him in a fury. Watch out with mothers who have their first child when it's almost too late to have any at all. They're savage and possessive and for ever frightened something might happen to it. Karlien could sit for hours drooling over her infant, and sometimes she seemed lost and helpless in her role as mother. She was so used to prim virginity, she had always been so indignant at the clothes the young girls wore, that now she hardly dared undo her dress to feed the child. But Toon, from his long years as servant to His Eminence, knew what he should do. He pulled his chair round and sat with his back to her reading his paper.

From the time he could walk Rik was at the Steenackerses' more than he was at home. Then, of course, he got the measles, mumps, and scarlet fever, and the rest. After all that the Steenackerses doted on him as if he were their own child, and it was nearly time for him to start school. What a spoilt little brat the sister got in her class! She couldn't raise a finger to him or the same day Karlien would be along to see her; sometimes it was the two old maids themselves. Then the sister was given to understand that he was such a reasonable boy and if he was a little difficult occasionally it was only because he was tired or maybe it was from his weak stomach or because he hadn't really got over some sickness or other. Or he must have been eating red cabbage again, the two old maids would explain, it always upsets him and Karlien just won't see that that sort of food is far too heavy for a delicate child like him. And he can be so sweet, Sister, if he's treated gently. But you have to be gentle with him, Sister.

It was the same story when Rik went to the boys' school, but there his teacher was young and still full of ideals, a fiery defender of the principles of education. This earned him a dressing-down from the headmaster, who used to play cards every Sunday with brewer Steenackers, and the fuss the brewer made nearly cost him his post. So he wrote a short article called: 'Theory and Practice', and signed it 'A Teacher', and all the readers agreed he was right, but did that make any difference? He'd find out soon enough that he just couldn't put the theory into practice, and Rik didn't care if he was always at the bottom of the class—he had brewer Steenackers to stand up for him against the teacher.

The next year his teacher was the headmaster, and in that class he discovered that you didn't have to bother learning anything either. Because the headmaster was friendly with the brewer, Rik was always amongst the first five with the best marks. He was the ringleader in any mischief and he never got a thrashing, no matter what he did. Once the teacher was standing at the blackboard with his back to the class and Rik threw a marble that hit him hard on the head. That sort of thing always meant a good caning, but this time the teacher only said: 'Get outside!' It was fine weather, in the shady porch you could catch the sparrows with your hands, so one of the others tried it too. But what a mistake he made! The teacher turned round and saw him throw it and he was sitting in the back row of seats so he couldn't dodge out of reach of the cane.

The Steenackerses treated Rik more and more as one of the family, and so the celebration after his first Communion was, of course, held at their house. Toon and Karlien had been in service long enough to accept that; they were even glad and proud of it. It's nice for him to be treated like that by the Steenackerses, they used to think, and it could help him a lot later, they haven't any children of their own.

Once Toon forgot his servility and really lost his temper when the little brat ran off to the Steenackerses after he had done something or other Toon was going to make him sorry for. Madame said not to get excited and go home, he was too angry now, and to hit a child in anger was very, very wrong. And they would deal with him. By God, was it his own son, or not? But Toon was so used to folding his hands and giving a little bow: Very well, Father, Yes, certainly, Your Eminence, Yes, Madame, that his rage subsided. He even gave a smile to show he wasn't angry any more, that he knew his place, that all these twenty-nine years he hadn't had a will of his own weren't wasted.

After Rik's first Communion the brewer strolled into the kitchen and said to Toon: 'We'll send him off to college.' He didn't even ask if Toon could pay the fees, he was paying it all himself. That too, and for twenty-nine years Toon had saved his wages and every half-franc pressed into his palm. For thirty-one years Toon had been reading edifying stories in which the devout mother stitched and sewed day and night in her attic so that her son could study for the priesthood, and the grey-haired father worked his fingers to the bone with the same end in view. Later he would clasp with those scarred and horny fists the white and blessed priestly hands of his newly-ordained son. Then a boundless joy filled the heart of the simple and honest man. What inspiring examples for all Christian parents!

2

The first term he had a bad report, the second term he wouldn't say who had thrown a stinkbomb in the prep-room and he was put on bread and water for two days, in the third term he was nearly expelled after he had stolen a bottle of wine and drunk it all on his own. He was tipsy as a lord. He staggered up to the proctor and he gurgled: 'Mijnheer, we're friends, aren't we?' and insisted on shaking hands with him. In the first term of the second year he was caught one night standing on his bed throwing rotten oranges over the partitions into the other cubicles. The proctor dragged him by the hair through the dormitory to the principal's office. Here no one knew brewer Steenackers, here there was no nonsense about sparing the rod. Rik began to hate that proctor so deeply that he used to have dreams about shooting him. He did throw stones at the man's head once or twice when the class was out for a walk, but he missed and his hopes of vengeance had to wait until the second term.

One afternoon he was allowed to go to bed with a sore throat that was only a pretext, and in the evening he gave an impressive performance of delirium. He yelled and screamed and banged with his fist on the partition, and when the proctor came running to see what was wrong he tossed and turned gasping as if he had pneumonia, staring and rolling his eyes, while he watched for a chance to slam the proctor hard on the nose, just by accident, in his delirium. The proctor thought it was genuine and he tried to hold Rik down without being too rough. But the delirium couldn't be calmed with just a bloody nose; there had to be at least a black eye as well. Then the proctor noticed that the delirium wasn't affecting the left arm of the feverish patient who was trying to get his right arm loose because that was the arm he could punch best with. So if it was that sort of delirium the proctor knew how to cure it. With the back of his hand he slapped Rik's face hard, a good dozen times. You'd have a bad fever if that didn't cure it right away. Rik realized that the game was up, but he didn't lose his presence of mind. He lay still and played the mystic, he breathed slowly, whispering about the Sacred Heart of Jesus, he pointed with a trembling finger to the stars he really did see and babbled: 'There you are, little angels, come here, come here to me.' He sank back exhausted against the pillow. The proctor left him alone with the Sacred Heart of Jesus and the angels and went to see if there was still a light on in the principal's office. The light was still on. And so that same night the principal wrote the letter that Mijnheer Antoon van Oepstal received two days later. We consider it advisable that your son Hendrik should terminate his studies immediately and we have arranged for him to return home.

It was a hard blow for Toon, for a father who had always respected authority and always served his betters. Toon made a grab at him as he came unrepentantly through the door. But Toon wasn't quick enough. Like a flash he dodged round the room, ran out through the shop and, of course, straight over to the Steenackerses'. He wasn't going to go home, he wouldn't go near there, he said. So they had to punish him themselves. They locked him in a room upstairs. The two old maids were loudly upset at the marks Toon's hand had left on Rik's cheek, and he could hear all that through the keyhole. Oh yes, he had to be punished, but all that trouble in the college was only because the teachers hadn't treated the boy gently, they'd heard such a lot of complaints about that college.

The two spinsters tiptoed upstairs with chocolates and a box of paints to the room where they had locked him in, they reproached him until they were both in tears themselves, and to get the box of paints Rik joined the tearful chorus and promised everything they asked, and he was given the box of paints and the chocolates. Then they went and fetched Karlien and left her alone with him like St Monica and Augustine who had started off as a black sheep too. Karlien wept just as copiously as St Monica to bring her son to repentance. She spoke as the mother of St Louis spoke in her favourite series of Catholic tales for family reading, and she almost convinced herself that she would ask Our Lord to take her one and only child away from her rather than see him fall into evil ways. And Mother and Father had always hoped he would be a priest when he grew up. Once again Rik promised he would be good and his promises were a wedge between his mother's heart and his father's unforgiving anger. Karlien asked him couldn't he just try to be gentle with the boy. But Toon didn't answer. In his thoughts Toon pictured the horror of His Eminence and the vicars if they could see what a monster he had brought into the world.

He kept looking at the stove not saying a word when the brewer came and sat on the corner of the kitchen table. We'll send him off to another college. Send him anywhere you want to—Toon was beyond caring. He would have been an excellent father for a child as docile as he was himself, but he became a father when he was old enough to be a grandfather and now he didn't have the strength to fight the devils of childhood wickedness, and he certainly didn't have the strength to defend his parental authority against the brewer's two meddling sisters who had worshipped the future priest from the day he was born.

Everything went well the first term, and in the holidays Rik was spoiled more than ever just because he hadn't done anything wrong. The second term went off even better, but in the third term it was discovered that he was the leader of a gang of six who had bribed the college caretaker and climbed over the wall to go and smoke cigarettes in the village and send letters to young girls. Rik and one of the others were caught in a bar, but it appeared that that was the first time they had been there. They used to smoke their cigarettes in the coal-cellar; they got the key from the caretaker. Rik was seething because one of the others had given them all away. 'Just you let them know at home,' he snarled at the principal, 'then you'll see: I'll kill myself!' The principal was a thickset, fat little authoritarian. 'You are at liberty, young sir, to do as you wish,' he said, white with anger, and he bowed. Then his face went even redder than usual, and he shouted: 'Now, get out!'

So Toon got a second letter. They deemed it necessary to terminate his son's enrolment. Furthermore, they would be obliged to notify the principal of any other college to which he might be sent of his deplorable conduct at this school. It was deeply regretted and so on, Yours faithfully.

Toon pushed the letter across the table to Karlien as if it were something that didn't concern him but only her and the house opposite. A few days later Toon caught a heavy chill, and for the first time in his life he stayed in bed. But he couldn't get his breath, he said. A fortnight later the doctor told him that it was his kidneys; he mustn't eat any salt and as little meat as possible.

Rik didn't ever want to go home again, but the brewer insisted he should now and then. Karlien always took care that Toon was out or upstairs when he came, and she sat alone with her son, sighing or sobbing that he would be the death of his father and mother. She ruined the last chance of making him mend his ways. That would have been to let Toon put him in his place. For Toon remembered that his own father never had to raise a hand to any of his children, but they all knew that he was someone to be frightened of and nothing would save them if they did anything wrong. One night as he dreamed he nearly pummelled Karlien out of bed. The more he thought about it the more he convinced himself he could, with one good thrashing, instil into the boy the fear which his prayer-book said was the beginning of wisdom. But Karlien knew what her little son could expect from his father and she shielded him more carefully than ever.

'I'll risk it just once more with him,' the brewer said, sitting on the corner of the table in the kitchen. He sent him to another private school, not a church school this time, and he paid one of the poorer teachers to keep an eye on Rik and send a report of his conduct every month. It suited Rik very well; here his freedom wasn't so restricted. He had a fine time without getting into

16

trouble, but at the end of the year he didn't get a quarter of the marks in any subject. At Steenackerses' they said: 'Oh well, not everyone can be brainy. It's not the boy's fault, we'll have to be patient, and, you know, the Curé d'Ars was the same, he wasn't very good at school.' The two spinsters were sure all that changing from one school to the other had kept him back because the boy was smart enough, at least he had his share of common sense.

Steenackers received no complaint the second year either. The principal noticed that they got at his fruit trees every day, but that had happened before. The maid got post cards, some of them with dirty rhymes, but they could be sent by someone in the village. One night her window was broken with stones, but it was easy enough to throw stones from the street, so there was no knowing who might have done it.

But one evening, when they were in the principal's garden, Rik was bitten by the dog. Two days later the animal was dead, poisoned. Up till then the maid had kept quiet about all the things she had seen, but she had brought that dog with her from home when it was a tiny pup and she doted on it. She'd seen one of them in the garden, she sobbed, and she'd recognize him if she saw him again. She was confronted with one of Rik's companions and he was the one. Don't try and wriggle out of it, I saw you, you dirty little poisoner. She avenged the dog but Rik and his gang avenged their friend. Twice a week, in the evening, while the pupils were in the prep-room, she used to empty a couple of buckets of ashes in the corner behind the lavatories. This was used to fill in puddles in the playground. Five masked attackers jumped on her in the dark near the ash-heap and the next day she pointed out Rik as the worst of the five. That was the first complaint Steenackers got from this school. It was more than enough for those two years.

When he was in the service of His Eminence the Archbishop Toon had always worn fine leather slippers, the best quality, expensive they were, but good value for the money, and in the long run the dearest is always the best. 'It's worth it,' Toon used to say.

'If you're handy enough you can mend them yourself.' All the vicars and the deacons knew that Toon was as handy as any shoe-maker, that he had bought himself a second-hand last and a shoe-maker's hammer at the market and that His Eminence couldn't have performed the rites of a Communion or a consecration with greater care than Toon gave to soling and heeling those fine slippers of his. Toon was in the kitchen, sitting at his last with his spectacles on mending his slippers when, in the house opposite, Steenackers was roaring at Rik that he could get out, he wasn't going to stay here, he could go and tell his father he'd been ex-pelled for the third time. By Jesus, if you try any of your tricks I'll break your bloody neck! Rik thought better of risking his neck; he did as Steenackers said, and that was how it happened that Toon, for the first time in his life, didn't hit a nail straight, and to cover his confusion he stood with his arms crossed in front of his son. Rik leaned against the mantelpiece without saying a word and Toon asked him what he was doing here. He answered in a jeering tone of complete indifference that he'd only come to say he wasn't going back to that rotten school any more and Toon felt himself shake inside.

Had he been chucked out again? Chucked out? Rik echoed, if that's what you want to call it, yes, he'd been chucked out.

He gave a shrug as well, and that was too much. 'Yes,' Toon shouted, 'that's what I call it,' and he grabbed him with both hands. 'Yes, that's what I call it,' Toon shouted again, and he shook Rik back and forth, banging his head against the wal. Toon lifted him right off the ground and he might have thrown him right through the door if a vicious jab in the stomach hadn't stopped him. His eyes swivelled round with the pain and the next second his son was holding the shoemaker's hammer ready to strike. That same shoemaker's hammer that Monseigneur the Vicar-general had once balanced in his hands: 'A nice hammer you've got there, Antoine,' he'd said.

Yes, Monseigneur, a nice hammer, he'd been using it for

thirty-five years and now his son had found a use for it too.

'Now then,' Toon said. He felt cold and numb. He shivered at the vision that flashed through his mind; he knew it was more than just imagination. 'That's enough of that, lifting a hammer against your own father. You can put it down now, but mark my words, as sure as I'm standing here, your own son will take a hammer to you. I'll be gone by then, thank God, but that day you'll remember me.'

Toon gulped back a sob, he turned round and there on the other side of the glass door he saw Steenackers and Jan van Uffelen from next door. Jan thought Toon had called him by knocking on the wall as he always did, and when the banging kept up he supposed it was something urgent. How was Jan to know that this time it was Rik's head Toon had been banging on the wall with?

Toon asked them both to come in, they were his witnesses. Jan shook his fist in Rik's face: 'If you were a son of mine, my boy, I'd give it to you, you wouldn't sit down for a month.'

3

From then on Rik didn't live at home any more. He stayed at the Steenackerses', and the two spinsters lectured him and remonstrated with him. His parents, he gathered, had only got married out of piety so they could present one more priest to the Holy Mother Church, and Rik mustn't hinder God's plans. Hahaha! But when he wasn't there the two spinsters told each other that he wasn't the sort of lad to keep shut up in a college. What else could they say now that no college would have him? They let him come and go as he wished; they were keeping an eye on him, you see. Karlien didn't interfere because she knew that she and Toon couldn't do anything with him and the best thing for him was to be treated like a son by the Steenackerses. But the Steenackerses soon found out it wasn't safe to leave any half-francs lying on the mantelpiece and then the brewer said to him: Now listen to me, they'd given him the chance to have a good education but he didn't want that, very well then, one of these days he'd laugh on the other side of his face. He didn't need to put himself out to please them, they'd only done everything they could for him. He'd been here for a couple of months and they'd seen that he still hadn't learnt his lesson, but never mind that. Listen to me now, he was giving him one more chance, don't make any mistake, just one last chance, he could learn a trade. Did he want to go to the school in Vilvorde and learn market-gardening?

'Yes.'

'Very well.'

Rik went up and down each day to the horticultural school in Vilvorde. One single complaint and the brewer was finished with him. He lived at the Steenackerses', everyone called him Steenackers' Rik. Toon didn't count any more, a father ignored and despised. Toon the flunkey. All his life it had been the same, he never had any say in anything. The poorest cowherd could give his son his own name, but Toon was denied even that consolation.

He brooded and his kidneys got worse, but he always said it was a bad cold. Now he had another one of those bad colds that made him choke and gasp. For two weeks he had been vomiting up every mouthful he ate; he felt his strength failing and, looking up at Karlien as she sat at his bedside, he murmured the name of their son—how long had it been since that name passed his lips? That afternoon Karlien stood waiting for the train Rik came back from Vilvorde on. Toon didn't realize it but he was waiting for the solemn moment of his son's visit the way it happened in those devout Catholic books when children who had gone astray were brought back to the path of virtue by the pious last words of their dying father. He would leave this world content and comforted. He would ask his son if he could die in peace, his heart at rest, or whether he would have to turn over in his grave from shame and grief.

Karlien let Rik go upstairs alone, Toon wasn't so very sick, she told herself, and, besides, it was better if the two of them were left by themselves.

'How do you feel, Father?'

Toon's pious hope made his eyes bright and gave him an air of dignity. He said he was poorly, that he wouldn't last much longer. With a last gleam of hope in his eyes he stared vaguely at the hat-box on top of the wardrobe. He could hardly breathe, if he had to cough he twisted and turned and nearly choked. It was five minutes of agony. But he managed to say in a tired voice, without rancour or irony, that he hadn't had much pleasure in his life so he didn't mind so much if he died.

The question he had rehearsed, his final plea, was only a soundless movement of his lips; his eyes wandered vacantly. He made a feeble gesture with his hands. He might have been trying to point to the cup of milk next to the medicine bottles. Rik held up the cup for him to drink, but that wasn't what Toon meant, he'd done with milk and medicine bottles. He made a vague sign again with his hands, he whispered ... wanted ... to ask, but Death gave him a jolt in the stomach harder than the one Rik had given him a year before, a jolt that closed his eyes for good and the Lord spared Toon a last heart-breaking disappointment. Toon folded his face back into its well-worn familiar crease, as if dying had been the oversight of an unguarded moment. Now he was dead he was his old self again, with that same patient, obliging expression he had worn on his face for so many years, that servile smile of thirty years' bending and bowing: 'Yes, Father.'... 'Very well, Your Eminence.'... 'A fine hammer that, Antoine.'... 'Yes, Monseigneur.'

There he was, dead; his was a lonelier death than dying alone.

Rik shivered. Here in this room his father was being judged and received into heavenly bliss, and from now on his father's soul could haunt him. Out of here, Rik, out of here as quick as you can. He looked back once: Father lay there as if he was only sleeping. He shut the door firmly to lock in the soul that still had something to ask him.

Karlien was busy in the shop. 'He's asleep,' Rik said, and he went off for a walk not bothering about his supper. The farther he went the faster he walked. A dog ran in front of him as he crossed a field. It looked black. He didn't believe in ghosts but he turned round and made his way back.

At nine o'clock Karlien tiptoed upstairs to give Toon his medicine, but he was still fast asleep so she decided she might as well wait till she came up to bed herself. If only she'd taken a good look then with her lamp—but who had ever thought Toon was going to die? 'Toon,' she called softly, 'are you still asleep?' When he didn't answer she said to herself she wouldn't bother with the medicine because a deep sleep meant he had taken a turn for the better. But when she wriggled into bed in her nightdress her foot caught on his rosary and knocked against a hard, cold thigh. She clasped him and shook him, sobbing, but he brushed her kisses off indifferently with the bristles of his walrus moustache. Every day as long as she lived she remembered what a fright she got from that moustache of his. Well, you should have come and looked at me sooner, stop that noise now, I'm dead and gone.

Rik wasn't the sort to spend much time thinking what Father had wanted to ask him. He was more interested in all the things he used to ask the girls who took the same train as he did to Vilvorde. He wouldn't miss that daily train journey for anything, and so there weren't any complaints from the school.

In any case they weren't so strict there. The technique of growing flowers and vegetables doesn't exactly require a great deal of study. Most of us, after all, could plant a cabbage or sow a bed of radishes even if we haven't a diploma from Vilvorde. To show what he could do Rik grew a few plants in the Steenackerses' garden. The two spinsters gurgled and cooed over the flowers as if Rik had made them himself, and he only had to say that it would be better to have a couple of glass frames for those beds near the wall and the next week the frames were there. They had sense enough not to sing his praises any more, but they raved over the magnificent blooms and how wonderfully the garden was kept, not a single weed anywhere, Rik was still the little tin god, and he got everything he wanted. Let him stay with us, Karlien; he'd only twist you round his little finger and that would be the worst thing that could happen. Karlien knew it was true and she used to tell herself that it was probably better for him to stay with them. At least he was always welcome there; anywhere else he was sent packing. Toon's sister's children would have been good company for him, but when Toon was still alive their mother had forbidden them to have anything to do with him. Since the funeral she wouldn't let him set foot inside their gate.

For a while Rik kept out of trouble. The brewer was beginning to admire the flowers, too, and when Madame had two big pots of hortensias put in the church under a statue of Our Lord the Steenackerses acted as if Rik had lovingly cultivated those beautiful flowers for that very purpose and they interpreted it as a sign that he had returned to the fold. The elder of the two spinsters nodded sagely and said Toon's death must have made a deep impression on Rik. And you've read the life of Father Corstiaens, haven't you, Karlien, you remember he died a martyr in China, he worked in his father's business until he was twenty-three, and it was only then, at that age, that he started his studies for the priesthood. So you never can tell, Karlien....Karlien said prayers morning and night, but now in the hope that sooner or later Steenackers would have to find someone to take over the business and why shouldn't Rik step from the garden right up into the brewery itself? What would Toon have said to that?

There a mother hoped and prayed, but at Alsemberg God's will was done. In Alsemberg Steenackers' youngest sister lost her husband. For thirty years he had suffered from an ulcer of the stomach and now at last he had died from peritonitis. It was because of his stomach trouble, the two Steenackers spinsters always insisted, that they couldn't stay in the same house with him. But his attitude, and he didn't care who knew it, was that he wasn't obliged to let them wipe their feet on him just because they'd never been able to find husbands for themselves. So they went to live with their brother the brewer and for eight years they sent their sister letters in envelopes marked 'Strictly Personal'. Every time their brother-in-law found one of these envelopes in the mail he wrote under their 'Strictly Personal' in large letters 'Return to Sender Immediately' and in front of their name on the back of the envelope he wrote 'The Two Misses'. The longer he lived the more the two misses clung to their dream of 'spending their last days together with their younger sister in their parent's house in Alsemberg'. They used to write that in their letters and their brother-in-law knew it, and when he doubled up with the pain of his ulcer he called on all the angels of heaven and all the fiends of hell but he never wished he could die, he wouldn't give them that satisfaction. All his life he battled with his ulcer and now this peritonitis had caught him unawares. As he lay dying the two spinsters decided to visit him. His wife told him they were there.

He was too weak to shout and storm, but he asked if they couldn't have waited till he was dead.

After he was buried they came back to pack their things, then they moved for good and Rik had no one to shield him any more. They did say that they would see if they could find something good for him there as soon as he had finished the course at Vilvorde. So he must keep studying hard and he'd have a fine future. They gave him a medallion that carried ever so many indulgences; he had to wear it in the to pocket of his waistcoat, near his heart, he would, wouldn't he? At the station they both kissed him as if he were their own son, but he would rather have had a kiss from some young girl than the slobber of the two moustaches. They gave him a handful of pocket-money. They waved to him until the train was out of sight, but that didn't help; it was a bleak prospect without those two old maids who had always stood up for him. His luck had run out. Then the same year he lost his mother.

Karlien, who was so strong and looked as if she'd live for ever. She was sixty, and she'd never had a day's illness. It wasn't till she was over forty that she had become a mother and she hadn't blossomed into maternal fullness from having a child at that age; she stayed as lean and scrawny as she'd always been, her flesh taut over her bones and not a wrinkle. Now, all of a sudden, she had a cancer somewhere in the stomach. In a few months she shrivelled up, and she lay there dried out like a piece of old wood. For Rik it was an inopportune moment. Eight weeks more and he would have got his diploma from Vilvorde, but now he had to stay at home to look after Mother.

All he did was slouch around the house. Jan van Uffelen's wife from next door did everything, and Madame Steenackers came over once or twice every day. Rik certainly wouldn't have given up the pleasure of the train journey to Vilvorde just to see those two, but sometimes Madame sent the maid with things for Karlien, and that was worth staying home for. All that fumbling and fondling in the passage from the shop to the stairs.

He was in the passage with the maid when Jan van Uffelen's Liza shouted hoarsely to him to come upstairs quickly, and the maid, red-faced and dizzy, ran off to get Madame and Mijnheer. Before they came Karlien had asked Rik what Toon hadn't had the time to ask: whether she could die with her mind at rest and not be worried about him, and Rik had lied and said yes. The priest came running to administer the last sacraments. 'Pax huic domui,' he said in the shop. *Pax*, as if that could be in this house. They were all in tears, all of them except Rik. He was thinking of what the maid had promised him and he was wishing that his mother would hurry up and finish dying. She lay there trembling and gasping: If only I could be sure, if only I could be sure... He was thinking to himself: The quicker you die the less time you'll have to worry about it. She could have been a stranger for all the concern he showed; he was still thinking of the promise the maid had whispered in his ear. They sponged Karlien's forehead and parched lips, and standing by the bed they bowed their heads murmuring prayers for her to say with them. Madame Steenackers leaned over her, sobbing, Karlien, Karlien dear, didn't her Karlien know her any more? No, Karlien didn't recognize her any more, Karlien was sinking away, she wasn't repeating the prayers with the others, her mouth twitched, shaping the words she didn't know she was saying... if she could be sure... if only... What is sadder than the anguish of a dying mother?

There are men, rough and ready by nature, who take cover in anger because they feel it is weakness to show any pity or sympathy, but it is a man without a grain of human feeling who can stay indifferent to the sight of a woman weeping. At first brewer Steenackers had coughed and gulped, but before long he couldn't hold back his tears for the mother who, even in her death agony, was tormented by a foreboding of her only son's wickedness when she was gone. Steenackers trembled with rage. Instead of praying he ought to give that young wastrel such a kick in the pants that he'd land on the other side of the room. The dirty little swine, not a single tear, didn't he just need a flogging!

Behind him the maid stood wishing that Karlien would die and leave that big bed empty for her, and while the brewer glared at Rik and cursed under his breath and the maid looked covetously at the bed, Karlien's soul was delivered from the torment of her foreboding, Karlien, widow of Toon the servant of Monseigneur the Archbishop, gave a last gasp and breathed no more.

[4]

The Lord knows well what He is about; we only see it later, sometimes not at all. The blessed peace the curate prayed for came not to this house, but only to the poor creature who had to die quickly to be spared a greater burden of misery. What a blow to her if she had been there a few months later to look accusingly at the maid from behind the counter! The maid would have snapped at her: 'Don't look at me like that, Karlien; look at your own little son.'

When the maid undressed herself in the evening she knew that Rik was sitting behind the window of his room watching. Deliberately, enticingly, she let him see her naked, but she drew the curtain when she looked at her own body sideways in a little mirror she held in her left hand.

She was an orphan like Karlien. The Steenackerses always got their maids from the orphanage. She had been tempted by the shop and the house. She pictured herself standing behind the counter by those well-filled shelves, and lying in Karlien's bed, suckling her baby. The wallpaper was so rich. One day Madame said to her that Karlien was getting worse, run over later with this bottle of wine, Alphonsine. That afternoon she had let Rik grab and fumble. She had heard all the stories about him, but she was only a maid, and an orphan as well, so how could she expect to hook herself a husband with a house and a shop and not have something to put up with. In the dark she used to lie smiling to herself, oh, of course he would love her. She whispered to herself all the things he had said to her, breathing hard as he held her close to him; she knew that her body was a kingdom he wanted to conquer and she was content. Then she was not afraid. She'd get married, she'd make him marry her. She lay in bed, limp with happiness, beautiful, desirable, like a jewel in a satin-lined box. She would try and frighten herself with the thought that he would beat her, but she wasn't afraid of that. He wouldn't be able to do without her. His flesh would want her flesh and if he had beaten her his embrace would be all the fiercer, his kisses wilder. She would have that hold on him, she was so sure of it. She wouldn't let him touch her until he had begged her to forgive him and he had promised he would never hit her again. Then she would yield to him. Every time it would be like that. Think of the lovely bed Karlien was lying in, and Karlien had only been a maid and an orphan too, and that beautiful wallpaper in the bedroom. Her hands felt her body; she must get married quickly, there was no time to lose.

But that wasn't the way he thought about it. Now mother was gone he was free, and did she think he was going to let himself be tied hand and foot? What sort of fool did she think he was? She wouldn't catch him like that, she should have been more careful and she'd better try her tale on the others. Her heart and the child she was carrying inside her turned over together; she swayed dizzily against the banister.

He shouted: So it was all his fault, was it, and she cried out: Who else? He said he wouldn't take the blame, and that was that. Her face, pressed against the banister, was taut and pale, it was a long minute before the tears came, and then the smile that was a cry. No, he didn't mean that, she said, it was only because he was angry. Her tears streamed. Kiss me, she said, you can kiss me and do all you want to. They could go upstairs, now, come on. She smiled at him with the tears still streaming over her cheeks and her eyes enticed him. Then he pushed her away, roughly, she stumbled, helpless and humiliated, then enraged. She could have flown at him spitting and clawing, and she would have get her first beating. But she ran out of the shop over the road to the Steenackerses', moaning. She flung herself on the chair by the kitchen table and sobbed. There Madame found her, when Mijnheer came in she was still slumped on the table sobbing.

That was just what you could expect from that Rik, and the Steenackerses were waiting to see whether he would be the rotter everyone said he was or whether he would marry the girl. In the beginning they had had such high hopes of him, but he dashed every hope one after the other. Up till then whatever he'd done had harmed himself most of all. This time the brewer would see, by God!

What are you going to do, by God? I want to know, and I want to know now. Don't look all over the place like that! Are you thinking of your hammer? Rik hadn't been thinking of the hammer, but the hammer would do, as long as he had something in his hand. He was going to say he wouldn't marry that little bitch, and the brewer had a temper, too, watch out for yourself. He saw his mother's scissors on the window-sill. He said: 'I won't marry that little bitch!' They both leapt at the same moment, the brewer sprung at Rik, and Rik jumped to get the scissors. They faced each other only a few inches apart, breathing hard, and it could have come to murder. But it came to nothing. The brewer went off home.

Rik wasn't going to marry that red-head and the red-head couldn't stay at the Steenackerses', and she certainly couldn't go back to the orphanage. The Mother Superior would send Madame another orphan, and as soon as the new maid came Alphonsine would have to go. Madame explained all that, and so sweetly that by the time Madame had said her piece she was even grateful. As she went through the kitchen door Madame turned round and said she would give her a half-month's wages more than she was entitled to, my dear. *Merci*, Madame, and Madame closed the door. For months she had thought more about that lovely wall-paper than about the child inside her. Now she spoke to the flesh of her flesh with a defiant, savage love.

Day and night she made plans with her unborn baby. Sometimes she would think of how they could die together and then she would decide to live only for her little darling, but the evening she had to leave because the new maid was coming at seven o'clock she walked out of the gate with her bundle of clothes under her arm and her other bundle under her jacket and she didn't know where she should go, to the station or to the river. She chose the station and the train to Brussels, like most of the little red-heads from the villages when they get into trouble. The first night in the park or on a seat in one of the big squares. Then somehow or other they had to look after the little bundle they'd brought with them. They managed to earn a little working here and there, but they would be more careful now in passages behind the stairs. Once caught and that was more than enough. But in the city you could have your baby; no one would point at you as you walked down the street. They wanted to have their baby and not have to bow their heads in shame. Once they're in the city they aren't simple little village girls any more, and don't they laugh at the silly m'sieurs. Sooner or later they find themselves a butcher, or a messenger in one of the Ministries.

Rik didn't miss her. There were plenty of others, much better than orphans, who would like to preside behind the counter of a prosperous grocer's shop, and to get what they wanted they'd take any sort of husband that went with it. After all he owned the house, the shop was a gold-mine and he had learned a good trade. Besides, they said, you can't be too choosy these days: where can you find a husband without any faults? There were at least a dozen wenches in the village who would risk going for a walk with Rik. They didn't trust him far; they said it was no good unless he was serious and they all wanted to get married quickly while the shop was still doing well, but they all went meekly down the first dark turning. Then they said: 'Don't do anything or I'll scream'—but no one ever heard a squeak from them.

But if you take the train as if you were going up to Vilvorde to the horticultural school, and then go right on to Brussels, then it's easy to find girls who are satisfied with a lot less. They're not set on getting married, they haven't got an eye on your shop, and, not only that, they're so much better dressed, and so friendly. Oh yes, an afternoon with them costs a pretty penny because they like drinking wine, as often as not champagne, and that is much dearer. You had to go and have dinner in a restaurant they picked out for you and when the fun was over Rik's pocket was a lot lighter. Fun for his money—no, it wasn't fun any more for Rik, it was just a blind, animal orgy. The money Toon and Karlien had left was soon gone, and he borrowed money on the house. He was too deep in the mire to climb out. He had a look in his eyes that made everyone in the village turn away when they saw him, and he walked with an unsteady, drunken gait. The way he talked, they said, would make a Christian go cold with horror. You'd think the ground would open under his feet and he'd go staight to hell. The baker said once if there's a God He couldn't let anyone talk like that, and we all know he had a tongue in his head. But the baker shook his head and said you should have heard him, it couldn't be fouler.

When Toon and Karlien were still alive he'd had to hold himself in check, and he watched his step, so as to keep in with the Steenackerses. But now it was finished, and after the way he'd treated the maid his name was dirt with everyone. Now he let the devil in him loose and what a devil it was! The women standing at the doorways went inside if they saw him coming; the girls kept out of his way; the children knew from what they had been told at home that he was wicked, don't you ever speak to him, don't ever go near him. They would see him and go pale with fright. Once Jan van Uffelen said at the bar in the café for everyone to hear: 'Wouldn't it be better to get rid of him? He's a disgrace to the whole village—break his neck and dump him under a dung-heap.' 'Yes,' they said, humourless and hard-eyed, 'a good idea, but then you wouldn't be able to live here for the stink it'd make.'

Rik still had a couple of drinking companions but he soon lost these friends too. Village lads are far from saints. At the fairs and on Sundays they can cut up rough, but it goes so far and no farther; they know when to stop. The last spree the three of them had together was in Grimbergen. They knew Rik had gone through all his money. He had borrowed some the day before and they spent it on champagne. In another café Rik had to leave his overcoat behind as security. In the next bar he ordered champagne again, but the other two put the proprietor wise. He brought a bottle of champagne to the table and said he would open it if Rik would leave his trousers with him and come back for them when he had money to pay. That caused their first and last quarrel; they set on him and knocked him down and went off singing. They didn't want to be seen with him again. They left him lying drunk and dazed, Rik, son of Toon, of Antoine, once servant to His Eminence the Archbishop, Primate of Belgium.

Wouldn't Toon be turning in his grave every night and pounding the lid of his coffin? they said in the village. And Karlien, poor Karlien, she'd be filling her coffin with her tears. Fancy having a son like that one. If a child was cheeky and disobedient the mother trembled, the father shook his head, they couldn't sleep. If he was going to grow up like that it was better that God let him break his neck or die of typhus.

5

Shunned and friendless, Rik looked more and more a wreck. The shop was dirty, cobwebs in all the corners and a stink of food gone bad. When he stirred out of his bed he shuffled round like a grimy, ragged tramp. On the mantelpiece there was an old photograph of himself, a bright-eyed little boy of eight or nine in a sailor-suit and on the band of his sailor's cap he could read the letters 'Avenir' as if a rosy future was waiting for him. If he went outside into the street he saw the Notice of Sale pasted on the wall. The price wouldn't pay off his debts by a long way, and what then—the lawyers always wanted the last cent of interest on interest. Now there weren't any young girls who would go for a walk with him, the bars where he soaked himself with cheap beer emptied when he came in. It was a Sunday afternoon and as soon as the beer got working on his empty stomach he realized, even more clearly than he had in the morning looking at that photo of himself, that he was finished. He'd had his fling, and all that was left was a sour, sickening hopelessness. He'd come to the end of the road. He didn't feel any sorrow, he was past caring; what did it matter to him now? He went down the path that led to the railway line.

He followed the line, walking between the tracks. The rails glistened and flashed in the last light of the sun. He thought he might need another pint or two so he could lie down calmly with his neck on the rail, but he took off his collar anyway. At college he'd heard about a drunk who had lain waiting for half an hour but by then he was sober and when he saw the train coming he jumped up and he was off like the wind. Rik grinned to himself. He hung his collar on the top of a bush. It just fitted. He put his shirtfront next to it and lay down with his neck on the rail. By Christ, it was cold! The oath made him think of praying but what a stupid thought, praying for forgiveness with your neck on a railway line. Then he thought that someone might see him here, it was close to the village. He went farther on and came to a level

34

crossing. He went still farther and came to the hut where the Zaterdag family lived.

It was nothing more than a hut. Near the door a girl sat on a three-legged stool playing with a dog that was as big as a calf. She called it, took its front paws and made it stand up. Both of them were lithe and strong and straight, and the dog was taller than she was. She tried to toss it but she wasn't strong enough. The dog landed on its four feet every time.

'Can I try?' Rik asked. 'Watch out,' she said gruffly, 'or he'll tear you to bits.' But Rik came nearer. What did he care if the dog was dangerous? He leaned against the corner of the hut and spat out obscenities about the dog. Without answering she stood up, grabbed it by the collar and tied it to a post. Then she turned to go inside. He asked her to stay and talk to him for a while. She looked at him, suspicious and hostile. What did he want here anyway?

He didn't know himself. He'd come to put his head under a train, he wanted to be sure of dying. But he saw that girl by the door of the hut and he didn't know why he suddenly thought of the letters on his sailor's cap. He could see the rails from here, dull dark strips now that the sun was gone. He asked her if there was no one else at home. Any other girl for miles around would have shaken with fright and said that they were upstairs, father and all her brothers, lying down till it was time for them to go out for a drink, and they'd be getting up any minute now, and another brother had just gone out to buy some tobacco. But not her. She'd put the children to bed, she said, and her father and her brothers were down at the café drinking beer. For him that sounded as if she'd said: Come on then, and he sidled over to her, leering, but she gave him an punch that wiped the leer off his face, and he rushed at her.

Anyone who is going to lie in front of a train won't think twice about murder. His lips swelled up from the blow, he was red-faced from rage and from the drink. If only he had a knife to slash and kill with, a wilder pleasure that would be than he had ever had

35

with the whores in Brussels. A sharp knife plunged deep in a girl's body, in her breasts, in her stomach. Get a little of his own back and then go and lie on the rails.

But she was a daughter of Zaterdag, the poacher and road-mender, and like her brothers she'd been brought up on potatoes, vinegar and kicks and cuffs. Her hands clamped hard round his wrists. He didn't have a knife and he couldn't squeeze her neck. Twice she threw him on his back as she had done with the dog, and when he got up the third time and ran at her, doubled-up to grab her by the legs, she lifted the stool and swung it down so hard on Rik Steenackers's head that he reeled back, senseless, and toppled over like a wax candle at High Mass melted with the heat. The dog wouldn't come out of the turned-over barrel that was his kennel just for a little scuffle like that. If he was needed he'd be let loose soon enough; he stayed where he was, confident Mie could look after herself. Mie sat herself down again on the three-legged stool. If he was dead, she'd tell the gendarmes why. If he was only knocked out he'd soon come round and if he kept quiet, she'd let him be, but if he didn't she'd knock him out for good.

He came to. She watched him as he staggered to his feet. She didn't move. He could see the rails gleaming in the dusk. He stepped limply over the loose barbed wire round the garden and lay down on the track, this time without a muttered curse. The metal was even colder on his neck.

Did he think she'd start howling and yelling? Mie didn't give him a glance. She knew he was safe till eleven o'clock and you can hear the train a long way off. She just sat there on the stool, it was dark already.

It must have been well after nine when he stepped over the wire-fencing again and stood in front of her. She had her hand on a lump of wood so she wouldn't be taken by surprise, but all he did was to ask her to forgive him. Forgiveness, a far too high-falutin' word for any of the Zaterdag family. 'You're mad,' she said. He insisted he wanted her to say she would forgive him and he had wanted to lie on the rails and be hacked in two. She only jeered at him. 'Are you crazy or still drunk, or what's wrong with you?'

He didn't know himself. He'd been thrown out of one school after the other, his father and his mother were dead, the Steenackerses had disowned him, his house was being sold over his head, everyone kept out of his way. Bad enough, all that, but even worse when that vixen of a girl, the daughter of Zaterdag the roadmender, nearly killed him. Maybe it was the cheap beer and the soft warmth of that summer evening. 'I'll tell you what a rotten swine I am,' he said. He told her. But before he knew it the miracle was happening.

The evil of his misdeeds was no longer evil as he told how it had happened. All of a sudden, he didn't know where the words came from, he could explain it all. He wanted to blame himself for everything but every accusation came as an avowal that was reason for pity as much as reproach. An aching tenderness of longing for her welled up in him and he spoke the truth, saying things he had never thought of before. Till that moment he'd only thought of himself and his own pleasure, he'd lived in the darkness of his own debauchery, now the words of his confession were lamps lighting a long tunnel of remorse. His parents weren't young when they got married. They had spoilt him like an old couple with a grandchild. It didn't matter what he did, he could always shelter behind the brewer and his wife who didn't have any children of their own. They always took his part, and the two spinsters even more. So he never knew any authority or fear or love, and a child that can do as it likes doesn't care about anyone or anything.

As he went on talking he was wondering what it was that made him talk like that. That's why I'm what I am, a good-for-nothing, a rotten swine. He kept repeating it with a strange sort of satisfaction: a rotten swine, a rotten swine. But she cut him short: 'Shut your mouth, you rotten swine!' and it was like the sting of a whip. He didn't dare say it again. But he went on telling her about himself. So that was why he wanted to lie down over there on the rails for the train to run over him, he wasn't joking, he'd decided, and he'd taken off his collar and tie.

She heard the train in the distance, and without looking up, without even glancing at him, she said: 'If you want to get under the eleven o'clock you'll have to get going.' But he didn't move. The train roared past, the lights winked at him: No, Rik Steenackers, there aren't many who go that far. He felt no bigger than a grain of sand.

'Well, you better go home now,' she said. The son of Antoine, servant to His Eminence the Archbishop, got up and went.

But the next day he was back again, downcast and shuffling, and he saw now that there was nothing in the world so gleaming black as that girl's eyes, and what a body she had, so smooth and strong, and supple as a young beech tree. She asked him what he'd come back for and why he didn't go and find himself some work.

It was years and years since he had felt shy. That time at his first college, in the headmaster's study with Steenackers, he had looked up with a shamefaced smile. Ever since then he had stared back shamelessly or leered with a knowing brazen look, now he stood there dumb and sheepish. But he tried it once more to see if it would work with her. He hadn't come to listen to her abusing him; why didn't she start off by saying good day? She snapped back that just to start with he could keep away from here. Had anyone invited him? Had anyone asked him to come round slobbering last night? He needn't think anyone here wanted to see him, and she went on and on. A family in a lonely hut far from the nearest house learns that half a word can say all there is to say, even in anger, but if it came to talking back she could give as good as she got. She left him standing in the yard and he waited meekly for her to come out and sit on the stool by the door with her darning and let him stand six feet away from her, no nearer. Toon, may God rest his soul, hadn't been born in a castle—and neither had His Eminence for that matter—but if he'd ever imagined the day would come when his son would be treated like dirt by the barefoot daughter of Zaterdag, the poacher, he would rather have forgone the holy sacrament of marriage and the honour of fatherhood. The day did come.

The whole village was hooting with laughter: He's running after that Zaterdag girl.

'If you came and told me . . .' the baker started off one evening. The young schoolmaster was there with the others round the baker's door, he joined them because of his diligent interest in the folklore of the village, and sometimes he asked: 'How did you say that again, Baker?' and that was flattering. 'Now if you came and told me that Princess Sarlot had her eye on me I wouldn't run away, oh no, just the opposite it'd be. Those titled folk, you know, at times they've just got to have some common stock in their bed, and that's all there is to it. But that Zaterdag's daughter, that's something for a tramp or chicken-thief or umbrella man. No village boy in his right mind would ever think of it. He's cooked his goose and no mistake. If he'd just had a little sense Steenackers' brewery would have been all his own. In a couple of years he could have lined up all the young maidens for miles around, he could have picked out the prettiest and then ten others for a reserve, just a second, I've got to swallow, it makes my mouth water now my Rosalie isn't here. And there he is walking his legs off down to his arse, pardon, schoolmaster, did you say something? Now, mijnheer, don't interrupt, you don't know the whole story. He's had to mend his ways, I'm telling you, he's gone right pale from being on his best behaviour and all that, by Jesus, for Medemesel Mariette from the villa by the railway line! No, don't start laughing, he's mad about her. This afternoon the little urchins in the village were shouting out at him but he didn't hear a thing. Since his house was sold Jan van Uffelen lets him sleep in his attic, for the sake of Toon and Karlien, may God rest their souls, and when he isn't over at his pa-in-law's villa, I can tell you he's up in that attic counting his beads like a real monk, he's well and truly converted. Laugh if you want to, but can you explain it, I can't. Just explain to me why for Christ's sake that randy boozy young rip could fall in love just like a snotty-nosed choir boy, and with that Zaterdag girl, mark you. Now, you tell me why, mijnheer schoolmaster.'

'Ah, Baker, love is blind, they say.' 'Yes, I know that well enough, from the time when I was running after my Rosalie, I didn't know she was deaf and dumb and lame as well and crazy as a rabbit.'

6

Hold her hand? No, she wouldn't let him touch her, and endearments, none of that either. She wasn't used to that sort of talk. She thought he was making fun of her, and she'd soon stop that, do you hear? She acted as if she didn't believe he was in love with her. She didn't see why she should believe him, she said, what was there to show he was serious, and he had to admit there was nothing, but she saw the change in him. She said: 'We'll see.'

Once he took her a dress that he'd bought from the little bit of money unexpectedly left over after the sale. She wasn't pleased at all: how could he pay for dresses, how much had it cost—or had he bought it for someone else who didn't like it, was that it, and it's good enough for me? I'd sooner throw it in the fire. But he didn't dare shout back at her, her eyes judged him and he only hoped for mercy. She believed him, and she disappeared with the dress to try it on, and he felt a fine noose press slowly and tightly round his heart as she walked towards him, a vision.

She wouldn't have been a woman if she hadn't wanted to be taken out, but a dozen times he had to say tonight was the Saturday before the fair and the dance tent would be open at eight. A dozen times he had to plead with her and then they went. Neither of them spoke. He slipped his arm under hers, timidly, it wasn't pushed away, and that swing and sway of her hips! From under the trees by the station there was a shout then a chorus of guffaws. Her head went higher, she turned and looked every one of them in the eye. She didn't dance. He ordered beer. She just watched the crowd. She saw the winks and sneers without a blush, but she didn't look once at him. If he was serious with her, if he meant it, then he'd stay there and face them; if he didn't mean it he could turn tail and run off. It was a hard and bitter hour, and then she stood up. Let's go. She took him by the arm and led him through the throng of dancing couples. Outside in the dark she stopped, she took his head in her hands and kissed him, a strong, passionate kiss. It sent a shock through him as if she had bitten hard on his lip. She could have said: I'll kiss you like that just once more and then I'll hold you down on the rail for the eleven o'clock express, and he would have said: Hold me there on the rails, but kiss me again.

'I can smell perfume on you,' he said, that was all he was aware off. It was an advertisement for soap, a tawdry piece of scented paper, she'd got it for nothing and she hadn't wanted to tell him. What did it matter? She was the hope he clung to. At night he would wake up as if she had called him; in his dreams she came towards him and she always walked past him. He saw her a long way off and he waited, scarcely breathing, hoping each time she would take him in her arms, press his head against her breast, but she went past him.

'I haven't a penny,' he said. They were sitting in the grass between the hut and the railway track. She looked straight in front of her. 'If we get married I don't want you to have a single penny,' she said, 'then no one can ever say I married you for money. I want to start with nothing.'

'I can't even buy a suit.'

'So much the better.'

Sometimes she made him frightened. She would sit saying nothing; she saw the way her confident, obstinate intuition traced out for them. He didn't have the money to rent a house, he didn't have any work, he didn't know what he was going to do. She just smiled.

They were in the hut. He stood by the window looking out at the train rushing by. 'That brown suit,' she said, 'is good enough to get married in, and I've got that blue dress.' He felt small and helpless, too humble even for that bare shack. But she loved him now, tenderly and proudly. She stood behind him, she drew his head back against her body, their lips met, they both quivered, staring dazed at each other. She bent over the pots on the stove as if nothing had happened and she said: 'You'll see, we'll manage and very well, too.'

Sometimes a phrase, words as simple as a clear sky, can linger in a room, take form and grow large. That phrase that Mie Zaterdag spoke lingered in the hut, prophetic words that gave Rik strength.

If he lived to be two hundred he would never talk about his wedding day. The wedding was at half past seven in the morning so it would be cheap. His suit reeked of the ammonia she had used to clean it, behind him, the witness, the road-mender Zaterdag, stinking of gin. The altar boys giggled in the vestry. The verger ignored them, as they came out of the church there was a burst of shrill whistles from behind a hedge, a path of white sand led from the church door to a wheelbarrow, their bridal coach. Over the baker's door a flag was fluttering.

They had their wedding breakfast in the hut by the railway track. They ate soup and then the rest of the meal from the same deep plate. After that they drank beer and gin and played cards until Zaterdag couldn't tell a club from a heart. The time went slowly for Rik, his blood pounded heavy and hot in his veins. The road-mender sat hunched and silent by the stove. He was thinking of his own marriage. He pulled a face and said: 'It's a pity your mother is dead and gone.' Finally the darkness seeped inside the hut, the half-light made Mie even more desirable. Between two hiccups Zaterdag turned to his daughter, his eldest, and said with a drunken grin: 'You'll be going off to bed now, won't you, eh?'

'Yes,' Mie said simply. She stood up and they went. The whole village was waiting in the doorways, for everyone knew they had to come past. They were going to live in the house that had been sold over his head, and how would they ever be able to pay the rent? But according to the baker that wasn't any problem at all: the steward of the Zaterdag estate, he announced, had told him only yesterday, confidentially, you know, that the bride had got her marriage settlement and with the interest on all that money they could live like royalty. It's all fixed up I can tell you, Mijnheer Zaterdag himself had paid it all out.

Past those doorways, past all the titters and whispers, Mie led him to their marriage bed. The only house where no one was standing in the doorway was the Steenackerses', but as it happened, they had visitors. Yes, Madame, Alphonsine had cried and cried the first few days she was in Brussels, and she had often thought of you, Madame. There you are, all alone in a big city, with no one at all to turn to. But there I was and I'll have to manage, she'd told herself, and I was never afraid of work, you know that, Madame, don't you? She had found work here and there, scrubbing floors, she'd been quite a while at the Cosmopolite. Once she had seen you there, Mijnheer, but she didn't have a chance to say good day no it wasn't that, she just didn't dare. If you hadn't had any people with you, she might have risked it, she was so glad to see you again. She'd worked in the Bazaar, too, and one or two other places. Then she got to know Fons, didn't I, Fons? He worked on the trams, and when she first knew him he was in the forty-six line, that was the one she went to work on every morning, and the tram was often empty so early.

Fons explained to Mijnheer what hours he used to work. Besides, it's mostly the new men they put on the forty-six, and he'd only started in the service that year.

Before long they were married. Fons had a steady job and quite a good wage. They were living in a nice little flat, three rooms and a tiny little cellar, that was all they needed, there were only the three of them. Today Fons had a day off, and she had told him such a lot about Madame and Mijnheer, so she just had to come and see them. That was very thoughtful of her, Madame and Mijnheer agreed, have another glass. Madame and Mijnjeer were pleased to see that it was all for the best she had gone off to the city and that she was happy and whenever she was in the village she must drop in and see them.

When they were saying good-bye at the door they saw the light shining through the shop-window from the kitchen where Toon and Karlien of blessed memory used to sit, and Alphonsine asked: 'Oh, who is living there now?' That same one, he's still there, but of course they had nothing to do with him. They'd heard he was married today to the commonest sort of girl. They'd have to see to their own troubles themselves, Alphonsine, we're not bothering about them, not the slightest bit. Alphonsine was still a little bit interested. She was thinking of Karlien's lovely bedroom and that beautiful wallpaper. Tonight another woman would take possession of all she had tried to buy with her orphan girl's virtue.

Mie pushed paper in the stove, laid a few blocks of wood on top, put a box of matches on the mantelpiece ready for the morning, looked round the room once more, and then she called to him from the bottom of the stairs. Slowly, still uncertain of himself, Rik followed her. She wasn't prudish. No pretending she didn't know what happened on the wedding night. When she called him her call meant: Here I am, an untouched virgin and if I yield I am yielding because I want to be a woman and a wife, his woman, his wife. I am his for him to take.

He had hunted after women, driven by the urge of blind lust, tempting them, enticing them, seeking a restless, transient pleasure that never sated, that only quenched desire with tiredness, and set him seeking again. Now Mie claimed his passion, a woman without powder or paint, or false curls or corsets or high heels, but firmfleshed and strong-boned and fresh with the mystery of all nature. She had let him desire her for months. Now she threw off her clothes one by one, and she desired him as he had desired her.

Is that wrong or ugly, is that the dissipation of sunken-eyed debauchers? When he fell asleep in her arms late that night, tired, happy, she kissed him once again and then set the alarm for half past five. And when the alarm rang and he woke, so gladly alive with this happiness that would never ever end, she smiled and pushed him back on his pillow, and Mie Zaterdag, Madame Steenackers, was off to the station to catch the six o'clock train. She came back in the evening at seven. She had found work in the factory and she left something for him to eat in the morning and at midday; in the evening she cooked and they ate a warm meal. 'You just see to the shop,' she said.

7

That was the way she set about things. She could earn more money at the factory than anywhere else, and she was too proud to look for work in the village. So she went off every morning to the factory, while Rik tried to get the shop going again. Then in the summer she could take his place behind the counter and they would rent a piece of ground where he could grow vegetables. If it turned out as she hoped, so much the better; if it didn't, well, at least they wouldn't go hungry.

It didn't come off. There were no customers, and if anyone did come in whatever they might want wasn't to be seen on the nearly empty shelves. Besides, would a girl with any thought for her reputation or a respectable married woman think of being alone with him in the shop?

But he was a model of goodness. Each evening he stood waiting for Mie in the doorway like a farm-girl waiting for her returning soldier boy. She would come swinging round the corner and when she saw him she winked at him, and that sent his blood racing. As soon as she was inside he flung his arms around her, no she musn't bother mending or darning. He was always frightened she might ask him what he had been doing all day, because all he had done was wait for her, a bit of scrubbing and polishing isn't work, it doesn't bring in any money. She earned the money. And then caper about with him, did he think she had nothing else to do? Here, peel those potatoes, the quicker you're finished the quicker we can go to sleep. And how quickly he peeled those potatoes.

One Sunday she asked him wouldn't he like to drink a pint, here's two francs. Was she going to keep him altogether, did she think he'd never be able to earn anything himself? Could she spare it from the little she earned each week? He didn't dare ask her. In dumb surprise he took the two francs and went. For weeks he hadn't been out for a walk, not once even in a café, and now he was strolling down the street with two francs in his waistcoat pocket. There was Jan van Uffelen standing in his doorway and he was the first who said: 'Morning, Rik.' The butcher passed him and said: .Morning, Rik.' The baker was outside, as usual, and he called out: 'Look who's here! Hullo, Rik, how's everything?'

What was happening? It was as if everyone were coming to the door to say good morning to him. He kept on walking and what a fine sunny day it was; who wouldn't be happy on a day like this? The swallows were back again, there they were flying round the spire, it was worth all of two francs just to be able to watch them. He sneezed from looking up in the strong sunlight, four times one after the other, didn't that make you feel better? That blew away the sniffly winter, you were all new again. 'Bless you,' said the old woman who cleaned the church, and, would you believe it, he was crying, without any reason, at least, if the wish of an old woman who cleans the church isn't worth a tear.

Back home he held Mie close and sobbed. She had to laugh at him because he couldn't take his drink any more, but it wasn't from the beer, here's the two francs. He wept because he was happy, because he was determined to do something, and from God knows what else. That evening when she put her arms around him and asked him to tell her what really was wrong with him he told her that he couldn't just let her go on working for him while he sat at home. From tomorrow that was finished. That's what it was, dear, I swear it.

Rik Steenackers pushing a barrow with a few vegetables on it. Rik going from door to door asking wouldn't they buy a cauliflower. Rik, Steenackers' Rik. A miracle, more than a miracle, everyone just looked, open-mouthed. But there weren't any sniggers or jeers this time; after all, turning a new leaf like that, there must be some good in him. It was late enough, but still.

But still, that didn't help to sell anything. Once they've got used to going to a shop they don't change so quickly and by now Toon's shop was forgotten, there was another shop where everyone went. It wasn't the humiliation of pushing a handcart round the village, but the hopelessness of not being able to earn anything, that crushed him. He felt smaller and smaller and the pile of vegetables was bigger and heavier. He shrivelled up inside, he was sick with shame. Bent forward between the shafts he bowed his head and said: 'Mother.'

By the evening the cart was half empty and that, Mie said, was a good beginning. In his heart he would rather have heard her blame him for everything, and he thought that it was only because of her love for him that she didn't reproach him, that she was pleased with whatever he did. But Mie had never lived in a brick house, she had never seen a painted stairway, at home there was only a ladder, and she never slept in a bed with a knitted bedspread. She hardly dared to cook on the gleaming kitchen stove, all white with blue flowers; she would rather have kept it as an ornament. She was happy. She could never be so badly off as she had been at home. Even if he didn't earn a cent he had done far more for her than she could do for him. He had lifted her from the depths of poverty and she would show how grateful she was. They'd get ahead, she'd see to it. In the train she knitted stockings and sold them. She always bought a ticket in any raffles at the factory because you never know if you're going to be lucky and what can't you win for a few carefully saved francs. She never took more with her to eat than a few pieces of bread smeared with dripping. At home it wasn't every day she'd had that even. She wasn't embarrassed because she was carrying a child. She walked with that same lilting sway of her hips right up to the last day, and instead of looking tired and worn she was prettier than ever. She didn't hide the way she was by wearing shawls and drapes. She walked with her head high, tilted back a little, as if she was proud that her belly was getting heavier each day. I'm the daughter of Zaterdag, the road-mender, and I'm not ashamed of it, I'll soon be a mother and that I'm proud of, and my child will be born in a bed covered with a white knitted bedspread. And no one can point a finger at the father, not since he's been my man, and no one can point a finger at me either.

The girls in the train said it suits you, Mie. Then she would laugh, it didn't bother her a bit, she said.

But one morning it did bother her. Lucky for her she was not in the train, she was still waiting at the station. She had to clench her teeth hard when the first pains shot through her body. Those black eyes of hers burned just like the eyes of a wounded animal. Aah, aah, she thought, I'll have to go back. She went back and at nine o'clock she was lying there in the big bed with her child at her breast. When she came back that morning Rik and said she ought to have a real midwife at least, but the Zaterdags never needed any help from anyone. Rik had to take off all the soiled bedclothes and put them in a pile in the courtyard at the back. 'I'll wash it all the day after tomorrow,' Mie said. And she did, the third day after her baby was born. If a doctor had seen her up and about like that—but the Zaterdags only laughed at what the doctors said. Mie put the baby to her full large breast. She looked at the ceiling and listened to the gurgles of contentment. It was a fierce little fellow with a mop of black hair and eyebrows that ran together. He pulled a sulky face as if he had never been allowed to eat his fill. When Mie lifted him from her breast and kissed him he tried to suck at her lips.

But those were hard weeks, no money coming in, a lot of things to buy and the rent had to be paid somehow. Rik went out pushing his cart. Up till then he had knocked at the doors timidly and asked if they wanted anything, but now he saw Mie's pretty, flushed face lying on the pillows. He saw the baby next to her and he started shouting: 'Greens, any greens today. Cauliflower and cabbage, peas and celery! Any greens today.' The feeling of guilty shame was gone. He trundled his cart from one end of the village to the other, and at the last house his cart was still as good as full. But farther on there was another church spire, another village, we'll try it.

49

They knew him there too. Isn't that Rik Steenackers? It's not so long ago that he used to ride past on his bike as if he owned the world and now, I'll be damned, look at him, hawking vegetables. They laughed at first, but they bought, and that encouraged him. He went on to the next village with what he had over. He'd keep on until he had sold the lot. Then, at the café where he sold his last pound of onions, I'll have a pint, Missus.

Maybe she had recognized him straight away, but he hadn't even noticed her when she bought the onions from him. But as he called her Missus he gave a start, and what am I blushing for? Didn't he even know her name any more? Yes, of course, Maria. They got talking, a conversation of short phrases, casual and calm on the surface but it was a game of tease and taunt. He felt a fever flowing through him. It was like listening to a yapping poodle, it won't bite but the yapping sends you wild.

'Are you married now?'

'I've got a son.'

'Who with?'

'You don't know her.'

'I'm a widow.'

'Oh.'

'He had an accident. He fell asleep on his cart and got pulled under the wheels. He had a load of old iron on and he was dead when they picked him up.'

Silence.

'It's just as well I didn't want any children.'

'That hasn't made you any thinner.'

'You don't think I've got thinner?'

'No.'

'Why?'

'You've put on weight.'

'Do you think so?'

'Yes.'

'Oh, yes? Are you sure?'

'You know you have, you're laughing too.'

'Yes, but only because you saw it at once. That I've got a bit fatter.'

'How long should I take to notice it?'

'I don't know, you'd know much better than I would.'

She giggled. Another silence.

'Have you got a good wife?'

'Of course, I have.'

Silence again.

'I'm left on my own far too much. This week I've got to sit every night till half past nine with my mother-in-law who's stone-deaf. My husband's two brothers are away, moving furniture from Malines to Brussels.'

'Do you get on well with both of them?'

'Pig!'

'What do you mean?'

'You can act so stupid. You've changed, haven't you?'

'I don't know.'

'You're too serious now.'

'You only imagine that. What's the time now? I'll have to get back home.'

'Already?'

'Yes, I have to go now.'

'You never used to run away so quickly.'

'Bye, Maria.'

'Don't we shake hands? That's right. Bye, Rik.'

'What are you laughing at?'

'Shouldn't I laugh?'

'Why not? Well, good-bye for now.'

He could feel she was standing behind the glass door watching him go. The unexpected encounter had unsettled him; he walked quickly, breathing hard. His coat pockets were heavy with the money. A sensible tradesman must keep things rolling, so he called at a few other cafés and by the time he reached home he was filled with love for his wife and child, and with regret for his misspent youth, and he was determined never to see Maria again.

But Mie looked at him with a cold hard stare as he swayed across the shop towards her. She didn't give him a chance to start drooling over her, she pushed him backwards and he could just keep his balance by holding on to the rice- and flour-bins. He laughed. She didn't know how much he'd earned, look at that and that and that. He tossed handfuls of money on to the counter. She swept it away with both arms, she threw it at his head till there wasn't another coin to throw. There, and there and there and now get out of my sight with your money, you drunken sot!

I don't think you know what I'm like yet. She shook him by the shoulders, she was grim and pale Before she'd let him play the drunkard she'd take hold of him and put him in the butcher's sausage machine and cut him into little bits till there was nothing left of him but his two heels. He shuddered at the way she said it, so slowly and so mercilessly, with her teeth clenched. His eyes were wide open with fear and when she packed him off to bed like a little boy he didn't think of a hammer or a pair of scissors, he just went upstairs without a word.

He lay in bed thinking of Maria, of those dark, long evenings with her behind the mill, but again and again his thoughts ended with the admission that Mie was right. He thought of how Maria had looked at him that afternoon, lustful, tempting. He realized what it could mean, that this unexpected meeting was just a chance to snatch a taste of the sordid pleasures he'd turned his back on. A woman left a widow too soon, a marriage cut short. A lonely, unsated animal, an easy prey to him and to her passion. Am I going to take this animal and leave my wife? He didn't think any further, he would rather put his feet against the soft flesh of Mie's legs. But she drew away from him. The next morning he stood ready to set off with his cart she said in a no-nonsense tone that he was old enough to know what he was doing, but if he ever got drunk again then he could stay away and stay away for good. She could look after her two children.

Two? He gaped at her.

Yes, two.

He bent over the shafts, he pushed his cart into the street and swore to himself softly: Two. No, he wouldn't see Maria again. Later when he went by she waved to him from the window. He nodded as if she were a stranger. It wasn't easy to keep straight on, not stopping, but he was thinking to himself: Two.

8

The third was announced casually one morning. 'We're going to have another one,' Mie said. That same day Maria bought the last of his load of vegetables, after all he couldn't refuse to sell her anything. Come inside, I'll get the money to pay you. She asked him if he'd like a young goat as a present. Had she guessed that he'd been thinking all day of a pair of rabbits, a goat, a pig, anything that would eat garbage and scraps and bring in a little extra? Now that there's another one on the way, and how much do you think it takes to keep a family of five.

The goat stood in a corner of the stall, her two kids stumbling round on their ridiculous long legs. Maria started talking about the goat, how it had been mated. They didn't look at each other. He answered with a vague mumble. Her words were coarse, he felt himself trembling, she spoke gazing into the darkness of the stall. Their blood raced hotter than if they had touched each other. In a daze he thought of Mie. He said: 'You ought to get married.' 'Yes,' she gasped, inviting, shameless. He ought to know he'd taught her to like talking about those things. If you only knew what you used to make me feel like. You devil, I couldn't stop thinking of those dirty words, sometimes my legs were so weak I had to lie down. And she started talking about the goat again. Was it the earthy animal smell of the stall or a sort of drunkenness? Her eyes were bloodshot, his head was spinning. They went back inside, they still didn't look at each other, they forgot the young goat she had offered him and when he left, pushing his empty cart, he found himself wondering what was it all about anyway? He stopped and wiped his clothes with his sleeve, but there wasn't any stain to rub off, he only wanted to wipe away the unseen traces of something that he didn't want anyone else ever to know about.

The next day he came to fetch the young goat. She told him that her brothers-in-law were moving furniture for some rich old boy whose family had got a lawyer to look after his money to stop him from spending it all. He'd gone through more than you could count and now the lawyer lets him have just so much every month. He had rented a house in the village. They said he had a sore above his hip that wouldn't heal, brrr. He'd be able to tell a tale or two, all the things he must have done.

Rik asked her was it his fault that she liked that sort of talk. She didn't answer him, she told him she wished she could get married again, but if she made a choice between her brothers-in-law there'd be trouble, the one would murder the other. They were so jealous that neither of them would go out with the wagon and leave the other alone with her. She wasn't fond of them but she didn't have a home of her own and she might do worse than marry the younger one, but she didn't dare think about it. She had to be so careful if they were both at home, she was so frightened. She had no chance of finding anyone else; in the village she had a bad name. That was why she was so glad Rik had come by. My mother-in-law doesn't suspect you, or she'd come and sit in the room with us. Now I'm glad this old fellow is coming to live here.

She looked up at Rik and said: 'If you hadn't gone and got married...' They were both silent.

Months later, when the fourth was on the way she said to him: 'That wouldn't have happened with me. Two babies and no more.'

He drained his glass but he didn't leave. He let her fill a second. They could talk to each other by now without embarrassement, without the tension of their first meeting, and her remark set him thinking. Mie had been out of sorts for the last few days. She had even asked him if he was bringing home all his money. He had known for a long while that they didn't have enough for the housekeeping but he said nothing, and Maria thought it was just one of his usual silences, for he never spoke about his wife.

For five whole years, five years last week it was, he had worked for the smile she gave him when he came home in the evening and the way she put the smallest one on his knee. And the way she would stand there made him forget all his tiredness, come here and let me kiss you. She had the habit of putting on a Sunday apron in the evening and fetching a bottle of beer from the cellar, pouring two glasses and laying the paper on the arm of the chair for him. He would read the reports of the trials at the local assizes and she delivered her fierce and fiery comments. As a boy he had been lectured and pleaded with; the two old maids had harangued him for days on end. All that had made not an inch of difference, but when she said what she thought of the witnesses, the judges, the lawyers' speeches, and the verdicts he was filled with a sense of justice and respect for uprightness and honesty, for thrift and work. Prison wasn't enough, she said, for a murderer, the father of seven children, who cut his wife's throat. They should have pulled his fingernails and his toenails and rubbed pepper and mustard in the raw flesh, and after that skinned him alive and tossed him into a barrel of brine. She took such a delight in thinking up gruesome tortures and her wrath was a gauge he could measure his own past worthlessness against. When he thought back on what he had been like himself...

'You're just sitting there dreaming,' Maria said. He gave a start, he stood up and left. He must have something on his mind, maybe it's his wife. She could never believe that that marriage of his would last and she used to picture to herself how they would spend hours together as they had behind the mill.

It was that evening that Mie told him what she had done. It would always be a riddle to her how it happened, but a few days ago she had suddenly discovered there wasn't enough money to pay the rent. She had worried and worried until her head ached, maybe he'd noticed, anyway she was at her wits' end and she'd gone to the Steenackerses. Oh yes, Rik could have married some old hag of ninety, or gone and worked as a farm labourer riding round all day on the dungcart, it wouldn't have mattered, but that he'd married a Zaterdag, that was something the Steenackerses would never forgive him. Madame made it clear enough, yes, but when you look at her from close by you can see she's getting old, she won't last too long. But never mind, there she was sitting opposite Madame, and Madame had an expression of what do you want here. You know how it is, Madame, a shop can be short of money all of a sudden. Of course there are customers who owe something, but they are customers and how could she go and make trouble about their bills? Anyway that wouldn't help; if they didn't have the money how could she pay the rent?

She waited for Madame to answer, and Madame just didn't answer. Ugly old bitch, say something. But she didn't open her mouth. Mie explained it all again, how she hadn't expected to be short, and how she could pay it all back in less than a fortnight, but then all of a sudden she was angry. She wasn't going to say a word more and she was thinking I'll sit here like you and you'll have to say something, you'll have to say yes or no.

Yes, yes indeed, Madame could understand quite well how it was. What a pity Mijnheer wasn't at home! Madame couldn't decide anything without asking Mijnheer first, but as soon as Mijnheer came in Madame would...

Mie stood up, she was at the door before Madame had finished. *Merci*, Madame. But yesterday the maid came into the shop. Half a kilo of sugar and a packet of potato flour. Mie had told her without wasting any words to go and get the money first, and tell Madame from me that I can't risk any credit. Of course the maid didn't come back, but Mie had her revenge.

Rik asked her if she had paid the rent. The rent was paid. He wouldn't believe it, she said, how she had managed to scrape all the money together. The crease between his eyebrows deepened but she didn't notice. She'd never told him that she was saving up a little nest egg, she never surprised him now and then by telling him how much she'd saved because he might start treating himself to too many pints. He thought they were living from hand to mouth, and they'd be poorer than ever with the fourth baby. He'd

57

have to sell the dogcart and the three dogs. He'd go round again with the handcart. There was nothing, nothing at all he could think of to earn a little more. If he only had a patch of ground where he could grow a few vegetables. Without looking at her he said that he'd met the new gamekeeper and they'd talked a while and he wasn't going to have a big family, two was enough for him, he said. Mie answered: 'That's all a lot of nonsense.' He sat dreaming about Maria who had different ideas, and a few days later when he went into the café he saw her at a table with a customer who was bald and fairly old. That would be him, the one with the sore. Maria could hardly wait to say that Rik had four children. Without glancing at Rik, Maria's new-found friend said: 'From the look of him you wouldn't think he was such a fool.' Rik flushed, his face dark with humiliation and rage. 'Yes,' he said, 'all sorts of scum turn up here.' That pleased the old rake: 'Come on, sit down and fill up your glass.' Rik glared: 'Thanks, mijnheer, I can pay for my own drinks.' The dissipated face cracked into a leering grin. 'Come on, come on, sit down,' he said to Rik. 'You're my friend; we'll drink champagne if you like.'

They sat there together, a bald old roué, a young and still pretty woman, and Rik, the three of them with their cares and sorrows, a roving bachelor whose roving days were over, a woman without a man, a man afraid of nature's ways, a pathetic trio. In the back room the mother-in-law and the two brothers-in-law took it in turns every few minutes to peep through the glass pane of the door. The three of them in the café knew they were being spied on. It made them want to do something wild, something bad, each time no one was watching. If the conversation drifted into a friendly vein then old bald-head was all of a sudden angry. He jeered at Rik, Rik jeered back at him, and then he laughed and said: 'You're my friend, young fellow.' But no matter what they talked about, Rik went home bowed under the burden of his troubles, and the furrow between his eyebrows was deeper than ever. He was sick with fear and doubt.

For five years he had been happy and he had worked hard, now he felt helpless and beaten. He was walking on the sunbaked muddy bed of a river in the summer when the water is low. On the surface it is dry but if you stop to watch something your feet start sinking and if you don't move quickly you get sucked down in the oozing rubbery blackness.

He couldn't look Mie in the face any more. But she didn't change. When he came home in the evening and took off his boots she put his warm slippers by the chair and his pipe and tobacco on the table then went on making the supper. Her movements were deft; her body, even after bearing four children, was still graceful and firm. Just to be near to her did something to him; what a woman she was! Now he didn't dare look at her. She always let the children stay up so he could see them before they were asleep. The youngest was in his cot, the three others sat with their eyes stolidly fixed on him. Three little Zaterdags, they were nothing like Rik. Three solid, round, dark heads with black eyes that wouldn't turn away, not for anything in the world, and just kept looking at what they saw. If one of them was sucking his thumb and Rik told him to stop, the little Zaterdag just went on sucking his thumb without a blink. If it was one of them that was big enough to answer he said no and kept his thumb in his mouth. The eldest was going to school but they couldn't get him to learn a single nursery rhyme. But he could eat his own weight in food and Rik used to think to himself: How can I ever earn enough to keep them? He took two of them on his knee and a sharp pang shot through his heart. They were such sturdy, solemn little fellows. If there was no more food for them he would pin a note on his shirt and cut his throat from ear to ear. In the letter he'd say that they could pickle his corpse, that would make enough meat for the children for a year. Lost in these crazy day-dreams he squeezed them too tight and they both punched him in the face with their little fists.

9

But now the nights were long hours of dark loneliness. They lay beside each other and they were far apart. She felt herself lost in a silent uncertainty, an emptiness that grew bigger and bigger. He was moody and he couldn't sleep: an urge to go out on his own in the evenings and then again the fear of falling into his old ways, one day thoughtful and tender, the next day in a black rage. Driving on his dog-cart along the deserted roads between the villages he would sit staring in front of him, softly and sadly cursing. And the dogs ate too much and the price for cauliflower had dropped and he'd made a bad buy of fruit, what a bloody fool he was, the cart needed mending again, what was he going to do?

Madame Steenackers died and twice her two sisters made the journey from Alsemberg. They knew that Rik had given up his bad ways. They could guess that he wasn't living a life of luxury with four children to keep but because he was married to that Zaterdag girl they simply couldn't know him any more. They didn't even look at the shop. *Dans le temps nous avons voulu faire une bonne œuvre, comprenez-vous,* and they still wanted to help people wherever they could but they were people you couldn't really associate with. Rik brooded and choked with resentment. Soon after that the brewer sold his business, for half a million francs they said in the village, and he was going to live in Brussels: he'd be able to make up for lost time. Madame had never let him out of sight; now he could do what he liked. The thought flashed through Rik's mind: If I murdered him? But I still wouldn't have the money. He didn't know where the idea came from, he couldn't shake it off, he began imagining himself what would be the safest way to commit the murder. He would go and see the brewer with a revolver in his pocket, he would talk casually about one thing and another, about the sale, about Brussels, and whether he had got the money already. Yes, Rik, it's all safe in the bank. So you've got it, Mr. Brewer, well, I want a hundred thousand francs and you're going to write a cheque here and now, or else. You know I'm not afraid. I'm going to kill myself anyway, but you won't get the chance to enjoy that money of yours.

Then he had another idea: get the maid to help and he would share the money with her, 50,000 francs each. She could frighten him by playing the ghost at night or else she could get into bed with him and Rik would catch them and ask for 100,000 francs to keep his mouth shut. But he decided none of these plans was any good, and when he thought it over it was only a crazy notion, he wasn't serious anyway. Then he began to think it over seriously. Suppose I could get hold of all his money without being found out, would I do it? He had to admit that he would, yes of course he would, and if I had to kill him to get his money and be sure no one could ever say it was me would I still go through with it? It was yes again. He began imagining how it would happen. He had shot the brewer in the chest but the bullet had missed the heart. The brewer was on his knees, crying and coughing blood, pleading for his life, I did so much for you, lad, I paid for the schools you went to, don't kill me now. Would I kill him? The answer was yes this time too. He was enjoying the fantasy.

But it was only imagination, a morbid childish game and he tried to think of something else. But the thought of all that money kept coming back. Was it so childish? Was it so sure that he would be caught? After all he hadn't been in the Steenackerses' house for years. No one would ever suspect for a moment that he would murder the man who had done so much for him. And besides, five years ago everyone would have expected the worst of him, but now he had five years of honest work to his credit. No, it wasn't so childish. He trembled all over, it was just a question of being ready to take a risk, and he'd have to be quick because some of the furniture had been auctioned and the two brothers-in-law were coming to take the rest to Brussels. Oh well, he could at least take a small precaution, that didn't mean he had to decide anything, but you never know. He said casually to Mie that he'd felt he ought to go and say good-bye to the brewer. But he'd thought better of it. The brewer had done a lot for him, but he couldn't forgive the Steenackerses for looking down on Mie. No, he wouldn't go near the brewer, so there.

Then if the brewer did happen to be murdered Mie would never ask him if he hadn't noticed anything strange when he was there. She wouldn't tell him to see the police so he could help them to find the murderer who ought to have his nails pulled out and get pepper and mustard rubbed into the raw flesh and then be skinned alive slowly and with a potato knife.

Mie was just as unsuspecting as the brothers-in-law over there. They didn't know that while they were busy shifting tables and cupboards Maria was seizing her chance; she was off with that old bald-head, with his stinking sore and all. They were taking a big bed apart and they didn't dream that she had her own bed all ready for that very same night. It wasn't so long ago that she shuddered and said brrr; now she was kissing him. The glass panel in the door hadn't helped.

When they drove off early next morning in their two wagons for the last load from the brewer's house they knew. That was why they took a bottle of cognac from the shelf in the café. They sat together on the seat of the first wagon, the horse pulling the second wagon followed obediently behind, and as they hadn't taken a bite for breakfast, in their rage and disgust, they kept passing the bottle to each other. Then for the first time they talked about Maria.

'You wanted her yourself.'

'And you more than me.'

'A fine mess it would have been too.'

It was just as well that the best pieces of furniture had been moved already, for the two of them were far from sober by the time they reached the village. In front of the house they shouted the news from the seat of their wagon: 'That little slut our poor

René married. She'd gone when we came home last night, cleared out she had, the bitch that she is!'

At the baker's, where they sat down for their eight o'clock bread and cheese, they told the story with crude angry oaths. Run off with that old wreck of seventy, that worn-out goat, and he's got a sore on his hip that won't heal. He used to spend all day in the café and no one guessed what they were up to. The maid who cleans his house said that when he starts taking his clothes off she'll fall over from the stink.

At eight o'clock the baker had finished his work, then he was in a good mood and talkative. He teased those two big fellows who were chewing on their sandwiches as if the sandwiches had done something wrong, and they didn't catch on that he was making fun of them. The baker said that Maria had always been a respectable girl all the time she had lived in the village, but ach, there she was, left a widow at that age, hardly more than a young girl, and neither of them had enough sense to do anything about it, or were they too shy? Both of them growled like bulldogs; they snorted with their mouths full of bread: 'What? Marry a bitch like that?' The elder licked the beer froth off the ends of his moustache.

It was the talk of the village. The only ones who said nothing were the good souls who never said a bad word about others, or those like Rik who weren't so sure they mightn't do the same sort of thing themselves one of these days. And Mie was quiet and thoughtful. She heard the two brothers-in-law shouting the news as they passed the door and she thought of Rik. These last weeks he'd been acting so strangely, she felt uneasy every time he went off in his cart. She had saved and saved every single penny she could and it had to be this very morning that they went shouting out about Maria. Today a plot of land was being auctioned. If it hadn't been for all that yelling she might have waited; now she had a hundred reasons for going to the sale.

She sat there, one woman in that crowd of farmers, and she kept her eyes fixed on the auctioneer. Two of them were bidding against each other. She didn't care what the piece of land was worth, she knew how much she'd saved and that was how much it was worth to her. When one of the two bidders gave up and the auctioneer was raising his hammer she called out, loud and defiant, offering a hundred francs more. The farmer who had thought the land was his turned round. Did he have to bid against her as well? She didn't answer. He raised the price again, that would stop her, and straight away Mie called out a hundred more. The silence that followed seemed to be laden with sympathy for her. She was no match for the farmers, her naivety made them smile, they knew she was bidding with her hard-saved pennies. Going, going, gone. They watched her with ungrudging respect as she took the money from the pocket of her dress. She had two notes left over; she could have made two more bids.

Time isn't such a problem if you go round from house to house hawking vegetables. If you have to you can finish a whole day's run in a morning. There was no need to hurry that day, but the brewer was leaving in the evening for Brussels and he'd probably have a lot of money in his wallet. Rik hadn't worked out any plan at all, but Mie was out, so he might still call in to say good-bye. No revolver, no knife, no hammer. But at the first school he'd been expelled from the beams in the rooms were inscribed with virtuous mottoes in large Gothic letters and one of them was: Whatever you do, do well. So he put on his gloves. And why did he do that? He wore his gloves because he was going to say good-bye to the brewer and he wanted to wear the proper clothes for the occasion. If nothing happened, well, the brewer would be pleased at this token of respect and Rik didn't expect anything to happen. But if the maid was upstairs or if she went out or if the brewer turned his back, maybe to point to a picture that hadn't been hanging there before, there'd be no noise, no mess, no shooting or stabbing, he'd just jump up and close his gloved fingers round the brewer's neck. No chance to yell for help or struggle and rip off buttons the police could find. It would be over in less than five minutes. Then take that bundle of notes out of his wallet; he'd be sure to be carrying it in the inside pocket of his coat. All the police would find would be the gloveprints on the brewer's neck, and not even Mie knew that Rik had bought those gloves for the day he would be presented with the diploma he hadn't been able to stay and get at the school in Vilvorde because of his mother's illness. He could easily burn the gloves or throw them into the river by the mill where the current would carry them away.

A poor devil sick with the worry of keeping four can get ideas like that. But it didn't go further than wearing the gloves. The brewer said there was nowhere but the kitchen he could offer Rik a chair to sit on. The rest of the house was empty. But he was leaving the things in the kitchen, the Mother Superior could have them for the orphanage. He had bought new furniture for his little kitchen in Brussels, modern and practical, he said. As it happened the maid was in the kitchen as well—what was there to do in the other, empty, rooms? She was making mayonnaise. That would take a while. Rik took off his gloves. They sat opposite each other, Rik and the brewer, the one just as surprised as the other. While they talked their eyes darted round trying to search out the reason why they came to be sitting there together, and they hardly listened to the polite remarks they exchanged. When Rik came outside he gave a sigh of relief. He told Mie that he had dropped over to see the brewer, after all, ach, why not, and nothing had happened. He bit his lip, he'd almost given himself away, but how could Mie ever imagine the crime he had almost planned, it was something beyond her simple honesty. That 'nothing had happened' of his made her laugh. Did he think the brewer would eat him up?

Nothing had gone wrong today and the beer made the day seem even rosier. Rik got another idea. He'd drink down another two glasses. Then with that inside him, half drunk and bold, he'd say straight out what he didn't dare say any more when he was sober, that he'd sold four rabbit-skins to Vereyckens yesterday and

65

they'd said no more of that for us, they weren't having any more children. Mie heard him, but she took no notice. Now she was going to tell him while he was sitting there like a lord drinking beer, though it was only Thursday. Did he know the postman was moving to another village and he's sold his plot of land and it was that piece down by the railway line where she used to live, and it was up for auction today, and did he know who'd bought it? I did.

'You did!' Rik shouted, so loud that they must have heard him at the end of the street. He stood up, he sat down again, everything was spinning in front of his eyes. There she was, the woman he'd been blaming all his misfortunes on, the woman who had made a man of him. A look or a gesture from her would rouse him, she would solace him and the next moment she could rouse him again. Contentment and longing in turn—there wasn't another like her. When he turned away from her he was lost, alone in a maze of temptation and folly. A fierce light flickered in her eyes. Another bottle? While they drank she combed his hair with her fingers. Then she was holding his head tight and she asked what was the matter with him all these weeks and the only answer he gave was a sob. She could have said that the feeling of not being wanted by her man will break the strongest woman, but she only said: 'What, are you crying?' That was all. It seemed as though they hadn't seen each other for a long, long time. She had to tell him how she had saved to give him this surprise and he confessed: 'You have saved so hard that I thought we were done for.' Their blood pounded, they were clinging to each other again. In their embrace they found the fulfilment of their being.

10

One baby after another and it was not all a bed of roses. 'Oh well, God bless us, we'll soon have another one,' Mie would say. It was nothing to do with lofty ideals; it was simple faith, joy in living and courage. A family that kept growing meant hard work, and there was never an end to the cares and worries. Today measles, next week mumps, then whooping cough. Rik came home one evening and found the eldest screaming, he'd sucked at the spout of the coffeepot and scalded his mouth with the boiling coffee, and that was the hardiest of the lot, never sick. But if a child doesn't get some illness or other then it goes looking for trouble.

There was always work to to do. Sometimes in the shop Mie had a few minutes to herself, but never in the kitchen, and when Rik came home after he'd done the rounds in four or five villages, he could toss his rake and shovel on his cart and go off to work for a couple of hours on the plot of land. Mie would send three or four of the children with him to get them out of the house for a while. If it had been left to him it would have been different. Once he told her so and she just said that he shouldn't make so many, and she turned round to face him with an expression of surprise that turned to indignation: So Mijnheer thinks he's got something to complain about. Did he have to carry them and nurse them and run after them? Who had the worst of the deal? Not him. They could keep coming along as far as she was concerned. She didn't mind how many there were, but he ought to be ashamed of himself if he was thinking all the time: I wish we didn't have them. Then Rik didn't know what to say, that simple uncomplicated way she looked at things couldn't be contradicted. Her strength kept him on the right path. Worry and work held his thoughts in check and gave him no chance to philander.

It would be after the seventh or eighth that Mie was up and about too soon; next day she was back in bed, sick as a dog. Rik was sure she was going to die. The church bells were tolling for the vet's widow. Only a month ago he had been trampled to death by a horse and now she had died from a miscarriage. That would have been her tenth child; it was better that it couldn't live, now there were only nine little orphans standing round her coffin. The bells hammered out their dirge and Rik felt like sealing the doors and windows with wadding and strips of cloth to shut out the sound of it. Only yesterday he'd seen everyone standing outside in Maria's village talking about the newest scandal. That morning Maria and old Bald-head had gone driving through the village, fancy, the cheek of it, the little hussy. And what a fine carriage too! The pair of them looking out, all smiles, ready to nod and wave. Rik walked through the house, sick with fear. In the kitchen the two smallest ones were howling for God knew what. He hauled them upstairs, undressed them and shoved them into bed with their shoes still on. He ran downstairs again, walked up and down wringing his hands, went down on his knees by the stove under the image of St Anthony on the mantelpiece. He thought of what his father had tried to say before he died, and that hammer, and the girls behind the mill and in Brussels, Maria, Alphonsine and the gloves. He heard the voices of his teachers and headmasters. One of them had said to him: 'My boy, you'll realize later what you've done.' He bowed under the weight of it all till his head was by the ashpan and he prayed silently.

Mie was lying asleep, breathing quietly. He slid into the bed beside her, holding his mother's rosary. They had never bothered much about praying, but, after a while, when he was counting how many beads he still had to do, he found Mie's hand in his. He pushed his arm gently under her neck, rested his throbbing head against her cheek, and they lay there, Mie Zaterdag and Rik, son of Toon, one-time servant to the Archbishop of Malines, saying their prayers on the same rosary. All of a sudden the door opened and the doctor said: 'Well, if that's how things are, it looks as if I'm not needed any more.' But he happened to come by and the lights were on everywhere. Ha'd called hullo in the shop and in the kitchen and then he'd thought Rik must have gone upstairs for a moment because it's just after eight. But seeing you in bed you might as well stay there, young fellow, and if you like I'll see if there's anything wrong with you, but don't forget to turn out the light downstairs after I've gone. Now he'd have a look at the patient. It didn't take long and he nodded and said she'd soon be right again, ready to take all the knocks she'll get. Only a few weeks back he'd had the same thing with Jan the basket-maker's wife, and he'd said when Jan was there, too, that a woman who got up too soon after a baby was taking a big risk and she deserved to have some sense knocked into her. And he couldn't help roaring with laughter when Jan, as serious as you like, said as soon as she's better he'd knock some sense into her. But all you have to do is keep warm and lie quiet. You're doing fine, I'll drop by again in the morning. Rik walked behind him in his bare feet to the door of the shop, then he came back and lay down with Mie, laughing, crying, praying. Joy and fear and passion and piety, that was the way it went, that was life. Nothing much ever happened, and time didn't wait for things to happen, never stopped, flowed on and on.

'Before we know it we're old, we've had our day,' said Zaterdag the road-mender. He felt all alone, the youngest son had got married and lived in a cottage of his own, the eldest son, who had married and stayed in the old house, had two children. Old Zaterdag knew what it was to lose a wife and be left with seven children. Mie had kept house and looked after her brothers and sisters but since she had gone it wasn't the same any more. He'd been born in a caravan that came by the village every year in the spring. His mother used to go round the houses collecting the iron spoons and forks and his father put a shiny coat of tin on them. One spring he'd stayed behind courting, did odd jobs on the farms; when his parents came back the next spring they found him married, settled down, and almost a father. He wasn't afraid of hard work. On the farms it was too monotonous and the pay was bad. To earn a bit more, and for a change as well, he turned to road-mending and he set new cobbles on the roads he had ridden over since he was born, and he would have been more than road-mender if it hadn't been for his wife dying. One day he had started digging round his cottage and laying foundations. In the village they said he was building stables, that he'd saved some money and he was going to deal in horses and ponies. His father had always had a couple of hacks for sale tethered to the wagon, or if he hadn't, then he would sell the horse between the shafts and stay in the one place until he could buy another. No one ever found out what he was going to build on the foundations. When his wife died they were level with the ground, and Zaterdag came back from the funeral, put on his work clothes, took his spade and shovelled earth over the stone and brick. No more building. Grief, they said, he'll start again, but the foundations stayed as they were, covered over with earth, except here and there where the stones showed through.

Now he couldn't stand up to that hard work any more, he had to stay sitting round at home, the same as being dead. His son was away all day at the factory, he felt a stranger with his son's wife and the children, he counted up his money. Then he packed his few things in a bundle and put the bundle down beside his pick. He went to visit Mie in that house that was far too fine for him, he felt even more of a stranger. He'd just come to see her, just to ask Mie whether his children had always had what they needed. Ach, of course, Father, but what's wrong? Nothing, nothing, but if he'd worked hard enough for them then he was satisfied. He was old and he didn't want them working for him. They could get along without him, the seven of them, so he was going away and he just called in to say good-bye.

No, they couldn't talk him out of it, he'd made up his mind, and they shouldn't think he was leaving in anger, it was only because he couldn't spend his days dong nothing but sit around. Sitting around waiting to die, that was something he couldn't do.

He had a little money saved up, with that he'd be able to look after himself. He knew an old men's home on the side of a canal, and he said, though it wasn't true, that he knew all the boatmen who passed by there, they were friends of his, and he could stay on board with any of them whenever he wanted to.

They could see he still had the wanderlust in him, that there was no holding him. Mie fetched a bottle of gin for him, and the drink made him talkative. Moving round on a boat from one place to the other, that was the life. If only his father and mother had let him do that when he was young. But then he'd met your mother here, so he'd stayed here, and that was a fine thing, too. It's good to be married and settle down together, but it shouldn't happen that one of you gets taken away. That's why he was glad to see you were better, Mie. Keep together, that's what he always said, and it was a good idea of yours to buy that bit of land. 'It was a sad blow,' he said, 'that we had to lose your mother.' When they buried her he'd stood at the grave and promised: Don't worry, I won't leave them in the lurch; I'll look after the children, and had he looked after them or not? But tomorrow morning, as soon as the sun was up, he'd be off, he'd get a berth on one of those boats he knew. And when he felt it coming on he'd find his way back, even if he was over the border in Holland; back he'd come, he'd come back here to die, and you bury me next to Mother.

'Of course we will,' the eldest said, 'but now you just go off to bed if you want to start so early tomorrow morning.' They didn't think he would, but when the eldest got up early the next morning to catch the first train to his work Zaterdag had been walking along the road for a good hour with his pick and his bundle over his shoulder. Off to the canals, oh yes, he'd go sailing round a bit, wouldn't he? All that bluff about knowing everyone on the barges!

But what he had said about staying together and finding a spot where you can take root, that was something Mie had been thinking about for quite some time, but an idea is somehow strengthened once it has been put into words. The eldest Zaterdag felt the same way. The first morning he thought to himself what was the sense of having to get up so early and lose so much time in the train when his wife's parents lived close to the factory, and they'd be only too glad to have a man in the house who could work in their plot of ground as well.

That was soon settled with his wife's parents and another arrangement was settled even more quickly with Mie. Her eldest had at last been allowed to take his first Communion two years later than he should have, and then not because he knew his catechism, he'd never manage to learn it, but only because the priest said, after trying to din it into his head for three years, that if they were going to wait till the boy learned anything then they'd be waiting a long, long time. Mie invited all the family to a celebration for the occasion, and the best present was from her eldest brother, Rosse, though he didn't know it. Next week, he said, we're moving nearer to Vilvorde and for all he cared the cottage could tumble over behind him. Without a moment's hesitation Mie answered across the table that she'd go and live there. She was serious about it, but everyone else laughed. They had invited Jan van Uffelen in from next door as a good neighbour. He looked over his shoemaker's glasses at Mie and said, with his face all creased because he found it as much a joke as the others did, that she had a bee in her bonnet. But in any case, serious or not, Rosse promised he would leave the door open for Mie. A promise easily given because if he wanted to lock the door he would have to find the key first and then, as likely as not, buy another lock. As far back as anyone could remember that door had never been locked.

11

Bee in her bonnet or not, what Mie did have with everything she started, and with Rik too, was that obstinate determination of her father. Stick together and there was nothing they couldn't do. To Rik's credit it must be said that in those decisive days he was just as crazy as Mie, or maybe just as shrewd. Everyone had always called him Rik Steenackers, even though he wasn't the brewer's son, but even the son of Toon, the servant of the Archbishop, could have felt he was far too good to doss like a tramp in a hut with his wife and eight children. But that wasn't what he felt at all. He said he was all for keeping the family together, that it was better if there was work for the children at home, that for years he'd had the idea of growing on his own land the fruit and vegetables that he went round hawking and then later he could let the boys do the hawking. And Mie said: 'You know, I'd rather use the money I've got to put into the shop to buy a cow and a few pigs and chickens. We'd eat better and cheaper, and I wouldn't have to be polite to people whether I wanted to or not, just to sell a tin of syrup.'

Of course, the whole village laughed and laughed. Once a Zaterdag always a Zaterdag; that sort would rather live in a tumbledown hut and be poor than in a good house with a shop to it. But how can that Rik be such a fool? They were sorry for him, watching him as he went back and forward to the village by the railway with his dog-cart seven times, the furniture piled up high behind him. The seventh trip Mie herself walked behind the dog-cart, straight and defiant as ever, the smallest one on her arm and, would you believe it now, the ninth is on the way. In the hut everything lay in a pile, even the best and the newest of what they possessed looked old and dirty in that hovel. It was like beginning all over again right from the start; she felt the jeers of the whole village like jabs in her back and Rik stood beside her not knowing what to do. A lump filled her throat. She chased the children outside, with the tears streaming down her face she got busy sorting out the mess. That first night the children slept one on top of the other in the tiny attic on bags filled with straw, Mie and Rik downstairs with the cobwebs hanging over them. As she lay down beside him a strange feeling of unworthiness and guilt swept over her, a feeling she had never had before, that Rik could have done better for himself and that she had dragged him down into these depths of poverty. Here, at the very spot where he had made her his choice and where he'd followed her back to, a tenderness stronger than herself pressed her close to him. A need in her to make him feel that with her beside him he could never be poor. A longing of the heart and of the body. In each other's arms, everything else forgotten.

So he got up the next morning tired but whistling merrily. Oh Lord above, the piercing ache of her happiness, but she called out laughing that he musn't go round whistling so early in the morning: 'Cross yourself first, you heathen!' Laughing with her, he shouted back: 'You too.' They stood facing each other bright-eyed, and he stroked his wrists as if he were rolling up his sleeves. Right? Yes. In the name of the Father and of the Son, they swung their arms crossing themselves.

What a lot in this life happens by sheer chance! For years Maria had never known where her husband and her brothers-in-law went with the wagons; they never mentioned the addresses where they had to load up or deliver at. But when the old bald-head had sat whispering across the table persuading her to run off with him, he had a villa here and he knew the owner of the castle there, and we'll go to Nice, she'd taken a good look at the work-book the brothers-in-law kept so she could decide on the best day. Old bald-head had always wanted her to leave on a Thursday and she'd never been able to get that idea out of his head. In the work-book, under Thursday, she saw that was the day brewer Steen-ackers was moving and that he was going to live in such and such a street, such and such a number. She wasn't going to run off with

74

him to Brussels and take the risk that their coach would have to move to the side of the road or maybe stop and wait to let their two wagons pass. So if he was set on leaving on Thursday, then he'd better not forget which way the wagons would go and he'd better make sure their coach wouldn't be within half an hour of them.

I can imagine what would happen if those two saw me. They'd think nothing of pulling me out of the coach in the middle of the town and flaying me alive with their horsewhips.

But when she looked in the work book she had, without realizing it, stamped the brewer's address indelibly in her memory, and now it came in handy. For, as a rule, those sorts of escapades with an old dodderer aren't very exciting for a hot-blooded country girl and so they don't last long. She was just one of a long list of predecessors for the old bald-head, but for her this was the first time. After a while he was placed under the care of the lawyers, then finally sent to an institution, there he'd stay, he didn't need to worry. But she could neither go back home nor back to the brothers-in-law. All she knew was the brewer's address.

Well, you know, he said, he had a good maid already. In fact she was dowdy and cross-eyed and a regular churchgoer whom a priest from his village, who was now a teacher here, had been so good as to find for him. Now, the brewer hadn't moved to Brussels to have a maid like that in his house, but just try and get rid of her and then explain to a narrow-minded village priest that as a good Catholic widower getting on in years you wanted a girl rather, let us say, more attractive.

So, no sooner had the brewer opened the door to Maria than he wanted to help her with true Christian charity, and she must come and stay here, he said, of course she must. She knew, didn't she, that he'd always tried to help others and he was always ready to do whatever he could for anyone from the same village. Maria would know Alphonsine who'd been the maid at their house—she had to go away, you remember. Well, she often comes to help with the cleaning and she does my washing and ironing. So you just stay here, my dear. Maria made herself useful by buying the vegetables and meat at the market instead of from the shops, and in this way the Lord rewarded a work of charity by an immediate saving on household expenses.

There was the second coincidence at that market. Rik had always talked about going into the early-morning market in Brussels where it was so easy to sell everything he could load on the cart and none of this hawking from door to door. If he had ever done that he would have been sure to meet Maria. She would have invited him round for a cup of coffee and at the first step of the marble staircase he would have thought of the hut by the railway track. Anything could have happened, God knows what she might have started in those first months of unleashed passion. But he sent his eldest, a rough-looking lad but a schemer, along the road and at the market as shrewd as he was dull at school. He sold more and quicker than Rik and with a bigger profit, and the joke of it was that the buyers always used to think they were getting the best of him. If he got a better price than Rik would expect he often used to say that his father would flog the life out of him for selling so cheap, so won't you buy this and that as well or I'd be too frightened to go home. In the city they think it's so easy to cheat the lads from the farms, but don't be so sure. The lads from the farms make out they're even more stupid than they look, they let the townsfolk have the pleasure of feeling clever but they get the pennies.

Driving back from the market Noo kept his eyes open for anything worth buying. Once he came home with a calf in the cart. He bought it for next to nothing and it was Mie's first cow. He'd never ride past if he saw a goat skin or a rabbit skin hanging up to dry. Every time he'd manage, by playing the simpleton, to buy it well below the usual price, and he'd sold it before he got back home. Maria recognized him first from the way he spoke and then from his face, and it was from him that the village came to hear that Maria was now the brewer's housekeeper.

That didn't cause any surprise in the village. 'Now she's house-keeper to brewer Steenackers,' they would say, and give an under-standing nod. The baker said, without a trace of a smile on his face, that a man as old as the brewer who'd gone to live in the city to pass his old age in comfort after all those years with his wife, well, of course, he needed more than anything else a really good housekeeper. When the young schoolmaster said it was unkind to speak like that he brushed the accusation aside with a wave of his hand. No, he wasn't unkind at all; on the contrary, he was Christian charity itself. Old men have to have someone to look after them properly, and let's face the truth, the children are asleep anyway, we married men like to show the stuff we're made of. Now the brewer, poor fellow, in all those years he'd never been a father, so let the man have another try, that's how we have to look at this business, dear parishioners and other sinners.

The brewer certainly got someone to look after him properly. We know how it happened. At first she was so attentive and he was more than grateful, then she was friendly as well as attentive and he was more and more responsive. He took to staying at home most of the time and he'd paw her at every chance, but not an inch further, oh no, not until he agreed to marry her. Married, the thought made him shiver, but even so.

Maria had fixed all that in less than three years, this time it wasn't just a coach but a gleaming new motor-car, and she drove off with the brewer, this time back to the village to see her mother and father. They were an old couple, both of them a little older than the brewer himself, they lived with their son, the postman. The car went past the railway line and Maria would have liked to see Rik but that cottage looked so poor that she felt it was beneath her, and the groom didn't want to stop anyway. What they didn't see was that Mie had bought three more plots of land and now she had to yell as hard as she could to make herself heard from one end of her property to the other. With the wind against her she just couldn't do it.

'That Maria,' they said in the village, 'whore that she is, what does she think she's playing at, coming back flaunting herself like that! It's only a couple of years back that she dragged her dead husband's family's name in the mud and now she turns up here again.' All along the street they were glared at, and her father and mother were so ashamed that they went out of the house as soon as she arrived. They walked through the village, the two of them, the mother leaning on her stick, the father a little more bent, his hands behind his back, a pathetic pair. They were poor but respectable, the brewer's wealth didn't tempt them and because he was so rich the disgrace was all the harder to bear. When the car drove off they made their way back home. They'd drunk a beer at the café and the proprietor had, out of pity for them, stood them both another glass, so they went home with their hearts a little lighter, and they repeated to each other that they were poor but still respectable.

Let the cars flash past the villa by the railway track, who cares? Now two of the boys were off every morning early with full carts to the market in Brussels. Some of the others were big enough to help Rik with digging and planting, and there was always another little one on the way. Mie said she wanted a proper house built before the next one arrived. Rik looked at her with a face that said: Build a house—that's easy; but have you got the money for it? He knew she could work miracles, and no one else could have saved like she had done from the meagre profits of a village shop and what he made from hawking vegetables, but still there were limits to what even Mie could do. But he was wrong, she had saved the money for the house too.

In the spring they started building. They'd uncovered the foundations old Zaterdag had put down, but these weren't nearly enough for what they wanted. They pushed a lean-to shed out of the way and began digging along two straight lines. In the evening when they were all at home the whole tribe of them studied the site of the new house. Each of the six of them made a mark on the ground with his boot and said up to here, but once they were busy digging they dug on past these six different opinions. Look, you only build once in a lifetime, you need space, and they dug three yards farther.

They were all Zaterdags, big and broad, sullen, obstinate, they'd never learnt any catechism, or poems, or vulgar fractions, they just went their own way, never saying much, but watching everything with their lazy dark eyes. They didn't need any help because they were always satisfied with what they could do themselves, and they could always make do with what they had. But one of them was a little different from the others, and they noticed this when he left school after his first communion and he was at home all the time. He used to read, well, there are all sorts of fools in the world. He read everything that came his way, through and through to the very last letter, then he stored it all in a big box in the attic. 'He's got a lot in his top storey, hasn't he?' they said, and they called him our Top. If he could slip away by himself he'd wander off God knows where and come back with a coil of wire, nails, a worn-out kettle, a rusted nut and bolt, anything at all that wasn't too big or too heavy to pick up. This same Top went and had a look at the trenches for the foundations, he saw that there was still some ground to spare and he dug on, without saying a word, right to the edge of the road.

Soon they had the foundations ready for two long side walls. Rik had made a rough sort of drawing, but when they were going to start on the inside walls one wanted the kitchen as big again as it was in Rik's plan and the others wanted it bigger still. They'd lived cramped up for so long that they dreamed of a wide and spacious house and big stalls and barns and sheds. They had a mason build the walls, but whenever he wasn't there they did the work themselves, and their work was just as good as the mason's 'Hey, where's that window going to be?' they called out. It was a long, low building with doors up to the eaves. Under the roof they made one bedroom after the other, and the kitchen was an

79

immense room with four windows set far apart. They made with floorboards and trestles a table of dimensons in keeping with the length and breath of the kitchen, a table big enough for a village festival. At the top end Mie sat giving orders, at the other end sat Rik, tall and thin, the father. Through the windows they could see their property, a wide, flat expanse, they looked at it, proud. If Mie had to put in words what she had achieved all she could say was that now they kept the goats in the house where she'd been born.

12

Rik didn't think of that hammer any more and now that they had so much more space all that stolid, self-willed troop could go their own way, each of them could do as he wanted. The first to do as he wanted was Top. He took his boxes of odds and ends and tools, shut himself in one of the stalls, and from lengths of rusty wire he made two frames for photographs. He patiently rubbed them with sandpaper until they shone, and then he brought them inside and put them on the mantelpiece. But they didn't have photographs to put in these frames and the other eight stood round laughing at him. He saw that his mother, with the smallest on her lap, was sitting on the chair with her feet barely touching the floor, and he made a footstool for her. On each side he cut out the shape of a heart. Rik broke the handle of a shovel, and Top made a new one. He mended the pots and pans he'd gathered, and they were as good as new. After Top it was the eldest girl. With her it was an obsession for flowers and sand in the house, for curtains and cleanliness. She pounced on every piece of mud or dirt and she knitted woollen socks that were always hanging by the door so that her brothers didn't need to walk inside with their dirty clogs. The two that went every day to Brussels were away most of the time. They left early, they were back late; their work was done along the road, and at the end of their long day they sat slumped in their chairs smoking and saying nothing. The others who were old enough to work put their roots down into the soil. If they spoke it was about their work, and when they sat not saying anything they were thinking about their work, and if they got up to go over to the window it was to look out with an anxious eye at the weather.

In the winter Top cut a stamp out of wood: Henri van Oepstal, Market Gardener, and the name of the village beneath. He filled the edges of a newspaper with the imprint of the stamp and the others stood behind him, a stupid grin on their faces. Anything to do with writing embarrassed them. To tease him they asked what in God's name was the use of a thing like that, and then, for the first time, they found out what a no-good lot that Top really was, a pig-headed madman. If they were too stupid, he said, to know what a stamp was for that wasn't his fault. Oho, they growled, what's wrong with you now? And the madman got annoyed.

There was hardly ever any quarrelling and if there was neither Rik nor Mie interfered. They were all easy-going, big and slow, they wouldn't hurt a fly if they were left alone. Once the curate tried to get them to join the church club, it was good fun and respectable, but they said they had enough fun without joining anything. It was to keep young boys out of mischief, he said, but they said they didn't get into mischief. But it would be a good example for others if they came along, and they said no, and that was all. Their motto was: Leave me alone, and if they got angry they'd say: I'll smash your skull in, nothing less, but they never lifted a finger or maybe they'd just stick their hands in their trouser pockets.

But this time Rik had a strange feeling of fear. As if he had to be quick to stop a calamity he said at once, emphatically, that his father had always had a stamp like that too, it's something that often comes in handy. They looked at him, amazed, and they didn't understand what he was bothering himself about. How could they know that for no reason at all he had suddenly thought of that hammer, and that Toon was standing there in front of him saying those terrible words again?

That didn't finish the quarrel. Top bought an invoice book and twenty-five sheets of letter-paper and envelopes. He stamped them all with his wooden stamp, and then the jeering was in earnest. In all their life they'd never seen such a fool, now he's going to write out bills and write letters. The two who went to Brussels every day said if you sell something you've got to see you get the money for it, but if you can't remember how much this one and that one owes you then you better not try and do business. Top got up out of his chair, his face was white. For the second time Rik shouted that that was enough now, and none of them could make out what was wrong with Father today.

Top was right. Writing-paper is useful. At New Year they got a postcard from Alphonsine Verberckt-Vermeulen, didn't that have to be answered? Isn't it handy to be able to write?

There was nothing on the postcard but a printed 'Bonne Année' and an address, but the intention was all too clear. Alphonsine wanted to get in touch with them. She was concièrge in the big block of flats where the brewer and Madame Maria lived on the second floor, and the brewer had done that for her. He was a director of the company that owned the building because he had such a lot of shares in it, and when he married Maria so unexpectedly Alphonsine had a feeling of power over him, and towards her he had a feeling of having done something wrong and been caught in the act. She gave him to understand, without wasting words, that she would like to be concièrge here and he'd seen she wasn't joking. A woman's tongue is long and dangerous, and he had to protect his reputation of being an exemplary Christian. Alphonsine wanted to be able to say to the brewer that she had visited the village because she felt that would worry him. He would be kinder than ever and give her odd little presents so that she would tell them all there how good he was. She wanted to be able to say to Maria: 'I've been to see Rik Steenackers,' because she knew how Maria had run after him, too. But Rik would be glad enough if he could say: 'I've never set eyes on that little stupid red-head again.' That went for her too. But if she could use him, what did it matter? Then, one day, a couple of months later, in the spring, she stood, unannounced, at the door, the only right she had to be there was that Top had answered her card. It was a Sunday afternoon. Behind her was an insignificant man with creaking brown shoes and an absurd, pointed moustache, but behind him a really fine-looking young miss.

'And this is my daughter Elvire.'

Rik felt as if a blow had numbed him. It was a shock to re-member again why Alphonsine had left the village. He didn't know what it was he mumbled when Alphonsine introduced her, but the girl, after hesitating for a second or so, called him Rik. Had she forgotten his name or was she just confused? In any case it was clear to him that she had wanted to say: 'Father.' He toyed fleetingly with the idea that it couldn't be possible. He laughed too loud and too heartily, he didn't know that Alphonsine had such a big daughter. If someone had calmly explained exactly how old she was to the month everything would have been cleared up in a couple of ghastly minutes, but Alphonsine wasn't going to start off this renewed friendship with the admission that her daughter was born long before she was married to this man, the man didn't like to admit it either, and there was an embarrassed silence. The girl nodded at him with a smile that sent a stab of fear through his heart. He wondered how he could send his sons out of the room, but when he looked at them they were feasting their eyes shame-lessly on the two city women. Rik took the man for a walk down to the fields. He had a habit of sniffling all the time as if he were smelling the hair-oil on that pointed moustache. When he spoke it was to explain that he hadn't said anything just now because Alphonsine had had the child before they were married. Rik didn't answer. 'A country girl,' the man said, 'an orphan, what could she know about life? Some dirty rotter promises her everything and so of course she thinks he'll see her through when it's gone too far.' Rik said nothing; at least the silly fool doesn't know the truth, he thought to himself, or he wouldn't talk like that. They walked on, both of them silent. To start him talking again Rik said that it wasn't safe in the city for young girls either, but the man wasn't so sure, in the city they soon learnt a thing or two. Or did he know the truth?

Rik had suggested a walk outside because he couldn't stand it any longer with the women in that room. But the girl looked all too knowing; he was frightened she might blurt out something.

Alphonsine was still the same as she was years ago, she'd still be up to the same tricks in Brussels, those capers in the dark under the stairways just like I'd be doing of it weren't for Mie. Her eyes asked him if he still remembered. As he looked back from the road at his long rambling house in the distance beyond the trees he shivered at the thought of what might be happening there. A chance word, a smile can start off a young love affair. He stepped out, hurrying back to the house. The past had come back to take its revenge.

All of a sudden Elvire was right behind him. She had gone out with his eldest girl Lisa, but Lisa wasn't very talkative and Elvire was soon bored. She squeezed in between them, taking her father and Rik both by the arm, leaving Lisa to follow behind. 'Here's the two papa's,' she said, and pressed their arms. To get away from her Rik said to the man that he hadn't seen his strawberry beds, and turned round to cross over the fields. But Elvire was coming too, she'd just love to pick strawberries. She presented the first strawberry to the man, the second she put into Rik's mouth. Rik's embarrassment only encouraged her. She tapped his cheek. 'Nice and juicy, aren't they, Papa?' The man shrugged: 'A little witch, that's what she is.'

Something happened inside Rik. This playfulness stirred up other feelings than fear. He blushed and clenched his teeth. He was still young, by God! Once he'd grabbed her mother and so watch your step, young lady. Daughter or not . . ., daughter or not, if one of his sons fell in love with her he'd be jealous, he knew it. With a breath of relief he thought what a gruff, slow lot they were, those sons and daughters of his, none of them had his wild streak. But that feeling of relief didn't last long.

He didn't know what he should do. The man bored him, talking nothing but news from the city that didn't interest him and a hundred times he said that as soon as he got back to Brussels this evening he'd know which rider had won the Paris-Roubais cycle race. In the Place du Nord he'd be able to buy a special edition of *Le Soir*.

Rik was thinking he ought to stay with the women, near Alphonsine to stop her babbling anything about him, and near Elvire to see that she didn't start playing the fool with any of the boys. But he would rather keep away from them; they were a danger he didn't want to face.

It was a little difficult for Elvire, too. Instinctively she kept apart from her mother. She had no success with Rik, it was impossible to keep up a conversation with Lisa, so she finished up with the boys. They stuck their hands in their trouser-pockets and looked at her as if she were some strange animal. They seemed to feel an urge to seem more stupid and more crude than they were, as if, by doing that, they would be able to relish the difference between her and themselves, and to make that china-doll genteelness of hers even more genteel. From their awkwardness and their coarse guffaws Rik knew that she'd cast a spell on them, and one of them, for no reason at all, said loudly and stupidly that by Christ it will bloody well thunder tonight! That was the first oath uttered in this new house. Mie stepped over to him and boxed his ears. Rik hadn't even heard him. He was watching Top, who had sat down next to Elvire.

Till then Top had never given a thought to a girl, but that didn't mean he wasn't embarrassed at all the boorishness that the princess had to put up with. Here was a wonderful opportunity for one of his brothers, if only they weren't all so thick-headed. If only one of them had been smart enough to attract her attention, if only there was a hope that she might marry one of them. What wouldn't he make for her, what wonderful long conversations he would have with her, because she had, she said, finished *l'école moyenne*. It would have been nearer the truth if she said she'd done the first couple of months. Top did his best to soften the humiliation she must be feeling. To impress her he said that they had two hectares of ground, they went to market every day with two big wagons and they had such a lot of milk, butter, eggs, meat, and all that. And that one, the eldest, he's a real businessman.

While he sat there next to her his brothers thought he was staking his claim, Rik shuddered and Elvire was thinking there was at least one of them you could talk to, Top, and his father too, for she'd heard from her mother that, in his day, the father had had his fling, but being married had made him strait-laced. She was going to find out just how strait-laced and respectable he really was, and as they were leaving she embraced Mie and Lisa the way they did in the city, and then, unexpectedly, she kissed Rik as well. She did it without laughing, without making fun of him. Then he knew that she was his daughter and that she knew he was her father. But why had she played up to his sons? Suddenly it dawned on him that her show of affection was too overdone to be genuine, it was hate. The hate she felt for the father she had never had, the father who had left her mother in the lurch. She would get her own back through one of his sons, and Top would be her victim. She would make him admit his shame and his guilt in front of his wife and his eleven children. Once, long ago, he had confessed to Mie how selfish and worthless he'd been, but now, after so many blameless years, to have to proclaim that this girl was his daughter, no, no, anything rather than that. But that was just exactly what this little she-devil wanted to make him do. Hate, the word wasn't strong enough. Two hectares of land, a house as big as a village hall, a thriving business, a wonderful wife, but the sins of the past had to be paid for; there was no escape from a father's curse.

13

Dear Miss. We received your letter and Noo will deliver the potatoes you order next Thursday, and besides we hope that you have got over your cold which is not serious at this time of the year and goes away very quick. I read your letter to Mother and she said you can come to visit us as much as you want to, and Noo said you can even come on the wagon but a joke. The oftener the better, and greetings to you and all your family from all of us, Yours, Isidoor van Oepstal.

While Top was wondering what else could he say to put Noo in her good books Rik walked in. He saw the enveloppe, already stamped and adressed. He read what Top had written, grabbed the letter, crumpled it up and threw it in the stove. There was an icy silence, Top didn't move, he was pale and tense. 'It looks as if you've gone crazy,' Top said. Rik sat down so his son wouldn't see how his legs were trembling, and Rop took another envelope, stamped the back of it with his wooden stamp, wrote the address on the front, then he took another sheet of writing paper, carefully stamped it and began: Dear Miss, We received your letter, and Noo will deliver the potatoes you ordered...Rik stood up. Top stood up too. Rik stretched out his hand to grab the sheet of paper, Top caught hold of his father's wrist. Rik made a swing with the other hand and Top caught his arm. Pushing against each other with all their strength, their arms twisted up to the beams of the ceiling and then down again. Their faces were red and set. Luckily Mie rushed in, she shoved Rik aside and smacked Top hard on the cheek. She could do that, none of them would ever question for a moment anything she did. Top sat down again, the pen shook in his hand but he wrote:...next Thursday, and besides we hope... Rik leapt out of his chair like a madman, but Mie was too quick for him. She thought so, she yelled, he'd started it, the boy would never go quarrelling. 'Don't you dare lay a hand on him,' Mie said, 'leave him be!'

Mie Zaterdag never bothered with theories about how to bring up children. She didn't hesitate, the father was in the wrong, the son was in the right. Her authority, acknowledged, established, undisputed, was enough, it had always been like that and it had always worked out well. She had turned a worthless, drunken, good-for-nothing into a respectable husband and father; she had saved up the money for the land and the house; she had brought up a sturdy, hard-working family. That's how it had been from the start and that's how it would be as long as she was there.

But that didn't solve anything for Rik. He realized he could never tell Mie why he wouldn't stand for a friendship or anything else between Elvire and Top, and so he cut himself off from the only help that might stave off the catastrophe. He saw the finger of God pointing at him. The hour of reckoning is come, the Lord was saying, let the curse that Toon spoke be fulfilled.

Everything was against Rik. Top would have given in for the sake of peace if he had any ideas about running after the girl, but he didn't have any such ideas, so they could just explain to him what was wrong with hoping that one of his brothers would marry such a beautiful, educated girl. Top was all too ready to say the others were stupid. It emphasized the difference between them and himself. If his father was too stupid to see that he wasn't in love with anyone and that he would never get married then there wasn't much he could do about it. But he wanted to know why he shouldn't write a letter to say Noo would bring the potatoes. So he finished writing the letter, he folded it, licked and sealed the envelope and, provocative and sure of himself, he walked past Rik in his chair to go out to post it.

In that moment the first strands of a drama were woven together. It might happen the next day or not for ten years, but happen it must. The explosion might come on one of those evenings when Top would ask the two who went to Brussels why they hadn't fetched Elvire back with them. Each time Rik caught his breath, but the two who went to the market used to answer that

Top could go and fetch his own lady-love. One day they said this, and added: 'We've found ours.'

'What's this?' Mie asked.

'We're going to get hitched,' they said.

It was as simple as that. They hadn't even had to put themselves to any trouble. Halfway to Brussels there was a busy inn they used as a sort of depot. Whoever wanted to sell them something or buy something from them knew where to go. Skins, chickens, old iron would be left there for them and the next day the sellers would come for the money that Noo and his brother left for what they took. At that inn there were three daughters. They chose the two prettiest with the same eye for a bargain as they did business with. But Noo miscalculated a little. He'd planned to go and live with his wife's parents. Her father was all for it, there was land at the back of the inn Noo could do something with and what with raising chickens there was a lot of money to be made. But Mie soon let him know that he could get that idea out of his head. She'd worked all her life so she could have her family near her and that's how it was going to be. He'd have to bring his wife to live here and he could raise chickens here as well. Down at the end of their holding there was still ground for sale, they could buy a plot and they could build a house on it that they could share to begin with. But it hadn't gone that far yet. First she wanted to see what they were like, these girls.

When they came they were scarcely inside the door before Mie had them sitting down to eat and she watched them. A good housewife can sum a woman up from watching her eat. The two girls were not only hungry, but in a busy inn they were used to eating quickly and having to get up and down in the middle of a meal. So they ate quickly enough to satisfie Mie, and when they had finished one of them, from sheer habit, stacked the dishes and the other said she would help with the washing up, oh, it wouldn't take long to get through that pile. That was enough to win Mie over in spite of their stylish dresses. She walked with them down to where the double cottage would be put up, and once they were settled in they wouldn't have any bother from her because she knew only too well that a woman must be mistress in her own house.

And she wanted to say something else too. On the seventh of August they'd been married twenty-five years, Rik and her, they hadn't celebrated it but now, if you two made it a double marriage, they could celebrate everything at once together, a real feast.

That was for six months ahead, by then a lot of water would have flowed under the bridge, not there in the village but in Brussels. The old brewer who had gone to Brussels, with all that fortune they said he had, saw Elvire for the first time after Alphonsine was well and truly installed as concièrge in the block of flats where he lived. His first thought was that his Alphonsine might have let him have a look at her daughter sooner. Alphonsine had her reason for this oversight. She knew, and it was her own fault, that she needn't expect anything from her daughter if Elvire ever got to be Madame Steenackers. So she counted on a scheme with no more scruples to it than a marriage between the seventy-year-old brewer and the twenty-five-year-old Elvire whatever-her name ought-to-be. Her plan was to make life with her unbearable for her husband so that she could get divorced and once again be the Steenackers' maid, this time with far better prospects.

But Maria was there first. That was because her husband was too patient with her, but then he'd been fool enough to marry her against everyone's advice and against the family's wishes. If he left her he would be giving too many others the chance to say I told you so, and besides what would he do if he did leave her; he had no where else to go. Instead he stayed and swung his fist, and whenever he'd filled himself with liquor, and that was fairly often, he'd start throwing crockery. More than once Elvire ran away with cuts on her face on her arm. That was a proof of what she had to suffer at home, and there is always much more sympathy for a young girl who can show an injury, especially a bleeding cut.

Oh yes, a caller who knocked and asked the number of M. Sieromski's flat or M. Steenackers' flat found himself talking to an attractive, smiling, friendly concièrge, and he would think: That must be a happy family. As long as you don't know what is going on. Broken plates and cups are easily swept up.

But Elvire had her problems too. After she had run away from home a few times she didn't know where she could go next. She was only young once, she said, so she'd have her fling, and in Brussels there was no lack of opportunity for that. As for marriage, she had seen too much at home not to shudder at the thought of it. What with having her fling she was soon over twenty-five, and then it is about time. At that age a girl starts thinking again, and a good-looking sturdy village lad of the van Oepstal sort, who blushed when he spoke to you and who had money as well, isn't to be sneezed at. Now she had another cut on her arm she had a good reason to run away again, and she ran away to the address on the letter headed: Henri van Oepstal, Market Gardener.

If it is God's will to punish the punishment will come. By a combination of circumstances, all as rare as miracles, Rik happened to be alone in the house. She burst in, in her usual manner, and she fell around his neck sobbing, dabbing her handkerchief at her eyes and then at the bleeding scratch on her arm. When Rik heard that she had run away from home he declared dramatically that she could get out of his house, she'd go back to her mother this evening, whether she wanted to or not, and a lot more in the same strain. That was his undoing. She clung to him, she kissed him as if she were a little girl and not a grown-up woman. Calm pleading wouldn't help, she knew; she would get her way by wailing and screaming and showing the cut on her arm. It was a hell that she had to live in back in Brussels. At least six times her father had threatened her with a revolver. Her mother had tried to sell her, her father had made suggestions even when she was still too young to understand what he meant. The room was silent and the setting sun slowly sunk behind one of the windows. The tale of the hell she had suffered went on and on, softly now. She was whispering. It was the things he said and what he wanted me to do, and he isn't my father either; you know that, don't you? It was sudden, bewildering, as a dangerous temptation always is. His hand had been resting with fatherly compassion on her shoulder when she showed him the bruise just below the top of her dress, that must have been the man's answer to her refusal, and the hand he had laid tenderly on her shoulder began to slip lower in a tremor of lust. As weak as that Rik was without Mie beside him. Next month we'll celebrate our twenty-fifth anniversary.

Rik stood up, wakened from a dream. In that case you can't go back home. He spoke in a brisk, matter-of-fact tone, as if nothing had happened. The calm reflection came later. Up till then he was the only one who had resisted Elvire's charms, and for a reason no one knew, a reason he had to keep secret. In a moment of weakness that wall of hostility was broken down and he himself asked her to stay. She had been able, in less than half an hour, to hypnotize him completely. With the tricks she knew she could do the same with any of the boys, or every one of them, now that she was there all the time. The catastrophe had to happen, he knew it, and he himself, who would have fought till he dropped to stop it, was bringing it closer. By inexplicable coincidence, but so surely, so relentlessly, did the avenging hand come nearer and nearer that sometimes he resigned himself to his doom: he shut his eyes, he held his breath and waited like a condemned wretch for the executioner's axe to fall. Sometimes, as he worked for hours on end bent over the vegetable plots and thought and thought until he couldn't tell a lettuce from a rose, he would remember his father who hadn't been able to finish saying what he wanted to say as he lay dying. If it was that curse you wanted to take back, Father, then the Lord will make allowance for it. That was his only hope, all too vague and all too unreasonable, for he saw he was trapped.

14

For the treble-wedding-feat Top made two immense trestle tables, you couldn't squeeze in or out, there was such a crowd. They were a strong breed, all of them. When the van Oepstals stood up straight you'd want to tell them to watch out or they'd bump their heads on the ceiling. and with the in-laws it was about the same. After the soup the bride's father hung his starched cuffs on a nail in the beam right above his chair. Elvire sighed that all they needed was a piano. Then she could have played something. At that Noo said they'd wanted to wait until the coffee, but if they wanted music...Top, you go and get it. Top went and got the gramophone with ten records, the silver-wedding present from the eleven of them. It was a shining cabinet with a big loudspeaker on top. Rik bent his head and rubbed at his eyes, Mie said: 'God knows how much that must have cost!' The gramophone had a stateliness to it that gave the room an atmosphere of solemnity. They talked, repeating the wise and time-honoured proverbs, of life's trials and triumphs, of marriage, love, birth, death, happiness, misfortune, honesty, work. When Mie spoke, but she didn't speak much, they all listened. Her authority was acknowledged tacitly, unquestioningly, and she sat with her face towards the fresh red brick of the new house and with her back to the railway line and the trains rushing past in futile haste. There's still space over there for another twenty houses and anyone ready to work a bit could make a living, but if they worked the way they'd learnt from her they'd prosper. And they'd be independent, there's nothing better than that.

When all the ten records had been played and the wine made them sing as well, they wanted amusement of their own making. The innkeeper started it off with a song, tararaboomboom and then they began calling for Mie and Rik to sing 'The Three Drummers', the two of them could harmonize so well together. There was no getting out of it and for the duet the fair lady had to be a little higher because in the song she was sitting at a window. It was Rik who stared limp and openmouthed at Mie as she climbed the steep stairway to the attic trapdoor, the others had seen it already, Mie was expecting her twelfth. The eleventh was already a lusty young fellow of seven. What a woman she was! She'd make your mouth water, the inn-keeper was thinking. Maybe it was the wine, but it was from the remorse and fears of the last two months as well, Rik was suddenly filled with a crazy happiness. As he was singing: O lady fair, he reached out his arms to her, awkwardly, and for all that the more sincerely, there was a quiver in his voice, every few seconds he gulped. He gave her his hand to hold as she came down the stairs, put on another record, Top, Father and Mother are going to dance. More in love than the two newly-wed couples he twirled around with her and in the noise of the gramophone no one heard him whisper in her ear: 'So there's another one on the way,' and she answered him: 'Hadn't you noticed? That's my present for you, and don't squeeze my arm so hard.'

In the evenings Rik sat dreaming that it would be a girl, the comfort of my old age. I'll be old and I won't be able any more to get out of my chair. She'll fill my pipe and warm a stone for my cold feet. She would say: 'Father, I'll never get married, I'll stay with you.' But the living symbol of his wickedness was there in the house, the sight of Elvire seared and purified his innermost thoughts. He began to dream of a son who would grow up and enter the priesthood. That was what his father, Toon, had dreamed for him and he'd ruined it all with the evil life he'd led. But perhaps these years with Mie would earn him God's forgiveness and if he could give his twelfth child to the Church, if that blessing was granted him, it would be for him a sign that he had found favour in the eyes of God. His thoughts were more and more devout and he shut his eyes to the stealthy glance of that trollop from Brussels who didn't have the remotest intention of starting anything with him though he was sure she did. He had convinced himself that she followed him round, that she wanted to have one more proof of his badness, and after that she'd play her tricks with Top. And if he interfered she would only pretend that she didn't know he was her father. He knew how touchingly she could pose as the young girl tragically wronged, and she would do it again. 'You're my father and you know you are,' she would shout and sob in front of Mie and all his children, 'and still you wanted to put your filthy hands on me. That day I came here you took advantage of me when I was so upset, and after that too, there and there you tried it again.' With her lies she would destroy all that he built in those twenty-five years with Mie. Mie would kick him out of her bed, the children would spit as they walked past him. He wouldn't be able to bear it and he'd leave, he'd wander off and go round from door to door with a box of shoelaces and maybe he'd have a sore on his hip that wouldn't heal.

These sickly fantasies were an escape from the storm that was slowly gathering and he waited for the twelfth child to be born so he could offer it to God as a bribe. Once Mie said that they'd had eleven and there wasn't a Judas among them but if it had to happen it would be the twelfth. But Rik knew his Judas had been born a long while ago, there he was all the time with Elvire.

Top wasn't sure if she would get used to the way they lived here. If there had been fifty in that family, all able to do a hard day's work, there wouldn't have been one too many, but this young lady didn't find anything to do here. He thought of letting her do their correspondence, but if they wanted something to write she would have to go to Brussels and post a letter and then come back to answer it. Next Top started talking how necessary it was to have an accounts book for a business as big as this, and now with these two new households, he said, it was more involved than ever. But Mie just laughed at him. Don't worry, she didn't miss anything.

Meanwhile Elvire knitted things or made curtains, and besides that she could help Top with his French. He'd bought himself a book on photography called *Manuel du Photographe* and if he was only able to understand all those difficult words he'd make a camera in no time. Elvire helped him. Every evening they sat next to each other while Top slowly deciphered the text. At school he hadn't learnt much more than *mère*, *père* and *tartine*. He wrote the meanings of the words he didn't understand in the margin, and it was a torture for the father to see that she leaned too close to his arms as she bent over the book and that her curls bounced up and down too close to his cheek.

Once Mie felt a little concerned herself at all this, but she didn't brood over it for days on end, she simply asked Top how things stood. But, Mother, he hadn't any ideas like that, he never even thought about girls, and if that's how it was Mie knew there was nothing to worry about. She had taken that girl in because one mouth more or less didn't make any difference, and as an act of kindness, out of pity for her. But she wasn't the sort of girl Mie wanted as wife for any of her sons. Top didn't say that he still had hopes for one of his brothers—or would they all be too stupid to see the advantages of having a wife who was cultured and well-educated?

But Rik was racked with fear and worry, and he had to keep silent so he wouldn't provoke Elvire. All he could do was go to Mass every morning and try to soften God's wrath. His piety was the final proof of his repentance, he was an example for all the village. A respected member of the community, he strolled from his house to the church, from the church to his house, and no priest would ever pass him in the square without stopping to chat with him. Wasn't such a father a living sermon? Where was there a finer example of hard work and thrift than van Oepstal, the market gardener? In all the villages round about everyone knew what a wastrel he was in his young days. The girl he married didn't have a penny but she was a good, respectable girl and she put him on the right path again. What a marvellous family! Didn't it prove that true Christians who did their duty and raised a family to the glory of God were rewarded here on earth too? They were blessed with happiness and even with a fullness of wordly goods in this life. They're well off, every bit as well off as the miller; we couldn't do better than make him a member of our church council now that the miller's lying at death's door.

For Rik this offer was the first sign of God's forgiveness. God had heard his prayers. God was saying: 'Be my faithful servant and I will guide you and protect you.' And so he'd just watched, not saying a word when the two of them sat together reading that French book, after all nothing could happen in the kitchen under the eyes of the rest of the family, but, now they'd started sneaking off into Top's workroom, Rik would have something to say.

Top had never let anyone else into his workroom; he always kept the door locked. He said that she had to be in there with him to translate the French instructions if he wasn't sure of something or other when he was measuring the pieces of wood. Elvire had never been able to make him out. He always came and sat with her and talked with her, and when she let him see she was willing he didn't seem to notice. If they were alone and her hand happened to be on a saw or a plane that he had to use he even showed how well-mannered he was by saying Excuse me, instead of clamping his hand on hers. A bit of playing around, she reasoned, and it will all work out. She could never have guessed how far away his thoughts were from playing around. But Rik wandered up and down past the door tortured with uncertainty and fear. He remembered her mother, who was only too willing to be grabbed and cuddled. If it was quiet inside the workroom he imagined to himself scenes of incest. If she giggled Rik could see Top grabbing her, and then her pretence of resistance to encourage him all the more. Once he rushed at the door but it wasn't locked, and he realized, all confused, that his intrusion was far too hasty, if they wanted to get up to mischief they would make sure first that they couldn't be disturbed. They looked at him astonished. Her face was red as a tomato. But that could be from the fright she got when he burst in on them. Anyway they were at least six feet apart.

Once he asked Mie if she wasn't worried about all that sawing and hammering in the workroom. Isn't the man just plain stupid! Why, a mother who had to stay in bed for years on end upstairs would know more about her children than a father who ran around spying on them like a detective. She would be suspicious of a girl who walked past the house every now and then and never came inside, but she wasn't worried about one who was in her house all day. She knew her children. Even if they said nothing they told her everything with a silence that her instinct understood. 'No,' Mie said, 'there's nothing to worry about,' and Rik answered: 'Yes, there is.' That stung her. She had never said anything so cruel to him as she did then. My children aren't like you. She pointed to the railway line and asked him if he had forgotten.

For days afterwards those words burned inside him like acid. He knew if it came to the point the children were hers, if she had to choose between him and them she would take their side, and he knew she would be doing right. It was only because of her that they were his children and he himself wasn't worthy of them. She meant everything to him but this one time there was a gulf between them. She didn't know all the facts and so he couldn't tell her the truth. For twenty-five years she had managed everything and solved every single problem, but this one, that could topple all that she had built up, he had to contend with himself. O God, give Rik strength and courage, save the good name of our church councillor—what, for heaven's sake, if she had a child by her own half-brother?

Just when he made up his mind to do something, there the camera was ready, a solid and carefully finished piece of work, every bit homemade, standing on three sturdy legs. It still needed a glass plate, but that would have to be bought in Brussels, in a day or two he'd have it. Elvire had to pose in the doorway; Top aimed the lens at her and then the others had to bend under the black cloth. The first two somehow stopped themselves laughing, but the third one swore loudly as soon as he was under the cloth, Top, you great fool, didn't he know he'd put the glass plate in upside down, she's standing on her head.

They all guffawed together and howled Top down when he told them they didn't understand anything. Gusts of laughter in chorus, and that didn't happen so often at van Oepstal's, the hilarity lightened Rik's heart. He was gentle and generous and defended the two he feared. After all, that thing there proved, didn't it, that they had been working in the workroom and not playing the fool. Now then, listen, the lot of you, Rik shouted jovially, Top's right and the rest of you don't know anything. The glass plate was just as it should be, and he bent under the cloth. Her gay printed dress. That slender waist. Those young breasts. And that laugh of hers. If only I could destroy you just by looking at you like this, you wicked tempting vixen.

'Give it to me then!' Top said. He grabbed the camera, legs and cloth and all, he shoved it under his arm and stormed into the workroom. Fortunately Elvire rushed after him while the others went back inside, for Top had his heavy wooden hammer in his hand ready to smash it to bits. She reached up and gripped the hammer and held on to it until his arm was limp. The hammer came down slowly and hung loosely by his knee. He was standing with his back to the work-bench, staring fixedly at the thin strip of light at the bottom of the door. Two big, slowly gathering tears started to run down his cheeks. She went and shut the door. The others would hear a key in the lock but she could turn the wooden crossbar without a sound. Then she jumped up on the bench behind him. Her hand stroked his hard bristly hair and he didn't move. Her other hand slid under his unshaven chin and he let her do that because it made him feel so soothed and rested. Her chin rubbed along his shoulder and turned slowly up to his cheek. The two hands and the two arms closed tight around him and her head pressed against his and neither of them saw that Rik had pushed open the door an inch or so, as far as it would go against the crossbar. But they did see him pushing the bar up with two fingers. He leapt inside, pulled Elvire by the arm across the bench, and, as Top still had that big wooden hammer in his hand, though he'd probably thought better of smashing the camera, the prediction Toon had made that day so long ago was fulfilled. The blow fell above the forehead just where the hair begins. While Top was swinging the hammer down—it lasted only a second—Rik saw to his surprise that it wasn't ending with his disgrace but with his death, he saw that he still had time to make a clear and reasoned choice between the two and gratefully he choose death. He fell backwards with his arms spread out.

If Toon was set on having his way, then it had to be, Rik would be struck down. But not the mother. If Toon had wanted that, too, may he be damned a thousand times over! While they were carrying Rik into the house Mie doubled up, writhing, her mouth open with blood-chilling shrieks from the pain that tore her apart inside. The first one to shake off the bewilderment that paralysed them rushed to the door, turned round, pointed at Top, and told the others to see he stayed where he was, he was going to kill him when he got back. Wait here. I'll fetch the doctor.

The doctor said he'd take a good look at Father when he came downstairs, we'll try and save your mother first. The only sound was the frightened whimpering of the youngest. Top kneeled in front of a chair and folded his hands. Noo gave him a kick that sent him tumbling over the chair. Top stood up, he put out his hands and said: 'Finish me off.' Then Lisa remembered something they had all forgotten, that Elvire, the cause of it all, had to be thrown out of the house for good, and she would do it this very minute. But she needn't have bothered. Elvire had gone, it was as if she had fulfilled her mission and now she could disappear, just as Rik had always expected.

15

We can truly thank the Lord that nothing had been announced about Van Oepstal the market gardener being made sidesman, nothing official anyway. The only ones who knew anything were the parishioners we'd talked the idea over with because they were concerned with the affairs of our church and they probably let some others know. That's not our business, though it's a pity it got round at all. As far as we're concerned the main thing is that he hadn't sat in the sidesman's seat in church and he hadn't been round with the plate, so he hadn't actually taken over as successor to the miller, and the least said the better. Seeing it hadn't gone that far we can just quietly forget we had ever suggested anything of the sort.

In any case, it looks as if it will be a few weeks before he's up out of bed again, and in the meantime we've had a word with Carlé, the chartered surveyor, and next Sunday he'll take the miller's place. What a relief it was that we were able to stop a scandal before it was too late! What a lot of trouble we had with the miller that time settling what should be done with the estate his brother, who was deacon of Westerloo, left when he died! The police were up at the mill, five times they came. Everyone in the village was sure he was going to be marched off any minute by the gendarmes. That was sixteen years ago, but we'll never forget it, it was indeed an ordeal, there's never been the like of it before or since.

That business with van Oepstal the market gardener could have been just as bad. One of our curates who had been to the house told us he had the impression there was something wrong. We said nothing, just kept our ears open, and we heard a thing or two, then only yesterday we were in Brussels to see Mijnheer Steenackers who used to be brewer here. We had to see him about a calvary we're hoping, with his generous help, to have finished, God willing, before the end of the year and set up level with the end of the aisle by the high altar, oh yes, on the outside, of course. Everything costs such a lot but it's quite a large donation, and when the statue is finished and once it's put there by the side of the presbytery garden, what a fine spot that will be, especially in the summer, for our priests taking a turn around the courtyard reading their breviaries, to stop and kneel every now and then. It was from Mijnheer Steenackers, and so you can be certain it's true, that we heard a thing or two more about the whole business. When we first came to the parish van Oepstal was barely making a living for his family of five or so by hawking vegetables. Later we heard that he'd been a bit wild in his younger days so there would be some truth, we were thinking, in the tales they told in the village about him and that girl from Brussels. Now Mijnheer Steenackers happened to know who she was: she was his concièrge's daughter; she had run away from home and she wasn't all she should be. That seemed to explain it all because we were sure that none of the sons, and certainly not Isidoor, the one they call Top, would ever do anything to be ashamed of. They take after the mother, she came from a poor family—very poor they were, her father, I believe, was born in a tinker's caravan—but honest, hardworking, and respectable. So there we have the reason why van Oepstal turned so devout all of a sudden. No peace with a bad conscience. *Quos vult perdere Jupiter prius dementat*, as the Romans used to say. Right from the start he must have been afraid he'd be found out, and he was using his piety as a cloak to cover up his sin. Ah yes, the wickedness there is in the world, but who of us can cast the first stone? Well, it's not for us to sit in judgment, and we know that God is merciful. Thank the Lord we were able to avoid a scandal, and just in time, too. Well, we can console ourselves with the words of St Bernard: *et etiam hoc transit*—this too shall pass away.

Mie van Oepstal didn't have time for philosophizing. A mother can't just resign herself in one day to the certain knowledge that she is going to die, and it wasn't the doctor who told her but the intuition that had never failed her. Childbed sicknesses had never worried her, but now something inside her body was worn out and broken, something that was her impulse to live, her reason for living. She knew now that she had to settle everything for good, and quickly, and she asked first for her father. At every death-bed there is something unexpected, mysterious; here it was the sound of a name that hadn't been heard in that house for years and years. Why should they have worried about Father, hadn't he promised to come back, and they knew that he was able to look after himself. He had said that he had a little money put by, and he would have left it behind here if they thought he hadn't done his duty by his children. Besides, Mie had said to him, when he left, that unless we hear from you we'll know there's nothing wrong. It was strange enough that Mie should ask first for him, but, stranger still, a few hours later a barge captain knocked on the door, it must have been about the same time as Mie asked for Father that he'd started out, and he'd come to tell them that Grandfather wasn't too well. He couldn't come back, it was too late now, but he sent his greetings and this watch was for the eldest, his godchild, and he wouldn't let me ask you to come and visit him. He said: 'If anyone comes I'll be pleased, but don't you ask them to come.' Top stood up, Top, who hadn't spoken a word and who hadn't moved out of his chair for days. He stuck his cap on his head and said: 'I'll go with you.' No one moved, but they were thinking, all of them: 'He's going like grandfather went. We won't see him again.'

In that house the dramas were played out in a wordless silence, but in the village the news went round: Top's gone. So you see, the baker was right all the time. He knew better than anyone what a good-for-nothing Rik had been, but he'd always said: 'Now the man's changed his ways. And I'll cut my throat if that isn't true, all that talk about him and the girl from Brussels is slander and nothing else. Top had been playing the fool with her and Rik was going to put a stop to it. Anyway if it hadn't all been Top's fault he wouldn't be running off now. If it hadn't been all his fault the others wouldn't have let him go away. But none of them have bothered about him.'

No, but Mie was asking for him as if her instinct told her that he wasn't there. Just as she had asked for Father, now she asked for Top, though no one had told her he was gone.

Suddenly, without a word, Rik appeared in the kitchen, a long, thin Turk with a turban round his head. No one asked if he ought to be out of bed walking about and he didn't seem to have thought about it himself. What has happened had to happen. He hadn't thought it would be like that, that was all. He wasn't wailing or complaining. It had happened and there was nothing he could do. The hand of God had struck. Rik sat bowed forward in his chair, he didn't matter, Mother was sick. Their silence was an unspoken veneration, an awed awareness of what she was and what she meant to them. Nothing else mattered, none of them was important. Their work was forgotten. The only two doing anything were the girls, the elder one looking after Mother, the other taking Mother's place in the kitchen. The rest of them were slumped in their chairs. Each of them had always sat in the same place, now they sat anywhere, and without realizing it they were all facing towards the room where Mother lay sick, they were like a pack of big Saint Bernard dogs, silent, waiting. When the elder girl, the one who was nursing Mother, came out of the room and said: 'Some milk,' they turned their heads to look at each other to see who was going to fetch the milk. Even if every cow they had was dry they'd get milk from somewhere, somehow. The eldest girl came to the kitchen door and said: 'She's asking for Top,' and they turned their heads again to look at each other. Top had to be brought home. Even if he was a corpse in a canal by now he'd have to be fished out and they couldn't leave him to rot as they intended to. Noo stood up and the rest of them sat there with their faces turned towards the bedroom.

Noo would never forget that day. He found his grandfather dead and when he got back with Top his mother was dying.

She died as only a mother can die, no tears, no sobbing and sighing, none of that lamenting from the others either, no thought for herself, only for the others. Take stock, and if you're off on your last journey make sure that everything will keep going as it should. Call them all in now, and when they're all there, the first thing was for Rik and Top to shake hands so she could see them. And can Mother be sure that it is all forgiven and forgotten? Words don't come easily to any of the van Oepstals, but now, with a heart as sore as his, Top could do no more than sink on his knees, his arms raised above his head, not by the bed and not in front of Father. He didn't move, and they let him stay as he was; everything was in order. That was because she understood them all so well. Then Mie said they had to stick together and remember that Father is master, do as he says, there was ground and place enough for all of them, they were to carry on building and working, marry sensibly and respectably, and may my soul perish, but never, never any quarrelling again, ever.

For the last time she kindled the warmth of happiness in their hearts. With a lingering look she said simply, tenderly: 'Good-bye, Father, good-bye, children.'

She had taken care of everything while she still had time to say what she wanted to say and it was an hour too early. Peacefully she lay dying and when she had died Rik said: 'What are we going to do now?'

Man of little faith that he was. They were going to bury Mother with regal honour, the service would be as late and as expensive as possible. And they'd fetch Grandfather and do the same for him because he was her father and she had asked for him. And they'd see that he was buried next to her. If only they could find their Grandmother's grave. They'd buy that plot of ground, too. That was the least they could do for the mother who had bought so much ground for them to work on and live on, for eleven families, please God!

Dazed and hopeless, the poor fellow just kept on asking: 'What are we going to do now?' He touched the corpse that was already growing cold, he bared it to the waist and bowed in grief-crazed, dumb wonder at the magnificent body he had loved so wildly. He walked behind that body as it was borne to the grave, he came home and huddled by the stove. From morning to night all he could think was that his life was finished, and at night, in the bed where he lay alone, a strange folly submerged him, a savage passion that should have died when she died. He hurtled down and down as sleep closed his eyes, falling endlessly through an emptiness, then he woke in an unfamiliar bed without her by his side. And he never shaved himself again.

But after they had sat for three days slumped in their chairs the van Oepstals started to stand up, one after the other, like sleepwalkers. They stretched their arms till their fists touched the beams of the ceiling, they felt for their pipes and tobacco, they looked out at the weather, they went to get their tools. Life began again, and before anyone had noticed it, the eldest girl had Mother's voice and Mother's firmness. The one they couldn't do without was scarcely gone when her ways and her voice came back in their midst.

What were they going to do? Tomorrow off to the Brussels market again and earn money from what they sold. Buying what there was to buy along the way and selling it all at a profit, pigeons, chickens, calves, cows, skins, hides, old iron. The parish clerk had died. His orchard was next to their land. His youngest son had just got an appointment as a schoolteacher. 'What's the daughter going to do?' they asked, and they hadn't even noticed that their own brother had been courting her. Their land spread out, away from the village, along the railway line where the trains still rolled over those same rails that shone and flashed in the evening light of the same sun.

The children grew up and married, Rik's beard grew long and grey, with the years his big house was more and more empty. But from all the windows he could look out and see in the distance the long, low dwellings the van Oepstals had built for themselves. That was where his children lived, chicken-farmers, fruit-growers, market-gardeners, dealers. They worked and prospered, some only moderately, some more than the others. Under those roofs they coupled with Rik's animal passion, with Mie's human tenderness. They built their houses, they bought more ground, and the fourth or fifth child would be born in a neatly papered bedroom. They had their triumphs and their sorrows, the death of a child, accidents, sickness, but that's the way life goes, and even Rik took it all calmly. He had paid the penalty for his folly; God and Toon had settled the account. Death struck but the empty places were filled anew; sickness and pain, all but the ache that is left by grief, were healed and forgotten.

While they were waiting till the eldest could finish with that nonsense of going to school they all needed extra help. There were young fellows among the labourers they hired. These young fellows saw there was money to be made if they did the same as the Van Oepstals on a piece of ground of their own. They got married and started off without a penny but with a will to work. Old-fashioned farming was out-of-date. The Farmers' League were saying that the whole country had to be turned into one big market-garden. There was no industry here, they didn't have to go and huddle in villages springing up around factories. Here it was not machines that triumphed but the strength of human hands, the strength that had stemmed from Mie Zaterdag.

Toon hadn't been able to give his name to his own son, Rik gave his name to this cluster of houses and the land they were built on, this thriving island of fertility. It wasn't the highest point of civilization, but it was the solid concrete foundation. At Den Oepstal there was work and more than enough for a baker, a shoemaker, a smith, a woodworker, a joiner, a wheelwright, and a flourishing trade for two shops and five inns. The masons who did all the building turned to building their own houses there too. Then they all started asking themselves why they were walking threequarters of an hour to the church and why their children had to go even farther to the school, and why they should be dependent all their days on those bald-headed stinkers in the village. By Jesus, we're sick of their meddling, let them shit in their own pot! We're going to have the say in Den Oepstal. Top can write a well-worded letter to the minister, and we'll all sign it. He can say we won't put up with any more of it, we're not going to have a lot of strangers telling us what to do here in Den Oepstal.

16

Yes, next Monday we'll be having the biggest funeral for many a
day. It's the founder of the biggest hamlet in the whole parish, and
he was chairman of our church council, you must have seen him
in his seat in the first row in the church, that tall, thin old fellow
with the bushy grey beard, Leopold II. Ah, a fine man, our Rik
van Oepstal, kindness itself, always calm and wise, and so generous
and helpful, never breathing a word about it. When I came here
more than twenty years ago his wife had died a few years
earlier.

Eleven children they'd been blessed with, the two eldest were
married by then, fine children every one of them, hard workers,
quiet, modest, thrifty, and good Catholics too. His eldest daughter
did the housekeeping and looked after him, only last year she
married a contractor in the village, a very nice fellow, he'd worked
hard and he'd put quite a bit by. I've heard he is going to build
another storey on the old van Oepstal house and divide it into
three. He'll sell two, keep one for himself and his wife and live on
what he's made. There was another son there too, the one they
call Top.

What I'm going to tell you now I heard from my predecessor,
God rest his soul, it all happened before my time. Even as a boy
this Top must have been the smartest of the lot, you can be sure
of that because he still is. There's something different about him,
I'd even say he was a little eccentric, but when he talks he knows
what he's talking about and he can turn his hand to anything. Well,
it seems that as a young lad this Top was something of a black
sheep, there's one in every family they say. There was a girl from
Brussels the van Oepstals had taken in out of kindness. I never
found out where they first got to know her, but I have heard that
she was an only child. There you are, it's always the same story
with an only child, and the parents couldn't have been any better,
you know how it is. So, to save her from that bad home influence,

Rik van Oepstal let her stay with them like one of the family. Just imagine, a fresh young thing from Brussels, with the bringing up she'd had, and then that Top losing his head over her. It could only lead to trouble. If you'd known our Rik, God rest his soul, a man of principle and honour, a true Christian. One of that sort for a daughter-in-law? No, never. The man was gentleness itself, but when it came to a matter like that he was as hard as iron. Tempers must have run so high that the end of it was Top took hold of an axe and hit his father on the head with it. A miracle that he wasn't killed. Not long afterwards the mother died, of grief, I've been told, but that may be true or not. In any case, it isn't important, why I'm telling the story is because it is such a wonderful testimony to our Christian principles of family life. The good old-fashioned ideas that men like Rik van Oepstal believed in aren't thought much of these days, but, you know, if we can't convince the young people that these are the only rules to live by, then, between you and me, though I wouldn't say it in a sermon, we can make a grave ready for our Christian civilization. In those days they had the right way of looking at things. They knew better than the young ones today. What do we hear now, all this talk about freedom and living as you want to, but our grandfathers stood by truth and obedience. That's how it should be, and there we have the proof of it. That black sheep finished by being the best of the lot, so kind, no thought for himself, ready to do anything for others, always helping someone, and, what speaks even more for him, he has been a comfort and a joy to his father. Many a time I've been in that house and, you know, the consideration that man showed for his old father was a wonder to behold. A devoted and loving son, and a big, broad-shouldered man of more than forty at that, well, it was a touching sight.

You knew, didn't you, that I was in Brussels for eighteen years, teaching for a while first and after that I was appointed curate, then I was sent here. I hadn't expected it; I was born in these parts, you see. But I had someone with a bit of influence behind me, look at that painting over there next to the door, the old chap with the decorations. He was the brewer here in the village and after he retired he went to live in Brussels...but that's not what I wanted to tell you. A moment, a moment, what was it now? Ah, Brussels, yes that was it, Brussels. Well, in Brussels I had hundreds of discussions about the Church's teachings on marriage and family life with all sorts of people, mostly of other persuasions, and you can take it from me there are some of them who are very well-informed and serious-minded too. When you're arguing with them it's no use just quoting dogmas or encyclicals. I always quoted facts, and the most important fact, I used to say, is that if we look around us we can see that our teachings, and no other, give a true moral guidance. In every single case, without exception, I used to say. If I were still in Brussels I'd tell the story of the van Oepstal family; what better proof could there be?

That's what I was saying only yesterday to one of my curates. Yes, he said, but what about the Goossen family, then, what does that prove?

Goossen was the parish gamekeeper, a good respectable, religious man. He had four children, a boy and three girls. I don't think there were ever children who had such a strict and religious upbringing as those four. With the little he'd saved and with the help of a benefactor he kept his son at school in the hope that he'd go on and study for the priesthood. The girls had to go and work as housemaids to pay the school fees. But when he finished college the son said he wasn't going to the seminary, he was going to Louvain, to the university. The benefactor stopped his help, but that didn't make any difference to our student boy. He got money from his sisters. Before the end of the first year he was expelled from the university, then he set himself up as a broker in Brussels and lived like a prince. That lasted about a year till the broker's business flopped, so then he lived by his wits with one thing and another, and now he's in the Congo, in one of the government departments, I believe. The father died of a broken heart. The mother sold the little house they had and rented a bigger one here in the centre of the village, and the furniture they've got, dearer than you'll see in any other house in these parts. I called on them and I talked to the mother about her daughters. I knew, of course, that they were kept women. 'Madame,' I said, 'if your husband were still alive it wouldn't have come to this,' and do you know what she answered? 'Oh, Father,' she said, 'I never had the same views as my husband about all that religion.'

So you see. Then people go saying: 'Look at them, brought up like that, every day off to church, and what are they now?' But if they talk like that they don't understand how it happened. It was because of the mother that the children turned out the way they did. Oh, no, in a family like the van Oepstals, every one of them God-fearing and devout, there's nothing like that; they have their trials and troubles but these little difficulties aren't a punishment.

But there's something else I wanted to tell you, every word of it as true as I'm sitting here. Rik van Oepstal, the chairman of our church council, passed away yesterday in the chair he always sat in in his kitchen. They all came running, his sons and daughters, and they had their children with them, that big house wasn't big enough for so many. When they saw their father there with that magnificent head of his they looked at each other and they said: 'We haven't got a photograph of Father.' Now, it seems that Top had made a camera a long time back, there's nothing the man hasn't made, but he never bought a plate for it. Straight away one of his brothers drove off to Brussels to buy a plate, and while they were waiting they carried their father, chair and all, into the bedroom, then they brought him back into the kitchen as soon as Top had his camera ready. Next Monday I'll show that photo. It's a portrait of the last of the patriarchs, Abraham, Isaac, Jacob, and Rik van Oepstal. They thought the head was leaning a little too far forward so the eldest crept behind the chair, he pulled his father's head backwards by the hair till the pose was just right. Ah, the dignity of death and the noble expression on that old face! You can see the eldest one's arm and shoulder in the background but Top says he can retouch the photo so you won't notice it.

Well, Father, I wanted to tell you all that because that's why I wrote to your prior this morning to ask if you could stay on after the triduum till Monday afternoon. One of my curates is off to a retreat on Sunday evening and you could assist with the Requiem Mass. Finish your glass, Father, you're not drinking.

ORDEAL

1

From out of the obscurity of village poverty a man climbed up above the others and prospered. That was long ago, when the villagers couldn't even write their own names, so far back that no one ever thinks about it any more. He was tall and lean and silent, and he had a thin, beaked nose that he could hang his cap on. A name on a certificate for a christening or a marriage or a death is nothing, but a name entered on a deed of sale drawn up by a lawyer acquires substance and importance. When this man's name was inscribed time after time on legal documents, for he bought land and more land and still more land, then everyone noticed it was a noble and ancient name. Once the man brought letters patent with him and the lawyer said admiringly: Well, now! The man put the papers back in his pocket without a word or a smile. Generation after generation of his noble line had done penance in dunghills and hovels, and now, strong again with new blood, this stock emerged from darkness and lowly anonymity.

The farmer had seven sons, no daughters. They were not as tall as he was but broader in the shoulders, short-necked, and they all had that same predatory, hooked nose. Two of them married. The others saw that the property could not be split up between the seven of them and they knew that their blood was too wild for the bonds of wedlock. They lay with servant girls and with the daughters of well-to-do farmers who dreamed of marrying a d'Hertenfeldt. They were self-willed and ruthless, misers and cynics who let it be thought that they accepted church and faith but believed neither in God not anything else. They had no use for gentleness or tender feelings. The wenches they brought to disgrace should, according to them, have been more careful. They would help in an hour of need if it would be to their advantage, or if they just got the idea into their heads, or if no one said they had to because it was their duty, or if there was talk that they didn't dare.

'You won't dare try and stop them,' one of their men said when the gendarmes came to arrest him because he had been poaching the night before. The eldest got up from his chair at the table and went and stood in the doorway so that the gendarmes couldn't come in. He said it was a mistake: the man had been with him all night tending a heifer that was calving. The servants of the law answered that the man had confessed and had even given his name, but the eldest said once more that it was a mistake. He glared at them and they didn't know where to look and they asked, confused: 'How is that possible, mijnheer?' 'Well it is,' the eldest said, and he lit up the cigar he had stuck in his mouth. The numbing grip his look had held them in only loosened when they were outside again, past the gate.

The seven brothers once bought from the Count land leased by two their enemies and then revoked the lease. When the two victims came and pleaded with them they shrugged callously. One of the two warned them not to forget that their luck could change too. They answered that their luck better not try it.

One autumn morning the Count forgot he had sold them the land and strode into the fields to go hunting. But one of the seven was watching. He put his hands to his mouth and shouted that no one could go hunting on their ground, then went on working as if he had just chased away a cheeky urchin. The Court could only turn round and slink off the way he had come.

When the last of the seven lay dying a twenty-year-old girl in a farm-house near by was howling and sobbing, crazy with grief.

Old and grey as he was, he had turned her head. The hour before his death he was jeering at the priest who, he said, should have brought along a scrubbing-brush to scour his soul white. Then the priest began a last offensive with dire threats of damnation to try and jolt him into a mood of seriousness on the threshold of eternity, but the heretic only replied: 'I don't believe a word of all that.' And he died.

But the inheritance his father and his brothers had left him lay round his corpse doubled four times over.

These were the founders of the d'Hertenfeldt estate that stretched over half the village.

From father to son the family became more and more distinguished, honoured and respectable. The sons were many, and those for whom there was no place scattered far and wide. The daughters were absorbed into other families, and the dross sank back into the anonymity of poverty. The village idiot was a d'Hertenfeldt. He rode round, cross-eyed and witless, in a donkey-cart. All the time he shouted at the beast and lashed it at every step. The children used to jump up and down in front of the donkey, and the donkey would try to do the same. Then Nooken d'Hertenfeldt would flog it, yelling a stream of shrill curses. The great d'Hertenfeldts from the Schrans didn't recognize this Nooken. If the donkey-cart passed by they didn't see it. It could have run over their toes and they still wouldn't have seen it.

After a century of flourishing vigour they softened from the refinement of learning. The great Jan Baptist d'Hertenfeldt, who wrote a fine, clear hand and could reckon shrewdly with figures—that's all a man needs, more than that is dangerous, he said—had six children and five of them wanted to study. He paid for their studies with an expression of indifference on his face but with a deep, sour contempt in his heart. The first became a Jesuit and was a famous preacher. His two daughters went into a convent. They were rich and domineering, and first one and then the other became Mother Superior. The fourth became an officer in the army and left for the Congo. The fifth became a wealthy lawyer in Brussels. With a sneer Jan Baptist let the sixth go off to college. For six years he paid the fees with that same grim fatalism of his great-grandfather who went to the presbytery to pay for his own burial, laid the notes on the table and asked if that was enough for them to shove him under the ground.

But in his sixth year at college this youngest one, the sixth,

Alexander d'Hertenfeldt, got to thinking of his future. All at once he understood his father who had never said anything to him, and he realized then the betrayal of his brothers and sisters. In the middle of the school term he went to the rector and announced that he was going home the following morning. That was not allowed, he was told. So he simply went to the gate, opened it and stepped into the street. Two of the proctors came to fetch him back at the station. He stood with his arms crossed and looked the two priests up and down, for he didn't understand how anyone could think of stopping him from going home if he decided to go.

Jan Baptist d'Hertenfeldt was standing on the stone pathway by the entrance gate of the Schrans when his youngest son, Alexander d'Hertenfeldt, arrived and said that he had come home to stay. Jan Baptist d'Hertenfeldt's teeth crunched as if he were chewing on sand, and his heart gave a few wild throbs. 'Go and tell your mother,' this last of the great d'Hertenfeldts said, and then, with a step far too brisk for his years, he made the rounds of his estate.

There, an extra stable would have to be put up, farther on, a pump with a drinking trough, and still farther on, a fence. He had let it run down, but a man didn't have the will and energy any more.

Alexander married and managed the estate under his father's silent regard. In those years it seemed as if the tough breed would survive the crisis, as if the devout and the learned had been cast out so that the old strength would return and live on in Alexander, who had come back to stay, and who rode a horse like Jan Baptist used to when he was younger, always with a double-barrelled gun slung over his back, for no reason, just as a habit. Alexander revived the traditional archery tournaments, and he had the ditches repaired and new roadways laid without being in the parish council. He said: No injustice. He held a protecting hand over the heads of those in difficulties, but he wouldn't stop at ruining one of them. It was again just as it had been in the days of d'Hertenfeldt greatness.

But his marriage was childless. That broke old Jan Baptist slowly and with a deep, searing pain.

One Sunday night Alexander was coming home in his small two-wheeled carriage from an archery tournament. It was pitch-dark and the wind howled. At the level crossing Alexander thought: I'll have to watch out here for the express from Louvain, and that was his last thought. The express from Louvain caught and crushed him. Like all archers, he had his pockets full of hazel nuts, and the wooden jay, used for a target on the top of the high pole, was in the carriage. What they could find of him they scraped together with a shovel and put it in a sack so that his coffin wouldn't be empty. They gave the battered wooden jay to Jan Baptist, and the best of the remains, the hazel nuts, were picked up by the children.

That was the end of the d'Hertenfeldts. Jan Baptist went to live with his son, the lawyer, in Brussels. The son sold the estate bit by bit to the highest bidders. The Schrans, with a quarter of the fields, was sold to the Van den Heuvels, another sturdy Brabant stock that had left the clay-soiled hills for the flat sandy ground. Jan Baptist died in Brussels as a fish dies out of water, not from any illness but tired, weary from the lack of any reason to go on living. He didn't ask for anyone, he didn't settle any affairs, he didn't speak any last farewell. He only gave a sigh of relief and closed his eyes and his wide, thin lips.

From these forefathers was descended the pale child that was the only son of lawyer d'Hertenfeldt. In him the forgotten, hidden vestiges of the strength and passions of a powerful breed flickered and sparked and smouldered with a foul reek. He was a flabby, pallid child, red-haired, with a head that was too big. Up to his seventh year he couldn't talk properly. He asked for his Sunday twousers, he found a bird's feawer, and anyone who stole was a fief. He never looked anyone straight in the eye. He couldn't learn anything at school. If the teacher spoke sharply to him he stuttered. But he never cried, and when he was nine he starved his canary to death by asking the maids twice a day for bird seed, so that they wouldn't bother to look at the bird, and then throwing the seed slyly down the lavatory. When it was dead he felt a deep, secret pleasure. Everyone asked him if he wasn't upset at losing the bird that he'd looked after with so much care. Oh yes, he was very sad. They all admired the self-control of this boy and respected his grief that was so genuine because he didn't show it.

2

His father had the habit of lifting him up and sitting him on his lap like a toddler. He had his fixed lawyer's ways of acting a part for every occasion. With wealthy clients he was pompous and bombastic; with the gentry he gave the impression that he directed his large office with a few brief instructions each day. He would ring for his chief clerk and say, without glancing at him: 'The file.' But if the butcher was there to settle the purchase of a new house on the corner, he would ask, through the clouds of cigar smoke: 'Could we have a look at the Caluwé-Peeters file?' When it was a Mother Superior he would say, smiling jovially, that he had drawn up so many documents for poor convents without charging them that he was glad now to be acting for nuns who were rich. Then the Mother Superior would pay up with a heavy heart, but proudly. He always said to children that they were already grown up, and that they were well-dressed.

André knew each time what Papa was going to ask, and he submitted silently but resentfully to the ordeal of being lifted up on that wobbling, puffy lap. He could see that there were more and more rolls of fat around Papa's eyes. When the bulging body leant back and the head rocked with raucous gusts of laughter, the child shuddered at the sight of the big wide mouth and the tobacco-stained, dirty, brown teeth. On birthdays and saint's days he made the present a torture by fussing and teasing. André had to guess what it was or beg to be allowed to see it. The child spitefully refused to do either. Papa thought this was a sign of a good and gentle character. He had never seen a child like this, always contented with what he got, never in a temper.

The boy was often sick. When he had to stay in bed he never complained. Everyone on the house came asking where it hurt, or if it still hurt. He would just shake his head or give a vague answer and revel in the concern he caused. Like all spoilt children, he never showed any pleasure when he was given a box of sweets or a new toy. Sometimes the oldest maid would leave his room with tears in her eyes: if that child wasn't a saint then she didn't know who was. The little saint, meanwhile, lay looking at the ceiling, diverting himself with the little bit of imagination nature had bestowed on him. He saw himself dying, surrounded by the whole family, all in tears, and he revelled in that grief.

The neighbour, a rich, childless widow, had two big dogs. Sometimes she had to go out and couldn't take them with her. Then they were shut up in the kitchen at the back, and all evening they kept up their heart-rending yowls. The boy was glad because it stopped Papa, Mama, and the two maids from sleeping. He lay in bed wide-awake, encouraging the dogs: Louder, louder! When Papa noisily jumped out of bed in the room next to his and banged futilely with his fists on the wall, the boy was in ecstasy.

Deep within him there was a need for malice and cruelty that made him hate, a raging bitterness at the timidity he was born with and could never conquer. It was only when he was alone in his room that he would put his hands in his trouserpockets and give himself that self-assured air that Papa had. He held imaginary conversations jeering at others for their stupidity, and he humiliated them without mercy. 'What's your father?' he whispered hoarsely, 'a miserable baker; you're only dirt.' But the most gratifying of all was to cross his arms, knit his brows, and snarl: 'You bastard, you're not going to play the bloody fool with me!'

But he wasn't a little saint, or even the boy who would get the prize for good conduct, in the eyes of the one who knew him best, his mother. She had nursed him and tended him, beset by a million fears, and she had sheltered him with unbearable care. She saw through the mask of his pretence. She knew that he went out and stood on the flagstones in his bare feet, when she had just the minute before warned him not to, because he wanted to make her terrified he might catch cold again. She knew he slipped away from her to run across the busy street alone and stand on the other side watching her as she trembled and went pale. She knew he couldn't bear the sight of her. She knew that he wouldn't put his arms around her and kiss her, and how she needed the kisses and embraces that his father so seldom bothered to give her.

Lawyer d'Hertenfeldt had put on flesh, while she grew thin and frail like an untended plant. It never came to an open conflict between them because he was by nature too indifferent, too complacently padded with flesh to quarrel. He was lost in dreams of dishes of rich food, of his game of dominoes in the Café Leopold I with his friends, a magistrate, Major Dutoy, and an old doctor, and of his hunting.

But the boy noticed the estrangement. He observed every hint, every sign, and she felt he was gloating over it. She could forgive all the countless ways he expressed his malignant nature in, but this incensed her. He could smile so mysteriously and evilly that she suspected he must be sexually initiated. When she drifted nervously through the house she had the hopeless, humiliating feeling that her twelve-year-old son despised her as a woman and hated her as a mother. It was then that the struggle between them became vicious. He realized he couldn't deceive her, and his hatred of her grew deeper and more real. The indulgent solicitude that had made him unruly was replaced with impatience, and she called this discipline. After all, the boy was growing up, she decided; he was beginning to show his real character, and that was the same heartless, coldly egoistic character as his father had.

It was a veiled, undeclared struggle they waged against each other, for neither of them wanted to acknowledge the real cause. Now and then she made a desperate effort to win him back. Never as a young girl in love had she so calculatingly resorted to a woman's weapons of tears, feigned illness, and unreasoned pleading as she did now, fighting for the love of her child. The most reluctant swain would have given in ten times over, but the boy was unmoved, and he had never felt a wilder glow of pleasure than

125

the thrill of knowing he was the stronger, of knowing that this woman needed him.

If André didn't love Mummy any more, then she would rather be dead. She pressed him against her thin, bony body that was scarcely thicker than Papa's arm, and in his mouth was the sweet taste of the words he never spoke: I love you. He savoured the words like a delicacy. To say them aloud would mean losing his supremacy, and so he let them glide slowly over his tongue. Whenever she took to bed for some little ache or pain he knew she was lying with her eyes closed, waiting tensely to hear his footsteps, hoping he might come to her and put his hand on her brow and ask: 'What's wrong, Mama?' He walked upstairs, deliberately coughing so that she could hear him, he stopped for a few moments at her door, then suddenly turned into the empty guestroom next to hers. The third time he came up the stairs she burst out sobbing, so distraught that the maid rushed to fetch lawyer d'Hertenfeldt. Madame was having a *crise de nerfs*. Another time she was sitting in the salon, ill, with her head in her hands. He came in and said nothing, just drummed his fingers idly on the windowpane. Then he went past her, so near that his legs brushed against her hanging feet, and as he closed the door he whistled a few bars of a popular song.

Sometimes she thought that his dullness at school was only indolence, for the interest he showed in the relations between her and his father was sharper than any normal child could have, and no idiot would ever be able to think up such subtle ways of tormenting her. Sometimes she spoke to him bitterly. When she was dead he would understand how good Mama had been to him. No other boy was so well looked after, and no mother got so much ingratitude. When he was older he would think of her, but then it would be too late. He didn't answer.

Other times she would rant at him. Did he want to make her sick? Did he want to send her crazy? Look me in the eye, you little hypocrite, and answer me. He looked at her coldly, and said he didn't know what to answer. Nothing was ever right. It didn't matter what he said, she twisted it round. Everything he did she found fault with.

She realized this was true, and in her heart she reproached herself for being so unreasonable. Often weeks would go by when they didn't say a word to each other. But even at meals lawyer d'Hertenfeldt didn't notice anything. His only thought was for the food, and since he felt that conversation went with a meal, just as much as wine did, he took care of the conversation himself. Asparagus is only right with butter sauce and hard-boiled eggs, Thérèse, my dear, nothing else will do. Today it's just as it should be. Yesterday it was perhaps a little too bitter. When he wanted to be jovial he asked when he was going to get a fresh herring, the ones you can buy for ten centimes. That was his way of what he called playfully teasing his wife. Where she came from they rarely had fresh fish and then only river fish, and none but the poorest families ate dried herrings. The very word herring made her so embarrassed that she almost blushed. If he started talking about what a delicacy a plate of herring was at the Schrans when he was a boy she had a feeling of shame. 'Please don't ever say that if we have guests.' Then he would burst out laughing. Every time there was trout for dinner he said it was nearly as good as a ten-centime herring.

3

Lawyer d'Hertenfeldt hadn't noticed anything until his wife, distracted, exasperated and worn out, told him that she was really worried about the boy. She said he was selfish and cruel and bad-mannered. He raised his hands in the air. And what else? A black-mailer, no doubt, a thief, a murderer, the leader of a gang.

He only half listened while she reeled off examples of her son's sly misdeeds. Once she had seen him sticking a pin in the tyres of three bicycles in the passage-way next to the office, and he did it so slyly. But when she voiced the suspicion that the child was aware of the coolness between him and herself, and that he gloated over it, he knew at once that this was all silly woman's talk. How could a child of twelve understand things like that? Did she really believe that a child of that age could be as subtle as she tried to make out? Impossible! She was imagining that André was far more intelligent than he was, and after all, Thérèse, my dear, he isn't clever, let's be sensible about it. But he's a good boy, and we can be thankful for that. He doesn't need to be brilliant. It's not as if he were poor and had to work his own way up. They didn't need to worry. The boy would go far with that character of his and the fine qualities he had always shown. That was how he saw it, my dear.

She insisted again that it was really serious, and then he looked at her. It was certainly serious with her. For quite a while she had been a little strange: she was nervous, and irritable, and she often had fits of depression for days on end. At the first opportunity he had a doctor in to see her, and his impression was confirmed. Not only was Madame badly run down and on the verge of a nervous collapse, but there was also some rather serious chest trouble. He ordered a long rest in the country, plenty of sun, fresh air, and nourishment.

When he had arranged for her to go into a sanatorium, lawyer d'Hertenfeldt asked the boy whether Mama hadn't been difficult these last few months. That was because she was sick, you see. But the boy said no, he hadn't noticed anything, Papa. Papa knew quite well that his wife would never have spoken as she did about the boy if there hadn't been repeated scenes, and nothing could have convinced him more of the angelic nature of his son than that gentle denial. Heaven knows what the poor lad had had to put up with from his mother in her moods and tantrums! In a burst of compassion he bought him a complete officer's uniform. He hoped this would have an appropriate effect. The boy needed a bold front as well as gentleness to fight life's battles.

The separation drew the mother and son together again. Each and every day she pined for her child, at night she dreamed of her child, and she talked to the sisters of nothing but her child. That, and the fear that she would lose her child if she died, for death was to her simply a final separation from him, made her forget the scenes and the anguish. The past was forgotten.

Her absence left the boy forlorn in his loneliness. For Papa and the maids he was André, the little saint. For the children of the families who came visiting, the chemist's three, the magistrate's two, and the only son of Colonel Dutoy, he was the weakling who mustn't be hurt. For the others at college he was the despised booby, and for the masters an unteachable dunce. But for Mama he was just what he was. When he was allowed to come and visit her it was as if the burden of humiliation and hypocrisy were lifted from him. For her alone he was someone. The bustling, matter-of-fact sisters, used to every misery and tragedy, were moved by this tenderness. Some of them watched, dreamy-eyed, and after that the ceaseless prattle about the boy never irritated them.

More than once she was discharged as cured, but she was never back in Brussels for more than a few months before the doctors insisted on her return to the sanatorium. In the seventh year they let her go home to die. It was André's last year at college and Papa had made it clear that there was no question of his not going on with his studies. A university degree, my boy. Not that he would really need it later, and, God willing, he would never have to depend on it, but these days a man of position had to have a background of culture and learning.

If his father could have heard that—Jan Baptist d'Hertenfeldt, who was proud of his copperplate script and never needed a pencil to tot up figures, and who knew how dangerous more knowledge than that was for a d'Hertenfeldt—he would have understood that André wanted a corner in the garden fenced off for chickens and ducks and turkeys. He would have understood why André, the first time Papa took him hunting, felt it was a pity the Schrans had been sold. Jan Baptist would far rather have heard these words than all the eloquent sermons of his famous Jesuit son. No d'Hertenfeldt worth his salt would stand up in front of a congregation pleading and arguing for a whole hour that they should be good. It might sound very learned, but for him all this fine phrasing was a sign of weakness and folly. The d'Hertenfeldts had always said in a few words exactly what they wanted, and they came down hard on anyone who didn't listen. A real d'Hertenfeldt in a pulpit would say: 'In the name of the Father, and of the Son and of the Holy Ghost, Amen. You all have to go to Mass and Benediction, and every now and then to Confession, and I'll soon know if any of you don't. Amen.'

But lawyer d'Hertenfeldt was of the many-worded sort. He didn't understand how his son felt about the Schrans, and his son didn't dare tell him how the books had humiliated him, how he hated the school and everything about it, and how he dreaded the formula on his reports: 'Marks insufficient for a pass.' The old deep-rooted urge of his breed to live close to the soil reasserted itself like a longing for deliverance. The wealth and position of his father could not give him any sense of self-confidence, but a stretch of land is something tangible, a reassuring and imposing possession: a house set in the middle of a big estate, and around this expanse a moat, and only one single bridge over the moat, and only one single gateway. Then everyone who came would know that his domain was great and where it began. He would shoot the birds that dared to perch on his trees. He would have a big horse, well-groomed and haughty and strong. He would go into the stable with a knotted whip and lash it round the legs and shout: 'Nondedju!' Three, four times a day he would do that. Then after a few days the horse would tremble when he opened the stable door, and that was what he wanted to see, that it trembled because of him.

A background of culture and learning, *mon ami*. A year or so at the university, that was all. His son looked down at the floor. The ash from his father's cigar fell just where his eyes were fixed. The boy said nothing, but he confided to his wasted, coughing Mama his horror of going to Louvain as Papa so obstinately insisted he must. What a happiness it was for her that there was something he hoped for with all his heart and that he told her and no one else of his wish! Of course, his father didn't listen to her. Anyone as sick as she was shouldn't be upset; she should get everything she wanted. But then his wife's health was one thing and his son's education was another, and no less important. He didn't want to have to decide which should come first. That would be painful and altogether indelicate. It was a question of not sacrificing the one for the other, that's what it amounted to. He tried to reason with her gently. André needn't choose anything difficult, he wasn't expected to achieve any distinction, and a year or so more or less didn't matter as long as he got a degree of some sort, you see. A boy in his position has to have a university degree.

She was glad, really, that her husband didn't agree straight away. It wouldn't be easy to get him to give up his obsession, and now there was something she could talk and talk about for hours with her boy. It was as if this man, whom she no longer loved, in whose shadow she had slowly languished and wilted for want of light and warmth, stood outside the bond that formed itself anew between her and her son. With her son she spoke of the father as of a stranger they had to get the better of. She had none of that pride that demanded a university diploma. All she had was her love, and her love asked nothing more than the happiness of her child.

When she began vomiting blood she didn't realize that this meant the end. She didn't notice that her son never showed a sign of concern at her sickness that grew worse and worse or that his only thought was for what she had to get for him. It was so wonderful to forget everything in the excitement of their conspiracy. Whenever he came into the room her sunken, dark-ringed eyes opened wide. We have to get him used to the idea that you aren't going to go to the university. Gradually, so he won't realize it. Leave it to me: I'll see that he gives in.

She looked younger and younger, a girl of twenty, his sister. Her face was paler with a wax-like lustre, her eyes had an unearthly, soft glow. There was nothing else but her child and the wish they both shared. Then the end came suddenly. She knew it and she was content, for now she would get her way. She wanted to speak to Papa alone, she said, and she gazed at her darling with a look of childlike happiness as he walked to the door. Now we can do it. The trembling fat man came to the bed and she made him promise not to force the boy to go to study at the university. The large body wobbled helplessly. *Mais, ma chère enfant*...But she wasn't listening, she didn't want to hear. *Je vais mourir, promets-le vite.* So, of course, he promised, and with a last smile of contentment she died.

Even the culturally-minded d'Hertenfeldts were too hard-headed to be serious about subtle considerations like promises given at a death-bed. That was only a token of sympathy that couldn't very well be refused, and just because someone dies the world doesn't stop turning. That was how lawyer d'Hertenfeldt thought about it. The world keeps on turning and the boy's future must be taken care of after his mother's death just as before. There were still seven months from the funeral to the beginning of the university term, and by that time the death-bed scene would be a vague memory. Besides, he had a strong argument in reserve. This was something Mama would never have wanted in normal circumstances, and so it would be wrong to do it even if it was what she had asked on her death-bed. 'We mustn't be sentimental about these things; we have to be realistic,' he said. 'You won't get far by being sentimental. I can tell you that as a lawyer.' This time the ash fell on his stomach. He was getting dangerously fat.

In the meantime Major d'Hertenfeldt came home from the Congo for good. He hadn't written to say he was coming, boy, but here he was. *Et voici ma femme.*

Out there he had lost the wife he had taken with him, but he brought this new one back, a young creature, not yet thirty. It was easy to see that he was used to getting his way. He filled the whole house with a bellowing cough and cigarette smoke, and when he spoke it was as if he were yelling from the bottom of the stairs to someone who was banging away with a hammer in the attic. He was going to buy a country house near Louvain and he would take his two sons to live with him there. The elder of the two wanted to study law, *quel sale métier, nom de tonnerre*, and the younger had another couple of years to do at college. When André went to Louvain he could come and stay with them. He looked at André, who couldn't sink into the ground, and despised him.

4

The first thing he bought was a car, and the first week he ran over a child. After that his wife wouldn't ride with him. She slept till eleven and she came downstairs dressed in a flowing peignoir to ask André for a cigarette. The room spun round before his eyes, and he had to admit that he didn't smoke and there weren't any cigarettes in the house. He heard her giggle, then he found himself out in the street, he didn't know how, and he went to buy cigarettes. At the shop window he stood sweating until he finally bought the dearest brand there was of perfumed cigarettes. He left the shop and stopped, wretched and dizzy, as he realized that it would look miserly to give cigarettes without a holder. He took out his wallet to see if he would have to buy something ridiculously cheap, then he went back in, bought something very expensive, and, at last, there he was standing in front of her again. She accepted it from him with both her hands. Her peignoir fell open and she said: 'Oh, pardon,' as she fastened it up again. He stuttered pardon, too, and stumbled out through the door. She called him back and didn't know what she had done to deserve such a lovely present. She thanked him with warm, soft words, sweetly smiling. She looked at him archly and asked, just to tease him, whether she should tell anyone that he gave her such marvellous presents.

He took that seriously, of course, and felt shocked that he had been so indelicate. No, he gasped, terrified, no, she mustn't tell anyone. Now she was more puzzled than ever. For a second or so she ran her eyes over him, thoughtfully gauging whether he was starting a game she knew only too well, and whether he might be interesting. She tapped him on the cheek and said: 'Naughty boy.' But he came out in a sweat, and he blushed so embarrassedly that she asked him if he wanted perhaps to be a priest, and that only made him feel worse. Well, he looked as if he did. A priest? No, certainly not, Madame. She laughed. Madame? He could call her Mouche. Or maybe he shouldn't. After all, I'm your aunt, don't forget. She thanked him all over again, and she leaned forward quickly to whisper caressingly that she would say she had bought the cigarette-case herself.

A month later the Major had bought and furnished his country house. It was just as if he had marched into the villa he fancied, shot down everyone living there, buried them all in the courtyard, and then taken up the telephone and threatened a couple of furniture-makers that they had the choice between an untimely end and delivering him what he wanted within forty-eight hours.

The two maids hated the sight of him with his cigarette-ash and his shouting, and if they couldn't dodge out of his way they backed against the wall, wide-eyed with fright. He used to barge into the kitchen at the smell of the cooking, grab a ladle, help himself to the soup, and give Marie a thump on the shoulder by way of appreciation. The only one in the house he never saw was André, who avoided him like the plague and always found an excuse to come to dinner either before or after him. Lawyer d'Hertenfeldt raised no objection because his brother's table talk was anything but edifying. The Major's young wife thought he was suffering from some sort of youthful feelings of guilt, that his conscience was troubling him because of her. This strange boy fired her imagination. She would sometimes spend hours lying on a sofa, smoking, possessed by a deep and urgent longing.

A sergeant's widow in the Congo is weak when a widowed major offers her a chance, but weakness is a far cry from love, and in the Congo it was easier to put up with the vulgarities of a military husband. Here, his boorishness was irritating, a humiliation. The Major still seemed to think that only the native boys could hear him bellowing, but in this lawyer's house Mouche didn't want to be insulted. If he wanted to stamp round in a temper then she went out shopping and forgot him. Or she would think of that shy boy upstairs. Her husband was ageing and coarse; he was young, innocent, and sweet. She was for ever bickering with the Major. Fortunately lawyer d'Hertenfeldt was there, and he could always smooth things over. Nothing was so unhealthy, he used to repeat, as getting excited at the dinner table. Fortunately, too, the Major found it rather entertaining, a wife of temperament. But how it made her long for that ruddy, freckle-faced boy who didn't dare look at her.

Sometimes she would sit near him for the amusement of seeing him run away, or go up and knock when he was alone in his room just to watch him standing terrified in the doorway, trying to keep her out. Sometimes she would ask sweetly: 'Can't I come in?' To keep up a conversation with him for more than two minutes was impossible, and so she used to say he needn't stop what he was doing, she would sit in the corner, if it wouldn't disturb him, and read her fashion magazine and the serial. Then it was fun to see how his hand shook as he tried to write, and how his eyes half closed from the blood rushing to his head, and how the drops of sweat glistened on his skin. After a quarter of an hour he didn't know what he was reading or what he was writing. He would take up a book and put it down again, and then aimlessly turn over the pages of a dictionary. Once she asked him what he was looking up and he didn't know what to say. She stood behind him and he realized with a shudder of self-pity that his neck was covered with brown freckles and on the left side there was a thin, hanging wart, a tiny nipple. She felt such a sudden surge of affection that she laid her two cool, slender hands on his shoulders and told him he was too nervous, that he had a very likeable character, that he would have lots of friends, and that he shouldn't get into a flurry.

She thought the touch of her hands would soothe him, but he shrivelled up in an agony of sickening dejection. So she was just like all the others: she made him feel the misery of his existence, and for her, too, he was just a poor fool. His first fleeting contact with a woman was a humiliation.

When he went to live with them in the villa near Louvain he noticed, with his over-sensitive awareness, that she paid more attention to him than to the two stepsons who would have been a far more natural preference for her affections. But now it was so obvious that the Major and the two sons noticed it as well. In his old age this grey-haired cynic was stung with jealousy. His young wife let him feel that Europe wasn't the Congo, and he knew that that was a sign she was tired of him. Until he had come back he had only seen his sons every few years or so. Now they lived with him in the same house, two sturdy young fellows who had dreamed of liberty during the six years they had spent shut up in college and who were exceedingly polite and deferential without ever saying the word 'mama'. They couldn't think of that pretty woman as the wife of their father, and they vied with each other in correctness.

That only infuriated the Major. He behaved more crudely than he usually did, and that was bad enough, and instead of putting his sons at their ease he only shocked them. They felt ashamed of the way he spoke to his wife and they tried instinctively to show that his bullying bluster wasn't a family trait. She did her best to stay neutral and keep a balance between her obligations as a step-mother and her duties as a wife. The four of them lived under a cloud of hidden conflict, three men with their eyes on one woman, the woman looking past the three men at the half-wit cousin they despised and ignored.

Twice it happened that she went shopping in Louvain and came back with her nephew. Twice she remembered she had to buy something just as André was leaving for an appointment with his tutor. Once she suddenly decided she wouldn't go out with the Major and she stayed at home all alone with André. Once she said that Willy and Jacques shouldn't forget to take off their shoes downstairs if they came home late and put on slippers to go up to their rooms as André always did. Another time she took hold of his arms from behind to make him go through a doorway more quickly. Once she spoke up to defend him as impulsively as a mother would jump into the water to save her child. She hadn't stopped to think it was senseless to take his part. He had said something hopelessly stupid that there just wasn't any excuse for. That was too much. From then on every day was for André a nightmare.

The Major, who had hated him instinctively from the start, now baited him out of jealousy. The sons who had left him alone, because it wasn't fair to make fun of a poor fool who couldn't hit back, spared him no longer. Neither of them could understand what a woman could see in that timid, pathetic weakling. Nor did the Major, who was guided by a few simple maxims. The first and foremost was: *Les femmes, c'est bon pour la nuit,* and as far as he was concerned women were just as unpredictable as they were irresponsible. The crazy way Mouche went on about this freak his brother had spawned only proved it, and by Jesus he would soon put an end to all that!

He was, as a matter of course, crude and brutal from his long years of army service, but when he made a point of being deliberately crude he went beyond all bounds. His own sons would have turned on him if they hadn't detested their cousin as much as they did. But Mouche didn't tolerate it.

The storm broke one evening at dinner, over a bit of vermicelli that fell on André's tie. The Major was just waiting for something like that. He pointed with his brown-stained finger: 'Dribbling again.' André could hardly get another spoonful of soup to his mouth, and every time he swallowed it was a noisy gurgle in his throat. The Major put his hands on the table, looked at him, and asked how he did that, and so loud, too. At the cadet school he had known someone who could do it nearly as well. The two sons coughed hard to stop hooting with laughter. Mouche fidgeted nervously and, when two drops of sweat rolled down the sides of André's nose, she imagined he was crying. Then a blob of sauce fell on André's sleeve. The Major stood up, took his serviette and tied it round André's neck as if it were a baby's bib, and pulled the ends up at the back like donkey's ears. Mouche shouted at him that if he wanted to act like a lout he should go and eat in the kitchen. He grinned and said she certainly did stick up for the young gentleman, but she yelled back that she was only insisted on her right to sit at the dinner table with a man who knew how to behave, and with that his pent-up resentment burst loose. '*Behave*, Madame—what the hell do you mean? Who doesn't know how to behave? It looks as if someone else here could tell a lot more than your husband about the way you behave yourself, or maybe you don't think I'm your husband any more.'

Now then, now then, Papa, Willy and Jacques weren't going to stand for that sort of talk. It might be all right to bawl out a regiment of niggers, but here in Europe ladies are respected.

'Ladies,' the Major growled, 'ladies, and we've got a lady here, have we?'

Willy stood up in front of him, big and furious: 'That's enough, Papa.'

Papa paled and took a couple of steps backwards and crossed his arms. He'd show them a major wouldn't stand any nonsense. 'Ah, *c'est comme ça*,' he said in a tone that implied he knew enough now to commit the whole row of murders he'd been planning for a long time, but when Willy, still in a fury, told him that was indeed *comme ça*, he didn't say a word. There was a silence, a sort of speechless amazement that it took so little to subdue such a fierce warrior. The silence lasted until Mouche burst out sobbing at the table, and that eased the tension.

They looked round and saw that André had disappeared. They opened the door and there he stood in the passage, turning round and round, the serviette still round his neck, the donkey's ears still sticking up at the back, and then it happened, something that he would never, never forget. Even if he was destined for Paradise this memory would destroy his bliss for all eternity. The pathos of the scene was shattered with hoots of laughter. Willy roared, then Jacques. The Major had to grin in spite of himself, and Mouche looked up and laughed shrilly, just as hysterically as she had sobbed. The noble scion of a noble family with a bib on, and those donkey's ears sticking up. Jacques said loudly that he'd better hurry up and go and put on a clean pair of trousers. André only saw Mouche laughing at him, laughing at him like the others.

5

He could see through it all now. It was a farce to make a fool of
him, and she had been in the plot as well. It was all a mockery,
those friendly smiles, all that attentiveness, everything, and the
others hadn't been annoyed because of her attentiveness that he
had always tried to avoid anyway. It was only a trick so they could
make a clown of him and jeer at him, and she had acted a part to
make it worse. How lucky he had been not to fall into the trap!
When she was tying his new tie for him the day before yesterday,
because he couldn't make a good knot she said, there was a look in
her eyes and her face came too close to his. He had felt a painful
longing for the tenderness of a caress. Now he was sure there must
have been someone peering through the keyhole to catch him.

Alone in his room he spat out his hate in whispers with the
foulest words he could think of, and he didn't know that she was
sitting behind the door opposite his, thinking how much more
she cared for him now. That he had skulked off, frightened, was
for her not a display of cowardice, but a reflection of his sensitive
nature, his delicate feelings. He just couldn't stand these ill-
mannered jokes. That sensitive nature of his intrigued her. She
hadn't been able to get him to respond, to draw him out of himself—but what would it feel like if he took her in his arms, how
would his lips taste as he kissed her? She tried sometimes to tell
herself that he was ugly and repulsive, but the yearning for the
passionate warmth she never got from the Major made her long
for him and long for him.

He started writing letters to Papa, for that was his only hope of
escape. He thought of putting down in black and white just what
had happened, but each time he would hesitate and sit staring
emptily at the wall. All he did was to hint that the lecture times
were so awkward that it would be easier for him if he could take
a room in Louvain near the university. He worded this explanation so feebly and so vaguely that Papa didn't even notice it, or,

if he did, he never mentioned it when he wrote back.

While he hoped for deliverance, Mouche dreamed of schemes to break through the barrier of his reserve. The more he kept out of her way, the more cunningly she pursued him, and every approach deepened his mistrust. The reason he was so aloof, she convinced herself, was his shyness that had got even worse after the incident. She wasn't discouraged, and that made him all the more certain that she kept on pursuing him not for herself, but for the pleasure of mocking him. It must have been clear enough by now that he wasn't interested. To reassure him she avoided any show of friendliness when the others were there, but she was all the more affectionate whenever she was alone with him, and he concluded that they had now decided to trap him with more subtle tactics.

But it seemed to the others that Mouche had been cured of her mad attachment for good by the exhibition of his heroism. So they left him in peace, and the change made him still more suspicious. In every single word that was spoken he looked for a double meaning. Once the two cousins asked him to go for a walk with them and he didn't because if he went they would only play some trick on him. Like a cowed dog he staggered through an endless labyrinth of fear and despair, and Mouche, who watched his every move, could only explain this baffling behaviour as a hopeless infatuation that he was trying to struggle against. At times the longing to know the secrets of his hidden, inner tenderness was too strong for her to bear.

Then, one afternoon, he came home unexpectedly with an excuse that seemed to her all too transparent. The professor was sick and the lecture had been cancelled. If he had known that neither the Major nor the cousins were there he would certainly have stayed in town, but for her it was obvious that he had been waiting for this chance, that he had got the better of his conscience at last. While he scurried up to his room in a panic, she sent the maid off to buy something to get her out of the house for an hour or two. Then, flushed and panting, she went upstairs and pushed his door ajar and whispered to him to come to her room, that someone might see them here from the driveway.

In her room she put on a light dress and waited, but his door stayed shut. His heart pounded so hard that he could hear it, and he flicked through the pages of a Larousse asking himself if this was a plot too. He couldn't find an answer, and he realized how stupid he was, for the others were always laying traps that he didn't see. How could he know that in the room opposite she was waiting, writhing in a restless suspense, taking off more and more of her clothes? The silence through the house was oppressive, unbearable. The minutes passed and she lay there with nothing on but a loose woollen peignoir. He must come in now, he must, and then she would show him what a woman was. Only two thin walls and a heavy, febrile silence separated them. In the Congo she had felt this ecstasy, the wild sensuality of yielding to the murderous tropical heat, when desire made the blood race with an animal lust. Then the rutting beast has the fury of a live volcano.

After she had dressed again for dinner it was a different Mouche who came downstairs, charming to the husband and the stepsons, and unaware that there was a fifth place at the table. He had spurned her and he no longer existed.

Lawyer d'Hertenfeldt ungrudgingly recognized his obligations to his brother. One way of showing this was to invite the whole family to come hunting, a gesture that was not without a quality of self-sacrifice, for at his age and with his corpulence it was only natural that he should prefer to confine his relaxation to the game of dominoes at the Café Leopold I and give up the more energetic pleasures. But he did his duty, and the Major's family came boisterously along. Farmer Van den Heuvel ignored Mouche, the scandalous sight of that woman in breeches stamping on the floor and the sand crunching under her riding boots. He called the four newcomers the Congolese, with a snort of disgust, because the four of them were all too brazen for his taste. But they had money and rank enough to be guests at the Koevoet. They came and came often, and he played the respectful host with wine and home-made biscuits. Besides, he had his Ursule and his Octavie to receive them with all the decorum they had learnt at the convent school.

By way of acknowleging their gift of the finest hares, he regaled them with an elaborate supper, and what a difference from the soup with dumplings and pork chops that his wife, may God rest her soul, always used to make. The dishes the girls served up were so special and so like city food—how did they ever manage it?

André sat opposite Ursule, and the company at table formed three groups. The lawyer, the Major and the farmer filled the long, low room with their deep voices. They talked of the Schrans, reviving memories of their youth, and the lawyer held forth on genealogies. Do you know where the Van den Heuvels come from, he could tell you their whole history. The Van den Heuvels had been weavers in Bruges, for a long way back. The first Van den Heuvel who took to the countryside about 1800 wasn't a farmer, he was a tanner, and it was this tanner's son, Franciscus Van den Heuvel, who bought the Kruishoef and I don't know how many acres of land, and that's where you were born.

The second group was made up of Octavie, Mouche, Willy and Jacques. They noisily filled in the occasional, brief intervals of silence the three older ones left open, and when the Major got to telling about the time when, as a boy of six, he had given an angry rooster that had chased him right into this room a blow with a stick and killed it, and, *nom de tonnerre*, didn't I get a thrashing for it, and I still don't know how I did it, then they waited patiently until they could make themselves heard again.

But the third group, Ursule and André, sat undisturbed. Now and then they said to each other that the weather was very good for this time of the year but last week it had been bad. They asked each other: Can I pass you the salt? *Non, merci*. She said that her brother wasn't there because he'd had to go to Ternat, and he answered that Ternat was in a nice part of the country, but when she asked if mijnheer had been to Ternat he blushed. No, he hadn't. Then he got round to mentioning Wavre, where she had been at school. How many girls and novices and sisters there were, and so many from other countries, there were one from Albania, and two from Egypt and two from India, and at every question and every answer they blushed without reason.

That night, back in his room, he felt more than ever that he had to get away from Louvain somehow or other. It wouldn't help if he failed miserably in his exams again, because when he failed the first year Papa had said nothing, hoping that he would scrape through with time and patience. He was too weak-willed to insist that the promise to Mama should be kept, and the burden of humiliations grew heavier, humiliation after humiliation from the Major, in the examination room, from the other students. There were young rips who got him to lend them money. He knew he would never get it back and they knew he didn't have the nerve to ask for it, but he didn't dare refuse them. They dragged him along to a café and flicked cigar-ash in his beer, and as he stuttered and gesticulated in an incoherent nausea of drunkenness he realized, with a vague flash of his feeble understanding, how deep was the abyss of folly where he played grotesquely his pathetic role of clown. The back of his head was, even then, at that age, going bald. They held him fast by the arms to his chair, four of them, and the others lined up to kiss in turn the bald patch, 'this noble scar, won in battle on the field of learning'. When they let him loose he was sobbing, a hoarse and helpless whimper of drunkenness, misery, and hate.

In the third year the news came that his father had had a slight stroke, and he was glad. The Major drove him to Brussels, and as often as the wheels turned the son repeated and repeated the wish that the father would die before he got there. But the cries of the devils within him were not heard, the corpulent lawyer stayed alive, but the son never talked of going back to Louvain and neither did the father.

145

6

Nor did the father ever talk of his deepest wish, his hope that André would take over his practice. He saw now that nothing could ever come of his hope. The shock of the sudden illness that had laid him low and foretold his end dispelled all his illusions. He would die just as his father, Jan Baptist, had wilted and died in this same house, spent and useless, the last of his line. The d'Hertenfeldts should never have abandoned the Schrans and all that it meant to them. The same fate awaited him, the wealthy and successful lawyer, as he and his brothers had inflicted on their father. Jan Baptist had had for him, the richest of them all, the veiled, unspoken contempt he felt for his own witless son, the simpleton.

The simpleton bought chickens, ducks, and turkeys. He had chickenhouses put up in the garden and closed in with wire netting, and he was idiotically indifferent to what happened to the legal practice that he was heir to. Lawyer d'Hertenfeldt was tired, a balloon that gave off puffs of air. That was all he had ever been.

He winced at the restrictions the doctor imposed. You'll starve me to death, doctor. The ten-cent herrings that had been all too plebeian to be eaten in that rich house were now too great a luxury. There was a meal list hanging in the kitchen with his starvation diet, carefully calculated to provide only an absolute minimum of nourishment and no more. He was served half an orange in a small porcelain bowl on a silver platter, an egg with a slice of bread, or a couple of paper-thin strips of smoked meat. Scarcely a taste, never even a single solid mouthful. He had the habit of opening one eye to squint derisively at the tray, closing both eyes and poking blindly at his 'nourishment'. The son saw him melting away under the blanket and hoped he would never get up out of bed again.

His heart was too bitter for any natural feelings. The old nun who was nursing Papa could see that he reacted with the same impassive calm whether the news was good or bad. She was soon

146

convinced he had trodden far along the path of virtue, and when he noticed that, he took a malicious delight in deceiving her. With a feigned casualness he would take a rosary out of his pocket, he put Mama's prayer books ostentatiously on the mantel-piece as if they were constantly in use, and he had the maid buy her fifty devotional works, and the cost was entered in Papa's accounts under the heading of 'miscellaneous expenditure'. It wasn't that he set any store by a reputation for devoutness; his only motive was the pleasure of deceit.

Once a plumber came to do some work in the house and he told the maid he was a socialist. Nothing, she thought, could be worse or more wicked. He had seen the nun on the stairs and he asked if the nun had to sleep with mijnheer—an ugly old hag, I wouldn't have her if she paid me. André heard him and he wished that the nun was young and that the plumber would seduce her.

The second maid was the youngest of eight children. Her father had a shoemaker's shop, a flourishing businees that was a small factory. He had sent his two sons to study for the priesthood, and the younger one was still at the seminary. This father of eight children, an exemplary citizen, honourable and prosperous, had suddenly become infatuated with a twenty-year-old village whore. The two daughters who were still at home were turned out so he could have the house for himself and the whore, and the youngest had, from poverty and shame, come to work here as a maid. The nun had told him the whole story, and she said the poor girl would probably enter a convent. As he listened he was wishing he could find a way to stop that. He gloated over the folly of the besotted father, grinning to himself, you're doing fine, aren't you? Such was his delight in human misery that he only read in the newspapers the reports of tragedies and accidents. 'The unfortunate victim is survived by a grieving widow and eight children,' but to make his satisfaction complete, the grieving widow would have to be 'expecting another child.' Then he chuckled.

He had other specialities as well, the secret vices of exemplary

147

Catholics, a wayward priest who had run off with a girl, or per-versions in a boarding school. To come by these titbits he bought anti-Catholic newspapers which he didn't dare show to the nun or the maids, but he left them on a seat in a park with the report ringed in red pencil. Then he walked on and came back after a while to see if he had had any success.

For him the misdeeds of his fellow creatures were never evil enough or numerous enough. When he counted up all the reports of one day's crimes and catastrophes, the murders, the railway disasters, car accidents, burglaries, poisonings, it was a sizeable total, but for him it was far too meagre. If he had only dared he would have ravished young girls, peeped through windows at women undressing, set fire to crowded cinemas, enticed priests into ways of sin, besmirched the honour of political leaders, but all he did was write obscenities in block letters on the walls of public lavatories, and once the cat went to sleep on his lap and he jabbed the lighted end of his cigarette hard on its nose.

The moments of normal reasoning became rarer. In his early years the thought of hell had always terrified him and curbed his malice, but maybe he didn't have enough imagination to picture in his mind the horrors he was told would be the reward of wickedness. As a small boy he had mused bewilderedly on the hereafter and eternity, until his bewilderment turned to an em-bittered feeling of helplessness, but now the effort of these reflec-tions was beyond him. The rest of his unbelief he got from Madame Dutoy.

Colonel Dutoy's only son had, with the years, got over his childhood ills to grow up tall and broad-shouldered. As children, André and he, both delicate and pale and timid, had been good friends, but as they grew older the physical discrepancy had weak-ened the bonds of friendship. Madame Dutoy was so attached to the villa in La Panne, where the sea air had banished those constant coughs and colds, that she still went with her son, now a student, for the holidays. There, on the beach that had so often brought

148

him back to health, he was suddenly taken ill with appendicitis. He was operated on in Brussels, and when he could get up and about the holidays were over. Madame felt it would be too cruel to send him back to his studies just after he had got out of bed, and it was better to have another month by the sea. When he was out rowing, in spite of all Mama's protests, the pains began again, worse than ever, as if the healed scar were being ripped open with a red-hot knife. Groaning in agony he was rushed back to Brussels, where he lived for another three days, and now and then he inexplicably asked for André. Twice his mother had his childhood friend fetched by taxi to his bedside, and the dying youth never knew that behind the timorous smile on that freckle-spotted face there were two conflicting wishes, a wish that every moaning breath would be his last, and a weaker wish that he would get better.

After the second visit to the hospital something came over him suddenly. A fellow creature, dying, had needed him, someone had felt an affection for him, not as a father or a mother would, but for himself as he was. He was grateful and he was gripped by the fear that this friend, his only friend, would die. He forgot his father who shuffled slowly through the house nearer and nearer to his grave. It was as if everything had changed, and he could become again as others were and be one of them and live as they lived. Lucien mustn't die. He forgot his fowl-run, and in a spasm of anxiety he forgot his timidity and took up the telephone. A hushed voice answered, and it was his friend's grandfather who was sorry to tell him the sad news that Lucien had died that afternoon at five o'clock. He hung up without answering, without a word of sympathy, and he whispered, resentful and bitter, that of course Lucien had to die. Just because Lucien was his friend and because he wanted him to get better, that was enough to make it certain that he wouldn't live. Now it was over. He shed no tears, he didn't grieve, he only sank deeper into the sombre depths of his loneliness.

But a mother doesn't get over such a blow so easily. The coffin was carried slowly out to the hearse, and the house was now so empty and still, so unbearably empty that she couldn't stay there alone, and before the Requiem Mass for her Lucien was ended she had wandered off to see André. She sat beside him, took his hand in hers and began repeating in a toneless wail that he had been his friend, that God should never let anything like that happen, that she had wanted another child after Lucien, that it wasn't her fault, and that she had made Lucien put on a warm singlet. With wide-open vacant eyes she mumbled to herself: 'Je ne pense tout de même pas que Lucien aura froid.'

Yes, this was grief, piteous grief, that he could neither share nor understand. He had nothing but his stupid smile with the flesh of his gums showing under the twitching upper lip.

That went on for a month. If she didn't come to see him she telephoned him and he went to visit her. Her monologues became metaphysical debates with herself. One day she would say that we had to believe in God because then we didn't lose our loved ones completely, but the next day she raged against the cold-blooded God who made a mother suffer like this. Then she would ask herself if it was true, and whether she would see her Lucien again. Nodding with deep satisfaction, she showed him the account for the expensive funeral, and said that Lucien would be pleased, look what she had done for him. Her final attitude was that she didn't want to be comforted, and so she cut herself off from all her friends and acquaintances. The only one she still saw was André, only because he had never uttered a word of sympathy. Do you know what a mother's suffering is? No, she didn't want to be comforted. What good would that do? Lucien had been taken away from her, and did they think she wanted something else in his place? No, Lucien or nothing.

Then she would forget Lucien and talk for hours about long ago when she was young, how she had believed in God up to her first Communion, and after that she didn't pray any more. Then Lucien came, and she would never forget it, he lay there so tiny and so weak, and even though the doctors came every day and her husband laughed at her, she started to pray and have Masses said. If Lucien got a little better she used to say: 'Don't you see, it has helped.' If it didn't help, she said nothing, and let him say: 'What did I tell you?' and she used to think: Now I can show I trust in God, and the next time God will listen. But now she kept thinking about the argument her husband always answered her with: 'Qu'est-ce que vous en pensez, chère amie?' 'If Lucien doesn't get better,' he used to say, 'then the doctor is giving him the wrong medicine and we'll have to call in another specialist. But if he gets better then it will be because of all those novenas.'

He wrinkled his forehead as if he were thinking up a case against unbelief, and she was suddenly stricken with concern for him. He mustn't start worrying about these things, she knew herself how unhealthy it was. You know, she'd had a bursting headache for these last two weeks, so be careful. Besides, prayers weren't any use for her now. If all her praying couldn't keep Lucien alive, then it wasn't worth much.

A last wavering hope drove her to spiritualism. The Colonel asked André to try and take her out of herself, he was the only one who could reason with her. He'd noticed, hadn't he, how thin she was getting, she hadn't had an hour's sleep.

As if he could influence her—it was the other way round. Without any reflection he had, out of bitterness and resentment, adopted her confused unbelief. He didn't resist when she asked him to sit opposite her at a small tea-table. He laid his hands on the tabletop the way she showed him, and closed his eyes when she told him to. Her foot began a nervous tapping on the floor, and it was a sight for laughter or for tears as she leaned forward, with her eyes shut tight, calling out in a delirium of fervour: 'Est-ce toi, est-ce toi, mon fils Lucien?' But he didn't laugh or cry. He only looked up startled at the Colonel, who had heard the tapping and come upstairs and saw that his wife was influencing this young man more than he was influencing her.

151

So I'll take her in hand myself. That would be wiser. He applied for leave of absence and took his wife away for a long trip. A mother's grief heals with time, but for the sicker of the two, the lawyer's son, there was no cure. As a souvenir he was given the expensive set of instruments Lucien had got as an engineering student, but he cherished more the impulsive godlessness of the mother who dropped out of his life except for a yearly letter on the anniversary of Lucien's death. His heart was filled with sorrow no less than hers, and his mind just as blunted and incoherent. He looked at his father who had shed fifteen kilograms, and he thought to himself, sourly and unpityingly: What a lot of bother just to have fifteen kilos less filth in a coffin! A lump of carrion in a wooden box, that's all he would be. There isn't any heaven, and the resurrection is a fairy-tale joke.

7

Twice lawyer d'Hertenfeldt was warned, the second time with a paralysis of the left side, and then came the final blow. No tears and no spiritualism for him. His son buried him and forgot him, and heard, with satisfaction, in the will that his father had more than doubled his own fortune and Mama's as well; and then he told Papa's old chief clerk that he wanted to buy an estate belonging to the Count Van Inghe de Corthout in the village where his father has been born.

The Count Van Inghe de Corthout had every reason to sell. He had only used the Koevoet as a hunting-lodge, and he hadn't been hunting for the last twenty years, for he was eighty-two. Since then it had served as a residence for his son, a prelate of no great distinction, who had died there of consumption in an aura of sanctity.

After that, the Count's family had kept away from the estate for fear of the germs. He had never found a buyer, and when he heard from lawyer d'Hertenfeldt's office that there was a likely taker, provided the price was reasonable, he was only too ready to oblige. Besides, he remembered there were favours for which he had been grateful to lawyer d'Hertenfeldt.

So the estate was bought and the surviving vestige of the great d'Hertenfeldt stock came back to the good earth of Brabant. It was as if the spirit of the glorious past had realized its sins and omissions, and had resolved to make amends. True, the Van den Heuvels flourished in their tenure of the Schrans and the lands that went with it, and there were other sturdy families farming in Brabant, but none could ever equal the glory of the d'Hertenfeldts. After the departure of Jan Baptist the lustre of the village had faded. The rogues felt themselves safe to cheat and swindle, the wronged and the needy felt unprotected. But the farmers who had bought or leased land that had belonged to the d'Hertenfeldts bestowed more than usual care on these fields, as if they feared that Jan Baptist might return and stand there looking at them, with his arms crossed, and say: 'What are you doing with my land?' Meanwhile, the sceptre of authority had passed to Father Claerebout, a dauntless guardian of his flock, who sometimes put obedience before justice. Woe betide the villager who missed a Sunday Mass, and that was the sort of thing the d'Hertenfeldts had never troubled themselves over.

But now a d'Hertenfeldt was coming back. He needed all the craftsmen in the village, masons for all the new outbuildings, carpenters for doors and windows and locks, painters to cover the inside and outside with two coats of paint, labourers to clean out the moat and the pond, and Seppen the verger brought along all his sons and daughters who were big enough to hold a rake or a pitchfork, because, damn it, you couldn't see the pathways any more for the long grass and the weeds, what a hell of a mess it was!

As soon as all that was finished the big vans came from Brussels loaded with old, heavy furniture of oak and mahogany. They could imagine what a house lawyer d'Hertenfeldt had had when all the rooms were filled with cabinets and tables and chairs, and half of what came in one of the vans was, for want of space, stored in the attics. The drivers and their helpers would have liked to divide amongst the four of them the surplus they carried up to the attics. And there were those chests of silverware.

When everything was ready, he arrived, the great d'Hertenfeldt. He came alone, by train, and he walked the mile from the station to the Koevoet, inches shorter than the smallest d'Hertenfeldt anyone could remember, and a good hand's-breath less across the shoulders, and that oversized head of his covered with a bowler hat that sat on his ears and must have been specially made so large for him. As he walked past the houses he began to smile, his thick upper lip pulled over the two crooked front teeth and the lumpy gums. The most pathetic of it all was the way he raised his bowler hat to everyone revealing that bald scalp and looking as if he were frightened of giving offence. There, in that same street where, for more than a century, the d'Hertenfeldts had strode along, proud without conceit, but always conscious of who they were. Anyone who had to pass Jan Baptist d'Hertenfeldt greeted him from ten paces away, and then Jan Baptist answered with just the name, Jef, Louis, Soo. That was all. Always the same brief acknowledgment, straight to the point, nothing more. I, Jan Baptist d'Hertenfeldt, see that you have greeted me, and I acknowledge this by saying your name, Jef, Louis, Soo. Anyone who dared could speak to Jan Baptist in the street, or even walk along with him. He made no distinction among farmer, tradesman, or labourer, priest or burgomaster, but whoever wanted to walk with him had to fall into step by his side, and whether it was on the left or the right no one could ever have the feeling that Jan Baptist wasn't given precedence of place.

Now this new d'Hertenfeldt walked along the old street with his hand on his bowler hat, peering timidly from side to side as if he had to come back the next day and go round from door to door peddling tins of boot polish that had gone hard. When he finally reached the corner, blinking and sweating, and turned out of sight, Seppen the verger called out to the tailor's open window to ask if they had seen him, the Little Lordie, and before he was inside the entrance to the château André d'Hertenfeldt had got his village nickname: the Little Lordie.

In the hall way the Little Lordie gave the maids each twenty francs and welcomed them to the château before they could wish him a long and happy stay. The eldest maid giggled over her broad bosom that everything was ready for the future madame, and what a park, mijnheer, big enough for a dozen children to play in. It's so lovely here, what a difference from the city. How could the master, God rest his soul, ever have thought of leaving here?

He went upstairs. From the window of his bedroom he could look out on the d'Hertenfeldt lands. The corn was stacked in sheaves, and heavy-laden carts went bumping slowly over the fields. The farmhands stopped their work a moment to glance up at his window. From so far away they couldn't see the difference between him and Jan Baptist, and it was good that a d'Hertenfeldt was there again to watch them at their work. But he didn't see them. It was the Schrans he was looking at, and Miss Ursule wasn't anywhere in sight.

So he went there himself a day or two later, surprised at his own boldness. Farmer Van den Heuvel had a bottle fetched so they could drink to their friendship as neighbours, and because every time the conversation flagged the Little Lordie, nervous and embarrassed, kept looking at the magpie that was fluttering round the room, he presented him with the bird as a gift. He mentioned, as a matter of interest, that the bird could say Anna. Later, his son Thuur discovered that it could do much more than that. There was another thing that farmer Van den Heuvel found it necessary to mention: 'A magpie is a fine bird, but dirty, I can tell you that. A magpie does nothing else but shit.' His two daughters hid their faces in shame, but how in heaven's name, he asked, could a farmer say anything else about a magpie! To break the embarrassed silence Octavie proposed another glass of wine, and as the Little Lordie clinked his with Ursule's their trembling fingers touched. He didn't hear a word more of what the farmer was saying.

'It doesn't matter where you come from,' the farmer said. 'Your blood knows where it belongs. A horse knows its stable, a dog knows its master, a pigeon flies back from the other sides of the world.' They had a horse, our big bay, that was foaled in Zellik. It had been here seven years now, but every time his son Thuur rode it anywhere near Zellik it lifted up its head and sniffed the stable where it came from. If you let the reins go it'd gallop back to its old home. Even the plants and trees know their own ground. Farther up in Brabant you have a lot of big orchards. Do you think you could get those apple-trees to grow like that in the sandy ground here? It's just the same with a man, he knows the place he's at home in and his blood feels the call of the earth. The Van den Heuvels come from the Brabant hills. I'm just as well off here as I was there, and you get settled where you've got your family, but I can't miss the big market every year or the fairs in my village, and the moment I see our old farm something goes soft inside me, and I say to myself: This is where I belong. That's why I've always said that when Thuur gets married I'll go back there; that's where I want to die.

It had surprised him that Ursule had acted as if she didn't know magpies shit all over the place, and as if she had never heard him use the word before, but now, when she piped up shyly and proclaimed that she didn't ever want to leave here, he took another look at her and he found that stranger still. It was only a couple of weeks ago that she'd said she would be only too glad to go. He looked at the Little Lordie, and he was more surprised. Now then, he thought to himself, be just as much a d'Hertenfeldt as you want to, and if you've got millions so much the better, but don't go taking my Ursule.

If you must have a Van den Heuvel, take our gendarme, our Octavie. She's more than enough trouble for us, and she's just what you need.

He was the sort Octavie would like, a timid weakling she could order round. Her sister was afraid of men, but she despised them. She would never marry unless she was sure she would be the boss.

8

Their brother Thuur had a bit of both, the fear and the contempt. A big strapping fellow, but never in a hurry. He was the eldest of the three, thirty-six, and it was high time he found himself a wife. Farmer Van den Heuvel used to announce at the table, and now more and more often, that he was going back to Cobbezele to end his days 'just as soon as our Thuur is married.' In the beginning Thuur had only answered that he couldn't run the farm yet without Father, and when Father asked if he had to keep on working till he dropped, then he wanted to know why, for God's sake, was Father in such a hurry to go and die. But that didn't stop the hints, nor did the argument that there were enough women in the house anyway. Oh, and did he think that Octavie was going to spend the rest of her life helping to look after his farm and ironing his shirts? Indeed. Just let him find a wife, and then he'll know how much patience she'd had with him. He'd been brought up the wrong way, my boy, spoilt right from the start, mother's only boy. If she'd had any say it would have been a different story.

The big clod, he can't put his collar on properly himself. Octavie, where's my white shirt? Octavie, where's my stud? His wife won't put up with his nonsense, wait and see.

That didn't encourage him to think about getting himself a wife, but they kept at him. On Sunday there was no more lying stretched out asleep under the apple tree. It was Mass, dinner, and then off out. The best of it was that the girls came flocking round him wherever he went. At every village fair, even before he had downed his third pint, and without even trying, he had a wench hanging on his arm, and it was always serious because the flighty ones knew they didn't have a chance. If he did set his mind to it, and went to visit one of the farms nearby to have a look at the cattle or talk about the crops they were planting this year, he was surrounded by all the young females of the household as soon as they saw him. From time to time he thought he had found his choice, but they were all far too eager to put up the banns. Now, now, Thuur, he would say to himself, watch what you're doing, and he could never make up his mind.

What with being prompted all the time at home, and then finding all too many opportunities, he became more and more wary. That family didn't have a penny, or there was a brother who had died of consumption, this one was too skinny, that one was ugly, and if he couldn't think of anything else he would raise his finger and say: 'You can see from the look of her that she has a nasty character.' But just when he was feeling that it was hopeless, that he had looked everywhere within three hours' ride from the village, and consoling himself with the thought that there was always some snag, just when he was reflecting that now he could spend the Sunday afternoons lying under the apple-tree with a clear conscience, and go and play a game of cards in the evening with old friends, then the magpie did the match-making.

He was lying under the apple-tree, and the girl who passed by was so trim and pretty that, in his surprise, he raised himself on his elbow to look at her again.

'Good day, juffrouw.'

'Good day, mijnheer.'

That was all. That was as far as it went, and it didn't go any farther when he asked Octavie, his eyes blinking as if he were still only half awake, who was that trim and pretty girl that had just gone by twice. Octavie could have hit him round the ears with her dish-towel. So, now he's found someone! He does know where to look, doesn't he? Lord above, these clever men, they can always pick out a girl who is nice and respectable. That was mijnheer André's parlour-maid, you idiot, and her father is Benoo Verstoopt, that shoemaker in Baldeghem, the one who's getting through his fortune with a little trollop no more than twenty. That child was chased out of the house by her father and mijnheer André gave her a place as maid out of pity for her. She came to fetch the magpie for mijnheer, and if he wanted to know anything

159

more about that trim and pretty girl, then he might as well hear that twenty years ago her grandfather had been fished out of the canal in Vilvorde where he had drowned himself. Go back to sleep, you great dolt.

But he didn't go back to sleep, and from then on he slept less and not as soundly as before. Even if your grandfather was fished out of a canal, and your father's spending his fortune with a little trollop of twenty, you can still be trim and pretty. And she was, too. She had those eyes that looked at him and asked: 'Is it my fault, Thuur?'

He used to go and see how the magpie was doing, and he didn't call on the Little Lordie. He went round the back to where the kitchen was. How is it? Is it eating well? Did they give it worms? There is nothing so simple as looking after a magpie, but he found it necessary to spend half an hour in the evening twice a week discussing the subject. Were they teaching it to talk? 'Oh,' Elza said, 'it talks a little.'

'You talk nicely yourself, too,' Thuur said.

'Do you think so, mijnheer?'

'Mijnheer? What's my name?'

'No, no.'

'Oh, yes! What's my name?'

'Arthur...'

'See, you don't know. It's Thuur. Now, what's my name?'

'Thuur...'

'Elza...'

Octavie was so unsuspecting that she supposed he was going to visit mijnheer André, and once she reflected that it wouldn't be a good influence on mijnheer André if he got too friendly with a good-for-nothing like Thuur. They would get to talking about women, and that one of ours is just the sort to lead others astray.

But she saw that the wind was blowing from another direction one day when she was in the attic with Ursule putting the washing through the wringer. She saw them in a pathway in the corn fields saying good-bye, a little love scene, and that was something she always liked watching. The two down there hadn't a thought for attic windows. They pressed each others' hands and turned to go, then turned round and came up to each other again, held hands, let go, started to leave and then came back again. He pulled her close to him, kissed her on the forehead, shook her playfully, took her in his arms again, to give her a long kiss on the mouth and a longer kiss still on the neck. Octavie and Ursule looked at each other, their faces as white as the linen they were putting through the wringer: Thuur.

Then Thuur found out for the first time what a woman is. If he went and married a real witch he knew what was in store for him. He thought that the first torrent of abuse was the worst, and after this first attack everything would calm down. But that first flood was just a beginning.

The idea of it, running round with a servant girl, him, Arthur Van den Heuvel. Not just any servant girl, oh no, it had to be that one. He knew, didn't he, she'd told him already, how the grandfather had drowned himself in a canal, and about the father who was the scandal of Baldeghem. Then the mother, that poor thing, who did nothing but have one child after the other, with miscarriages in between, there was something wrong there too. Oh, yes, there was a brother at the seminary, but he would soon be sent away, and because Octavie didn't know where the other sister was, she must be working in a café, you can guess what at in one of those cafés. Mijnheer André's servant girl. No one less than mijnheer André from the château. Mijnheer André, the friend of the family. She didn't say that mijnheer André would never be able to have a high opinion of the sisters of the wastrel who married his servant girl, but that was what put her in such a rage.

He had had to weather many a storm of abuse, and he weathered this one with the same unconcern. The rebukes and scoldings had never changed him or improved him, and neither did this tirade. He came and went and they kept seeing each other. The Little

Lordie, who know nothing of this wooing, and still felt obliged to express his gratitude for the gift of the magpie, sent her with presents to the Schrans. At the Schrans they didn't have any ducks, so he gave them all his duck eggs. He had read in Larousse that duck eggs were used in Germany for sausages and pastries, and he recopied that in the letter he sent with the eggs. *Je suppose que vous voudriez, comme on fait beaucoup en Allemagne...* That suited Thuur —the eggs for his sisters, and for him, Elza, a smile, a blush, a word that meant nothing but said all he wanted to hear. She had never asked for a free day because she had nowhere to go, but now he got her to ask, and there were hours, all too brief, of delicious happiness.

'You aren't serious with me,' she often used to say. 'You're only passing the time.' Then he would give solemn pledges. She knew what an undreamed – of chance he was offering her, and the hope of rising above her modest origin made her more cautious than she was. Out of the hundreds of trees along the lane to Grimbogen he would always remember the tall beech tree she leaned against when, with a voice that shook, she implored him to think it over before he decided. She wouldn't have any money because Papa was throwing it all away. The disgrace of what Papa was doing fell on her as well, and he shouldn't forget that it could be thrown up at him, too, and she didn't want that, Thuur, it would hurt too much. Besides, she wasn't a farm girl, she couldn't even milk a goat. You can't overlook all that.

Think it over carefully, Thuur. She said it would be better if he didn't see her for a month, or maybe longer, and if he changed his mind he mustn't even write to her, because that wouldn't be good for either of them. She said she would understand, and she would always be grateful for the friendship that had made her so happy. Yes, she was serious, and now let us do that, we won't be sorry later that we stopped to think it all over.

She was too sweet and appealing to interrupt, but when she finished he lifted her up. There was nothing in the world he couldn't have lifted at that moment. He raised her mouth up to his own and their tears flowed between their lips. When it's like that there's nothing an Octavie can do.

9

That was why Father was let into the dreadful secret. They didn't know that he had had to wage much the same battle to marry their mother, who had been a schoolteacher, but he remembered it all too well. He looked at the ceiling, and why couldn't they leave him in peace?

Leave him in peace! Had Octavie bottled up her distress for weeks and weeks just to leave him in peace? Had she told him she could hardly sleep any more at night, and that she was worn out with worry, and look at Ursule with rings under her eyes and getting paler and paler. They'd pleaded and pleaded with that rotter of a brother of theirs, but it had done no good, and now when they asked their father to help he said they had to leave him in peace. You weren't always like that, Father. Mother spoilt Thuur and if you start letting him get his own way...

He knew she would go on and on if he didn't show he was getting angry—for they were a tough lot, women, he always said. He snapped at her, now had she finished, and then, at least, Octavie ran into the kitchen sobbing. He sat there as if he were still enjoying his afternoon nap, but when Thuur walked unsuspectingly past the back of the chair he said, wide awake: 'Thuur.'

Thuur stopped, and from his chair, with his legs stretched out on a stool, farmer Van den Heuvel growled: 'What's all this I hear?'

'Yes, Father, maybe it's true all this you've been hearing.'

'No, that can't be true!'

Behind the chair Thuur said: 'But true it is.'

How in God's name was it possible? It was with these same words that farmer Van den Heuvel himself had put his father in a towering rage, forty years ago to the very month. His father had jumped up, and he'd never heard of such a thing, and he wouldn't have that nonsense here. He'd see the farm in ashes first, he'd slaughter the cattle one by one before he'd leave it to a Van den

Heuvel with a schoolteacher. The farm was still standing, and the cattle bred from that same stock were grazing in the fields. The Van den Heuvel with his schoolteacher had farmed well and thrived, and all his children had bounced on Grandfather's knee. Farmer Van den Heuvel knew it was useless to fly into a rage, and Thuur didn't understand why Father, for the first time, let himself be contradicted, and on a matter like this. It was a strange silence.

Thuur shuffled uncertainly and, just to say something, he asked what they would do with the field behind the church, maybe plant it with clover again, the same as last year? Farmer Van den Heuvel answered: 'It seems that you're big enough and old enough to know what to do yourself.' The farm was Thuur's now; he wanted to go back to Cobbezele.

They're all the same, these men, Octavie lamented. But there was one who might be better than the others and might do what he should when he's told. It was discussed a hundred times over with Ursule, and they reached their decision after a whole night of mournful deliberation. They were so unhappy that they put their arms round each other, and Octavie held Ursule tighter and started sobbing. They had to go and tell him everything. It was better to do that than have to hang their heads in shame before the whole village and all the families round about. He'll help us, Ursule, he'll get rid of that little hussy. But they still had to decide which of them would ask him, and while they flattered each other, he'd listen to you more than he would to me, they started to feel jealous of each other. They turned over, good night, sleep well, and they forgot Thuur and they couldn't sleep for wondering which one of them it was that he would like to ask him to help.

The Little Lordie trembled and blushed by turns. He trembled at finding himself host to two young ladies, and he blushed for happiness because they had come to ask him 'a special favour'—that he would send that girl packing there and then. He didn't dare refuse. He always had visions of rendering them a great service so that Ursule would come to him and out of gratitude ask him to marry her.

But he would never dare to send Elza packing and then face Marie who sheltered the poor child in the shadow of her massive maternal bosom. Mijnheer, she's the best in the world, so good, and she works so hard, there couldn't be another like her. The father who turned her out ought to be flayed alive, mijnheer, he ought to be strung up on the nearest tree. The Little Lordie couldn't bring himself to say a word to Marie about the favour that had been asked of him, and a devil whispered in his ear. He had never even noticed the girl, neither in Brussels nor here, and the song of praise from Marie made him wish he could corrupt this virtuousness.

The first time he gave her some money was when she asked for an afternoon free. There you are, just to buy some little thing for yourself, but don't tell anyone. There were enough little things she needed to buy before she was married and she didn't tell anyone. The second time he said she had been used to having more than her wages here, and she was a good worker, and here was something for her. The third time he gave her money while she was making his bed in the morning. It was not a small amount and she stared at the notes. He stood there looking at her with his stupid grin; she didn't know what to say.

He was only waiting for a smile from her, a sign that she understood his gifts. He wished and hoped she was the sort that went and worked as a maid just to get into a rich household and make the most of every chance. She'd been able to snare that levelheaded Thuur Van den Heuvel, and if the Schrans could tempt her, then the château would tempt her even more.

He didn't even know himself what he wanted of her. Sometimes he would think it was sheer folly, that he was in love with Ursule, and that he must find some way to make Ursule his wife. Other times he would feel sure he could never win Ursule and that all he could expect was an occasional chance to paw in the dark at a servant girl kept quiet with generous tips. Now his only thought was that she must smile. Perhaps she would laugh knowingly and walk by too close to him. Then, in a daze, he would grab at her. But all she did was to thank him politely. She had to buy things, mijnheer, because it doesn't matter how careful you are, everything wears out so quickly.

Do you have to buy a lot? What are you going to buy? He waited for her to answer, to say the names of the undergarments so he could nod, leering at her. Even that didn't make her thaw out. Then he said quickly, but she mustn't tell anyone about it, he was going to give her double her wages for a month, she would be able to buy everything at once. She could read his purpose in his eyes from the signs that a woman knows instinctively. She refused his money, and that evening Thuur heard that she didn't want to stay any longer at the château.

Of course he couldn't believe the improbable explanation she gave for this decision. He kept at her until she finally admitted it was mijnheer. She hadn't said anything before, because he might think she was just making it up to tease him, and anyway, if she had said anything, it would only have caused trouble, maybe Thuur would be jealous and she would have been accusing mijnheer without any real reason. Besides, she was so glad that she could put a little extra in her money box, so she could give Thuur a surprise later when she showed him how much she had managed to save up all by herself.

This wasn't a harridan like Octavie, this wasn't the sort of woman he had always been afraid of. She looked up at him like a little girl and asked him what she ought to do. She would stay if he said so. Mijnheer hadn't really done anything, and she was sure she could look after herself. So Thuur had to decide.

Thuur looked forbiddingly at the ground, ready to break a hundred Little Lordies in two at the first misplaced glance at his Elza. Finally he decided she should stay until they were married, but we are getting married in two months.

'I don't know anything about a farm,' she said.

'We're getting married in two months' time,' Thuur said.

Octavie hit him round the ears, right and left. She rushed at him from behind and punched at the big round cushion of his back. She kicked his legs and before he knew what was happening she had whirled him hysterically out of the door. Farmer Van den Heuvel wasn't sleeping so soundly in the afternoons any more. He heard Octavie in the kitchen yelling that there wasn't a man in the house to say what was right and what was wrong, but she would throw him out and keep him out. When she opened the door to tell Father all this, Father's eyes suddenly closed and Father was snoring, and there was no waking him. Stop that shouting, leave Father in peace. Then she sat down at the table crying, and when that was over there was Thuur back again. And once again she flew at him like a wounded beast ready to fight to the death, but he calmly caught her by the wrists. Now then, Octavie. She gave him such a vicious kick on the shin, it hurt with such a pain, that he gave a roar, and it was as well that his fist only hit the table. The coffee bounced out of the three cups, and that's enough. He was getting married next month, do you understand?

And if they wanted to know why it had to be so soon, then they might as well know that it was because of their mijnheer André, the dirty swine. Yes, that snake who thought he could buy a poor girl with a handful of his money. He offered her money, twice her month's wages, if you please, and in his bedroom, if you please. Now say something, or put some vinegar on your forehead if you think you're going to faint. A respectable girl that no one could say a word against, and for months now they'd been telling tales about her and abusing her, but that whoremonger in the château, the way they ran round praising him would make you sick. And he wasn't ashamed of his Elza, she was his Elza, and if there was any more of that talk they'd soon see what would happen.

But he would hang his head in shame, and so would Elza, when one of his sisters twisted that fine fellow from the château round her finger. That would make him ashamed. That wasn't all, and their faces turned all colours before he had finished saying that he could just see his two dear sisters tearing each other's eyes out when it came to deciding which of them would have him: you're both running after him like a pair of bitches on heat. They didn't know where to look. Octavie put her hands over her heart. And now they could take it or leave it, but he was going to marry his Elza next month.

If only they had believed what their brother had shouted at them. Then they might have freed the Little Lordie from the fetters of his furtive shyness, the relationship could have been normal, and Ursule might have married him, not next month, but next year. But instead, they were tearfully indignant, and now they could see, they wailed to each other, what a wicked, wicked hussy that Elza was. Ach, but what could you expect, it runs in the family. Their sister-in-law-to-be would stick at nothing, telling such awful lies about mijnheer André who had picked her up off the streets and been so good to her. He had given her notice, and, of course, she knew that Thuur would forget her as soon as she was out of his sight. So she had got in first and played up to him, twisting everything round. That wicked baggage had been too sly for them. But it's always like that. No wonder they say that a whore has more luck than ten respectable girls.

When they went and told mijnheer André about his servant girl's despicable intrigue, he realized what thanks he had got for his generosity, and they saw with tender sympathy how he lowered his eyes in shame at such dreadful slanders. He said you couldn't expect anything else from folk like that. If Octavie was in his place, mijnheer André, she'd get the gendarmes to come and hear what she had to say for herself. And they could give her a warning she wouldn't forget, mijnheer André. He blushed and looked at his nails, and observed sanctimoniously that you didn't do good for the sake of a reward. Ingratitude, after all, that's the way of the world. They stared at him adoringly.

Of course Elza didn't get any wedding present, a disappointment for Thuur, who was only waiting to send it back. The morning of the wedding day Octavie stayed in bed 'sick', and from the look on Ursule's face, she was even 'sicker'. The most presentable member of the family was farmer Van den Heuvel himself. After he'd had a few glasses, he confided his opinion to his sister-in-law. We'll just have to be patient for another nine months, and then Octavie and Ursule would be fighting each other to nurse the baby. That's how it always turns out, Eulalie, and, as for him, he was going back to live in Cobbezele.

But he was wrong there. Thuur could get his own way, but he, an old man now, couldn't stand up to Octavie and Ursule. The fine house that stood waiting for him in Cobbezele was built even finer here, four wide windows in the front and a high attic, facing the Koevoet. Like the churches with their doors facing east, to the source of light and hope. *Ex Oriente lux.*

10

But for the next few months at least it couldn't be expected that that light would cast forth its beams. If mijnheer André should ever want to be the brother-in-law of his servant girl, if he does want to, we'll have to be patient.

Then the family from Louvain put in an appearance. First Willy and Jacques. It was the holidays, he could put them up, couldn't he? Then, a week later, Mouche. The Major had gone off alone in his car for fourteen days in Switzerland, that's the sort of crazy thing he does, and she had felt lonely. In the middle of the second week the Major himself turned up. He'd found the house locked up, and he called out from the entrance at the bridge that he thought that's where they would be. And there they were, *nom de tonnerre!*

They enjoyed themselves, except the Major. He didn't go sailing, he couldn't swim, neither animals nor plants nor flowers interested him, but since his boyhood days he had made a hobby of carpentry, and now he would make his nephew garden seats and tables. The rest of the time he was bored, and he left the three others to their outdoor diversions, rowing, swimming, fishing, cycling, shooting, and when they could think of nothing else they baited their host.

That was just what they could expect him to do, to go off and live all alone in a château like that. And they soon noticed that he was somehow interested in that big new house over there. He always sneaked out so that he wouldn't have to take any of them with him, and once Jacques offered to go himself with the parcel he had given the new maid to deliver, but it didn't come off. Once Ursule and Octavie came visiting, and he escorted them into the salon, passing Mouche without introducing her. That was too much. The same evening the four of them insisted on being introduced to the Van den Heuvel family, and he couldn't refuse.

Right from the start they took their revenge. The three of

them—for the Major had, out of boredom, taken refuge in a volume of old numbers of *L'Illustration*—were on their friendliest behaviour, keeping up a flow of lively conversation that completely excluded the Little Lordie, and when it was time to say good-bye, but only till tomorrow, they had arranged to meet again to go for walks and go rowing and Mouche had coyly asked if she could call in some time, just to have a talk. She could bring her knitting, and it would be nice to sit and chat, that's what we women like.

Ursule was four years older than the Little Lordie, Octavie six, and the Little Lordie himself was five years older than Jacques, the youngest. But Octavie couldn't help feeling that Willy had been attracted to her. Ursule thought the same about Jacques. They didn't discuss it with each other, but how exciting it was for the sisters-in-law of a servant girl to be flattered by these fine young gentlemen! That would help mijnheer André to forget what had happened, and maybe he would even be jealous. But Ursule tried to put this thought aside, so as to stay true to mijnheer André. Then she wondered why she felt like that, because there had never been any real sign of encouragement, and she suddenly realized with a thrill of consternation that, in her thoughts, she never said mijnheer André any more. Oh dear, she'd have to be careful, it would be so easy to forget herself. Hullo, André. She gave a dreamy sigh of yearning. He wasn't as ugly as she had thought at first.

But when they went rowing Jacques always found a chance to take her arm as she stepped into the boat and to put his arm round her if she screamed because the boat rocked too much. She was drowsy, she wanted to lay her head on his shoulder. He would sing, and his voice was warm and velvety, he spoke such wonderful French, the afternoons were hot and languorous. He asked her if she was a good swimmer, and she said helplessly, that she didn't know what was wrong with her, she could just lie down and go to sleep. Willy went to work even more vigorously on Octavie.

It wasn't difficult to sweep two country girls like them off their feet. The boarding-school had given them grandiose ideas, and it was only on the rarest occasions that they could mix with such distinguished company where they would surely find their Prince Charming. They spared no effort to be lively and gay, so as to show that they were at home in this milieu, they said they had been to Switzerland although they hadn't, they were so sorry that they couldn't play tennis here, and the Little Lordie saw a new Ursule, an Ursule he didn't know, and he imagined that he hadn't been able to make any impression on her. He saw her transformed by Jacques's glances just as a plant taken from a dark corner revives and blossoms in the sunlight. A sad, rankling bitterness choked him. She saw this and it was a proof that he was far from indifferent.

If he was just a little jealous there would be no harm done; that would make him all the more determined, and he would appreciate her all the more for rejecting Jacques. He couldn't, she told herself, seriously think that she would prefer Jacques if it came to making a choice. For a country girl the profession of lawyer could only be somehow suspect, as if he didn't earn his living by honest means, and who would stand a chance against the owner of the Koevoet? Her artless scheme to draw him closer to her created a gulf between them. As his despair deepened at the attentions Jacques showered on her, he gave up all hope, he realized the futility of his illusion, and he brooded in silent bitterness. So she smiled all the more at Jacques to rouse him and tempt him. One night Octavie confided that Willy had asked her if she was in love with anyone, or whether there was someone who had won her heart. Jacques was too considerate to take the joke so far with Ursule. She thought she hadn't been friendly enough and she flirted even more recklessly.

She wasn't serious, but Octavie was. Octavie was ready to follow her Willy to the ends of the earth. But for the time being she only followed him to the back of the aviary, where there was enough cover for a first kiss. The Major had, *nom de tonnerre*, noticed what was going on, but Mouche winked at him that it wasn't important, not to make a fuss, *tais-toi donc*, she would explain everything later.

There had to be a farewell supper to end such a wonderful holiday, the family from Louvain said, and the Little Lordie was prepared to spend half this fortune on it if only they would leave and never come back again. Mouche arranged the places at the table, putting the holiday couples next to each other. She took the Little Lordie for herself. She still had a score to settle with him, and her stepsons' jokes and jeers were childishly crude compared with the subtle ways she embarrassed him and humiliated him and prevented him saying a word to Ursule, who sat opposite. With a friendly, serious face she started a conversation about books. Not that she read much, but he never read anything at all.

On his right, Ursule and Jacques were talking literature. He began to sweat from every pore.

'Ah, Bourget, je vous crois bien, et Bazin donc!'

He rashly joined in: 'Oh là là, Bazin! *Le blé qui meurt!* Mm!' And he pulled a face as if he had been asked whether he liked caviare.

The three from Louvain weren't going to let this chance go, and they shouted together: 'Et *La terre qui lève* alors!' They laughed so strangely that he wanted to sink out of sight, but he couldn't imagine why they laughed. To cover his confusion he stood up to fill the wine-glasses, and in the mirror he saw a red, puffy, ugly face. As he slumped down again in his chair he thought he breathed the reek of his own sweat, and his toes pressed tight and cramped against his shoes. Cigars, he thought, the smell of tobacco. He grabbed a cigar as a drowning man seizes a stick, lit it, and groaned to himself as the maid came in with the chicken and apple sauce. Wriggling with embarrassment, he looked down at his hand, and saw a pea had fallen on his waistcoat, and there was dirt under one of his nails. The thought that Ursule must have noticed this dirty finger-nail made him tremble, and Mouche at once took a knife and gently scraped a blob of sauce off his cuff. When she put her hand under his sleeve to wipe the stain with a serviette she touched his wrist that was damp with drops of sweat. She asked him if he didn't feel too warm.

She leaned over, her red mouth too close to his; he pulled nervously at his waistcoat to make the pea fall out of sight, and he caught the reek of his sweat again. Hastily and awkwardly he handed her a rose to smell, then smelt it himself, and from farther down the table Willy said: 'Le baiser sur la rose.' Everything began to spin round. The sweat streamed. He eased his legs apart, he felt a shoe lightly tap three times against his. He said pardon, and all the others stared at him. The rose lay on the table, he didn't dare touch it again. Jacques was talking to Ursule, even more softly and intimately. The Major, who had been drinking in silent boredom all evening, just stared at them. *Quel idiot, nom de tonnerre!* The Little Lordie sat there doomed. He could see Ursule and Jacques already married, and suddenly he realized why they had laughed. The book was *Le blé qui lève*.

'Est-ce que je n'ai pas dit là tantôt *Le blé qui meurt?*

'Non, tu as dit: *La terre qui lève.*'

'Ah, tout de même, Je pensais avoir dit «qui meurt» et c'est «qui lève». Oui, oui, alors c'est bien.'

'Qui lève, qui meurt, qui meurt, qui lève, what the hell is it then?' the Major bellowed, and glared at him so that he didn't know any more which it was.

They went on teasing him, mixing the names of titles and authors. Had he never read *Les pas sur la neige* by Paul Claudel? He shook his head, guilty and ashamed at being made a fool of in front of Ursule. But Ursule had seen through the mockery, and as she got up from the table she took the rose and pinned it on her blouse. That evening Jacques asked him if he could send him letters to pass on to Ursule, but even that couldn't destroy the happiness that was his at seeing her wear his rose.

11

In his sleep she came towards him with the red rose still pinned on her blouse over her left breast. But his six turkeys began to hiss. They leapt at the patch of red, and when he tried to jump up to protect her he couldn't bend his legs. He jumped but he didn't move. Her blouse was torn, and the turkeys pecked at her left breast.

She was in a hospital, lying on Mama's lap. Mama lifted up the torn strip of her blouse and he could see a deep red hole where her breast had been, and in the hole her heart was beating. If the fog comes, Mama said, and the fog gets to her heart, then she'll die. We'll have to take off her clothes and wrap her up in rolls of cotton wool, but you mustn't watch; you call the young man she's going to marry.

He called out Jacques, and she groaned: 'Tu es là, mon chéri?' The Little Lordie answered: 'Oui, c'est moi, ma chérie,' but when he looked closely it wasn't Ursule, but the fat maid, Marie, and every time he tried to pin the rose back on her blouse he stuck the pin into her left breast. Her blouse kept bursting open, sixteen buttons all at once. Desperately he tried and tried to fasten the rose, then she shouted that he was jabbing the pin into her left breast, and he didn't hear the fog starting to boil in the heating pipes. He ran upstairs, and it was almost too late. The fog, thick and heavy like water, had risen up to the second floor, and it was forcing the windows open. He nailed them closed and glued them down. The glue splattered everywhere. He called out for help, but there was no one in the room. Suddenly the heating pipes were steaming like the spout of a kettle, the fog sprayed out in a sizzling, boiling jet. Weeping with despair, he put his mouth to the pipe and sucked up the smoke. He felt sick, then he tried to blow the smoke back into the pipe, but a stream of sparks and flame flew out in his face. He hadn't seen that the fog was smouldering, and when he had blown back into the pipe it caught fire.

He woke for a moment, lying across the bed, and vomited on

176

the carpet. When he fell asleep dreaming again he heard Ursule saying that she had to feed her baby, and she would show him how nicely it had all healed up. The only difference, she said, was that her left breast was a little heavier now than the right one. She weighed them separately on the scales Marie had in the kitchen, and the difference was just over sixty-five grams. Her husband took a rifle down from the wall and asked him—*voyons, cousin*, no nonsense now—if he loved Ursule or not. *Tant mieux alors*, he said, and shot him dead.

The Little Lordie sprang out of bed and ran to the window. In the garden below Jacques was calling him with a gun and a dead thrush in his hand. It was half-past five in the morning. By ten o'clock he had shot four more, and he took them all to the Van den Heuvels before they drove off at eleven. They left the Little Lordie behind, so tired that he stayed in bed all day. But the family from Louvain, all except the Major, had enjoyed themselves so much that they didn't need any sleep. Jacques and Willy hilariously assessed their conquests.

Jacques maintained that he had put up the best performance, he had got the Little Lordie to promise to be a *postillon d'amour* between him and his own heart's desire. Can't you see that jealous lover delivering his rival's letters, next week he would have the first of the series ready: 'Ma très chère amie, Que les jours de séparation me paraissent longs. Je ne puis oublier, ma chère Ursule, les heures trop courtes, hélas, mais si délicieuses que j'ai passées près de toi. Je ne puis oublier ce merveilleux crépuscule, où pour la première fois ton regard si doux, si tendre et si pur...' But Willy said the love he had awakened in a virgin heart was far, far deeper. They had scarcely savoured the first kiss together, natural-ly together, in meteorological and psychological circumstances that couldn't have been more favourable, than she had, with that resolute high-mindedness of hers, turned the discussion to the question of ideals. Sitting there, hand in hand, they had dig into this problem. Would you say that was well put, brother Jacques,

177

with all your literary talents, that image of digging, sitting down? She had immediately and most emphatically proclaimed her deep aversion to modern concepts of marriage. Now don't think that he bowed in submission, far from it. He had taken the standpoint of a modern young man considering marriage, and what is more, birth control didn't go far enough for him, he had told her without mincing his words, conditionally, Octavie, my dear, I am in favour of abortion. Of course she didn't understand that 'conditionally', but that he was in favour of abortion, and not just in favour of it, but 'conditionally' in favour of it, this was even worse than mere approval, much worse. That seemed to make her realize what a grave responsibility was hers. Not only the noble duty of bringing to fulfilment and fruition a truly Christian marriage, but first, before that could come to pass, she had to lead him back to the fold. 'No getting into my bed until I've banished these false and evil doctrines' was her motto from then on. But he had piled up this mountain range of difficulties higher and higher. Jacques, on the other hand, had kept to a purely sentimental approach, and we'll see if he can wriggle out of it with honour and dignity unscathed. Sooner or later Jacques would have to drop this mask of pretence and leave Ursule with a broken heart. Ach, so vulgar! His wife, if he ever found himself a wife, would get anonymous letters and telephone calls. But he, Willy, had established an ideological barrier, right from the start, and no compromising. When she had protested, all aflutter with fear and horror, that he simply couldn't reconcile those godless ideas with his faith, he had given her the second jolt, and that was a jolt. 'Oh, that,' he had answered, with a nonchalant cynicism, 'let's not talk about it.' Her hand went ice-cold in mine, ladies and gentlemen, her face turned white as chalk, her maidenly bosom heaved and quivered. 'Faith,' I said, 'I have just as much faith as my professors have.' Monseigneur the rector would never get to hear of it, he hoped, but he had held forth at some length on the crucial issue of faith and science, and in the heat of his discourse he had declared that there were professors—and he reeled off a few names he had made up on the spur of the moment—who had just as much faith, Octavie, as that stone there. Of course, she babbled about the danger of 'all that scientific talk' that these women are always so suspicious of. And so that's how it is, now his Octavie was praying for him every night. He knew now she would never ever give her hand, and all that went with it, to an infidel who was in favour of abortion, and conditionally to boot, and she was well aware, too, that, be it but temporarily until her prayers were answered, he was completely unsuited for a d'Hertenfeldt-Van den Heuvel combination dedicated to the unlimited production of truly Christian progeny. It was, at least, a clear-cut situation.

If the Major was sitting behind a newspaper, then it was certain that he saw and heard everything that was going on, for nothing absorbed him less than reading. He shouted over his *Le Soir:* 'Was that what Willy called a clear-cut situation? What sort of a game was that, faith and science, *nom de tonnerre?* On ne discute pas avec les femmes!' When he was young they didn't go on like that. A bit of flirting, just as there is nowadays, but that was all, everyone knew just how far to go, and there was none of this leaving a girl behind saying prayers and all muddled up with this faith and science nonsense.

And the Little Lordie, with less hope than ever, could start his wooing all over again, so timid that Ursule didn't understand him, and trembling each time the postman came riding through the gate on his bicycle. He didn't dare mar the idyll of young love that had unfolded before his eyes and had to be continued now by correspondence. There wasn't much point in visiting the young ladies or asking them to call, and so that he could at least see them now and then, he fastened like a leech on the old farmer.

He took to calling on him often, as if he valued him as a special friend, and as if that were the reason he kept in touch with the Van den Heuvels. He brought the old man to see the new stables, the poultry-run, and the lawns and gardens.

'Yes,' the farmer said, 'we have to make our living out of it, and for you it's just a lot of money spent, that's the difference. All these model farm gadgets cost a pile of money, but a farmer works his farm to earn what he can,' This remark gave the Little Lordie the excuse he was looking for. It wasn't his intention to throw his money away, though it didn't matter really if he had to invest something each year, but if he could just cover the expenses he'd be pleased, and it should be possible. So the farmer gave him good advice and, with the same authority he wielded on his own farm and with his natural disregard for formalities, he took things into his own hands and gave orders direct to Seppen the verger, who was now gardener and handyman at the Koevoet. The Little Lordie, who had dreamed of ruling at least over the domain of his fowls and turkeys, saw this dream shattered, too. The farmer told Seppen to sell these chickens, to keep these hens for their eggs, and the ones that had their best days behind them he just handed to Seppen with a knife. It's better for mijnheer to eat them than let them eat up his money.

Marie had always let him think that he chose the menu himself. 'Mijnheer, if we had roast beef with peas and new potatoes today...,' she would say, as if she were asking him. But no longer. Now she said: 'Today we'll have to have chicken.'

Once, just as an excuse for a visit, he went to ask the farmer where he could buy one or two incubators. This would be a fine way to pass the time, to put the lights on over the eggs, check the temperature every now and then, and watch the wonder of hundreds of fluffy chicks breaking through the shells. But to the farmer's way of thinking that was all too dear, and anyway you don't need machines like that. Why don't you do what we've always done, put the eggs under the old hens. So the Little Lordie had to give up his idea of incubators.

He went with the farmer to buy the horse he had so long dreamed of. There were two. The Little Lordie set his heart on the black one, but the farmer said that out of the two only the roan was 'a horse with character'. If he wanted to buy the other one, he could, but he shouldn't have taken the trouble to come here, he might as well throw his money in the moat. Reluctantly, docilely, he bought the roan.

12

The weeks passed, and still the dreaded letter didn't come. He began to imagine something far worse, a direct correspondence between them. She might have had a dozen letters and answered them all. Sometimes in his dreams these letters were read aloud to him, and once he woke up sobbing, and another time he was invited to come and watch their lovemaking. Jacques said to him: 'Just look at what I can do with her.'

These nightmares set his blood throbbing with a morbid excitement. He grabbed the hens and felt with his finger, the way he had seen the farmer and Seppen do, to see whether they were going to lay. They blew on the feathers and pressed with a broad, strong finger, looking thoughtfully sideways. He would shut himself in the stall with the three sheep and try to milk them. When they pranced around on heat he rebuked them with the crudest words he could think of. Those timid hands, that shook and sweated at the dinner table or when anyone spoke to him, were hard and vicious when he was alone with the animals. He spoke to them with the words he never dared to say. He breathed deep the heavy smell of the beasts and their dung, and the wild longing of male lust, that is soothed and made pure by a woman's embrace, was savage and depraved. In the evening when Seppen wasn't there he flogged the roan, lashing with delight where it hurt most, and cursing. A horse is a fine and noble animal. If it is in pain its eyes are almost human. The suffering in its eyes awakened in him a feeling of tenderness, and that was why he delighted in making it suffer.

He liked to play the philanthropist, though his benevolence was only weakness. Octavie and Ursule, Seppen and Marie would tell him about the plight of poor families in the village, and then he felt that they were thinking: You are rich and they are poor. So he gave money, and because he was afraid it might seem too little, he gave too much. The word went round amongst the poachers, and, since he could never refuse, he bought all the hares they came round selling, and he paid prices that were always too high, and he always bought so many that he had to send them to the Van den Heuvels and their friend, Father Claerebout.

When young couples married his generosity knew no bounds. They could come to Marie and order the pudding and home-made cakes for the wedding-feast, and Marie would say that they must go upstairs to see mijnheer. He never gave less than a basket with five or six bottles of wine. They didn't know that their kind benefactor was lewdly hoping the wine would loosen their tongues and inflame their passions, or that, alone in the evenings, he pictured to himself the intimacies of their bridal night. The poorest couples got princely gifts, a bed, a table, with six chairs, fine linen sheets. To his sick mind their marriage was an animal orgy of pairing, for he could not understand that a man and a woman could be drawn together by their love and by their trust in each other. He found his pleasure in spreading a nest for these two rutting animals, a mounting-place where the stronger would quell the weaker in the blind violence of lust.

When, after three months, Jacques's letter finally arrived he was plunged so deep in despair and uncertainty, so racked by his solitary obsessive fantasies, that he was glad to fulfil his promise to Jacques. But first, he tried by daylight and by lamplight to read it through the envelope. The letter gave him an excuse to ride on his horse past the Van den Heuvels' and to whisper to Ursule at the door that she must come alone, he had something for her. A love-letter would be sure to trouble her virginal serenity and arouse in her an eager longing that would make her ripe like a fruit ready for him to pluck if it ever came to a break with Jacques. But she only wanted to let him see that Jacques had no reason to write her secret letters. She gave a frown when she saw the address, then she opened the envelope and read the letter as if it were an ordinary message of greetings from an aunt or an uncle. If only he could have known how her body was throbbing with the thought that this was a wonderful chance to draw him out of his shell. Perhaps that was why he had asked her to come, any other time he was always so frightened of being alone with her or Octavie.

They sat opposite each other at the table that seemed to her now to be too wide, and the bright circle of light from the lamp enclosed them in their nearness to each other. He saw her black, wavy hair gleaming; he saw her fine, sensitive lips forming the words she read; he hoped she would blush, hang her head in embarrassment, that she would realize the blinds were drawn and the doors were closed, that no one could see them or hear them. He edged his foot nearer her chair. Just one touch of her shoe, then he would nudge back, clask her ankle with both his feet. She would reach out her hand to him, he would bend over the table towards her. The maids knocked and said good night; they went to bed at nine o'clock. That made his heart beat faster. Ursule dearest, love Jacques if you want to, but kiss me once, oh, just once.

She read the letter only to find out why it had been sent via the Little Lordie, and the reason he gave was anything but convincing. Cousin André could be trusted, Jacques wrote, and, of course, there was nothing to hide, but he was afraid that it might be the custom in her family to let everyone in the house read the letters they got. That was the rule in some old-fashioned families of good standing, and even though he was not confiding any secrets, this was a letter from a sincere and devoted friend, and it was not meant to be read by anyone else. And now, why was he writing to her— he felt he had to tell her now he still remembered with such happy thoughts that wonderful holiday, and how he was looking forward impatiently, now in these winter months, to the next summer. Did she remember that time they had . . .

The rest she only glanced at, a woman can always tell whether a letter is just so many empty words or whether the words are written with the warmth of affection. Her thoughts were with the man opposite her. He just sat there. She had read the letter through, but she still held it in front of her, and still he didn't speak. Finally, she pushed it across the table to him to show that there was absolutely nothing between her and Jacques. He would have to say something, and then she could give an answer that would start the sort of conversation she hoped for. But he didn't want to read the letter, he wouldn't have dared, not for anything in the world. She tore it up and tossed it into the stove, then adjusted her hair in front of the mirror, and said that she didn't like the way lawyers ranted and babbled.

What could be more natural than for him to ask what she preferred, what she really did like? Then she would be coy: I don't really know. With her, too, the path that led to cosy intimacy was long and roundabout, but it was for him to ask: Well, do you like doctors? No. Engineers, then? No. So it would go on, this childish game, until she admitted with a shy, playful smile that she liked a serious man, who was reserved and modest, kind and devout. What colour of eyes should he have? Blue. How tall should he be? So tall, and she would put her hand on his head. Now kiss me, don't wait any longer, don't be frightened to touch me. Hold me, crush me, I'll lie helpless in your arms.

She gave a start when his voice broke the long silence. She patted her hair again, and he said that there were good lawyers and bad lawyers, and he generously praised his cousin Jacques. When she didn't answer he stopped speaking, terrified that he had said something that might have displeased her. She said nothing, and he felt it was an unspoken reproach: What a conversation! You can't even keep a woman entertained for five minutes. He couldn't think of anything more to say, and the dreadful silence continued.

'How is Father, juffrouw Ursule?'

'Very well, thank you, mijnheer André.'

Silence.

'And is juffrouw Octavie well too?'

'Yes, she's very well, thank you.'

Silence.

185

'They'll be wondering where I have got to.'

This chance, the last but one, to insist airily that half an hour wouldn't make any difference, stay a little longer, as a special favour to me, he let go because he was afraid he would have no conversation.

At the gateway he muffed his last chance. He suggested he should walk back with her. Out of politeness she whispered that it wasn't far and she wasn't frightened. It was an unpaved lane, and he would have to take her arm. She could always easily stumble, or trip over a puddle so that he would have to catch her with both arms. She would take that for an embrace and she would put her arms around his neck. Come with me, André, I'll kiss you and kiss you.

But he said that he would stand at the gateway until she reached the street into the village. She went, and felt she was the sister of the man who had married his servant girl.

13

The ordeal of those last few months was scarcely over when he found himself under the shadow of a new threat, one that he had never expected: Father Claerebout. It was not those gifts of succulent hares, but the the fame of his good works that commended him to Father Claerebout, a rugged veteran of eighty who, for thirty-six years, had ruled the parish as spiritual guide, burgomaster, police-commissioner, sexton, and president behind the scenes of every club and society in the village, a man who had been rich and had given himself and his wealth to the church and the poor, and always had to contend with one recalcitrant and disobedient parishioner: his curate. 'The Bishop always sends me his mischief-makers,' he said to the dean. He meant his curates, and he wasn't wrong. The Bishop always had one of those pretentious young men who know everything, who feel themselves called to great things, and want to make all mankind so virtuous here on earth that there wouldn't be another mortal sin for at least fifty years, and he sent these hotheads off to Father Clearebout. After a year they would be biting their nails, unnerved and sullen, thwarted at every turn, and after three years at the most they were completely tamed, a little sceptical and disillusioned. By the time Father Clearebout had knocked them into shape and would be able to make something of them, they were taken away from him.

There had been one who surrendered with wholehearted conviction after three long years. 'I've fought you for three years, Father,' he said, 'but now I can see that you are right, and you have my respect and admiration. The way you do things is behind the times, and it wouldn't work out anywhere else, but you manage somehow, and here's my hand, Father. I'll stand by you in everything.' Then Father Claerebout fetched the best wine he had, a seventy-eight-year-old bottle, and he told the story of his life, his quarrels with bishops and vicars, his struggle with priests and deacons, his fights with dozens of curates, and the wars he had waged in the parishes. As he put down his last glass, empty, on the table he said: 'I've suffered, too, and, as God's my witness, I have never spoken a word to anyone of how I have suffered.' That evening he told of the grief he had known. Friends he had never had, never a kind word, never the solace of human sympathy. He was Claerebout, the strong man, and he didn't need that. He had given away three fortunes, his own and two he had inherited from his family, and not even a nod of thanks. He was silent a moment, then, with his head slightly bowed, he said: 'There is nothing you could imagine, no matter how vile, that I haven't been accused of: extortion, theft, slander, every form of depravity. In the Bishop's chancellory there is a photo of me with a naked woman on my lap.' He nodded slowly, and with his head bowed a little lower: 'I have wept, I have wept often.'

The curate stared at him, his hands in his hair: 'Is that going to happen to me too?'

Father Claerebout: 'Yes.'

Less than a month later the curate was replaced. Claerebout went off like a streak of lightning to the Bishop's palace. A vicar, who had once been his curate, rebuked him, but he rebuked the vicar and said he wasn't going to be any longer a sort of trainer of young cubs, and stamped out. Still the same old Claerebout, the vicar laughed, when he was gone, we'll just have to let him go on until he's worn out.

As if Claerebout could ever be worn out. For two years now, he had had another young cub, another one of those saints, he walks round six feet up in the air, I'll have to bring him down to earth. Besides that, Claerebout was displeased with his burgomaster, and he began thinking of the Koevoet. He was far from worn out; he was going to change a few things here.

He had written a letter of thanks for the hares, leaving it at that, but from far and wide, and most of all from the Van den Heuvel sisters, he heard of the good works and the high repute of the Little Lordie, whose existence he always ignored because this fellow had, contrary to the tradition of thirty-six years, neglected to pay him a courtesy call when he came to live in the Koevoet. This was another d'Hertenfeldt, and he knew what that meant.

'I haven't had the honour of making the gentleman's acquaintance.'

'He goes to church every Sunday, Father.'

'So it seems.'

'And he does such a lot of good.'

'So I've heard.'

'I thought you must know him.'

'I have not yet had the honour.'

They met by chance at the Van den Heuvels', and Father Claerebout saw that all he had of the d'Hertenfeldts was the name. With the condescension that autocrats show towards those who are clay in their hands, he said that the Little Lordie certainly merited his fine reputation. He was very favourably impressed. Next year we'll be losing our burgomaster. I don't think he'll be elected again. He meant: I don't want him elected again.

There was nothing that made the Little Lordie shudder more then the thought of holding a public office, to have to stand up in front of everyone, a centre of attention. If Octavie and Ursule had pounded his head with a hammer it wouldn't have made him any dizzier and sicker than their happy whisper that Father Claerebout was thinking of having him elected as burgomaster. That anyone could be so modest that he wasn't flattered or tempted by the prospect of being burgomaster was something they couldn't imagine. But he was as modest as all that, and because he was so modest he was the ideal choice, and because he had been chosen, and because it was him, they were determined to encourage him. Willy and Jacques just didn't exist any more, now that mijnheer André would soon be burgomaster.

He would rather die first. Before it went that far, he would sell up and disappear. Better to go to the Congo, better to go and live with the Hottentots, than to parade round for all the world to see him, wearing a big sash to welcome distinguished visitors, giving speeches, and not daring to do anything when the one says this and the other says that. For him it was the ultimate, the most galling mockery they could have heaped on him, to be used by a priest as a pawn to keep the village under his thumb, him, an unbeliever who would take a savage delight in destroying every vestige of religion on earth—if he could do it by just pressing a button here on this table, and be sure that it would only be found out after he was dead.

This news overshadowed everything. Octavie and Ursule forgot their feud with their brother and their sister-in-law, and he forgot the haunting fear that the family from Louvain would come again for the holidays. The village elections were coming slowly nearer, and that led to a renewal of a vague contact between the farm and the villa. The farmer wanted Thuur to take his place on the list of candidates, and Thuur didn't want to. Now they needed him they changed their tune, but he wasn't at anyone's beck and call. Once Octavie came over to him in the street to remind him it was his duty to take the load off Father's shoulders, and put his name on the list of candidates for councillor or, even better, alderman. But she could see him at home if she wanted to discuss anything like that, not in the street, and if she does come she'll have to be friendly to Elza or he won't think about putting his name on any list, and, in any case, they'll have to ask at least five times.

Just as farmer Van den Heuvel had so wisely predicted, little Thuur came along and resolved the whole problem. The two sisters kissed Elza, and what woman with her first baby at her breast could harbour unkind feelings? Her eyes glowed with a soft light and everyone who saw her shared her happiness. Domineering Octavie and gentle Ursule dreamed the same dream: lying drowsily in a high-ceilinged room of the château, with maids and midwife at the bedside, and a kind, gentle husband who blushed and smiled. Farmer Van den Heuvel lived again the birth of his son Thuur. He could see his Irma again, just as sweet and pretty as Elza, the years roll on, there's always new life, new gladness, and we're pushed aside. This gladness united them all again, a divided family joined around a young mother and a cradle.

With all that excitement, the family from Louvain didn't cause so much of a stir: they're so quiet this year. Like pleasure-seekers who had once had a fine time somewhere, then came back with high hopes, and it just wasn't the same, it was dull and dreary. This time their noisy presence found no response. They were unimportant intruders in this little world of happiness and ambitions. Besides, Willy had failed his exams, so that, for Octavie, he was scarcely worth the trouble of her missionary zeal, and Jacques had, after Ursule's answer, never found the inspiration for a second letter. The Little Lordie himself was so beset with the fear of his impending doom that he couldn't care what tricks they might play. They went rowing and shooting and swimming, just like the last time, but without any enthusiasm, like actors in an empty theatre. Mouche said it was because André had got dull and rustic from living here all alone; the sons said it was because the two girls were both in love with André; and the Major grumbled that it wasn't a pleasant atmosphere with that Jesuit around all the time.

But it wasn't a pleasant atmosphere anywhere any more for the Major, but not because of Jesuits. He had shouted and cursed himself more and more into disfavour; his wife found his gentler sons more agreeable company. She wore clothes that made her look younger; when they were travelling the waiters in the hotels called her mademoiselle, and spoke as though her father and her brothers were at the table. In the rowing-boat she curled up limply against Willy. In front of the others he was just like a big brother, and he kissed her on the forehead, but in the dark was that all he did?

While they were still there Father Claerebout strode through the entrance to give the château, that had now acknowledged his authority, proof of his good will. It was simply impossible for him to imagine that anyone could not be deeply grateful at receiving from him the office of highest authority in the village. It never occurred to him that he should first ask whether the favour he could confer was welcome. He had, he said, discussed the matter, and he had the impression that everything was as good as settled. The Little Lordie wished that Vesuvius would erupt under this black-robed meddler so he would be blown a mile high and come down burnt to ashes. There was nothing he hated so much as these self-willed order-givers. They fixed their eyes on him, and under that gaze he shrivelled up to nothingness. He stuttered that he would like to think it over.

14

But even if the eyes that looked at him were soft and inviting he didn't know what to do; he was just as helpless with Octavie and with Ursule. He longed for a woman he could make his own. The chickens he could grab roughly whenever he wanted, the sheep squirmed when he gripped them, the horse trembled when he came into the stable, closed the door and cursed. Bring him a woman in his room, then, in the dark, he would tame her, he would show her how strong and heartless he was. He would say to her: 'I believe neither in God nor devil, I'm frightened of nothing. I'm going to take you for my pleasure. Do as I say or I'll batter you to death. You'll come to me when I say: Kiss me, and slink away when I say: Lie down over there, and you'll take your clothes off when I reach out for the whip.'

And then she would be yielding and ardent. In the evening she would sit on a cushion by his feet while he read his paper, ignoring her, and she would giggle in a flutter of joy if he was good-humoured, and said: 'Come here.' If Father Claerebout came he would order her to get that black-cloaked busybody out of the door within a quarter of an hour. I'm not at home, and tell him that as far as I'm concerned he can put his slut of a housekeeper up for burgomaster. I'm no one's lackey. At the dinner table he would be difficult. Call Marie, the spinach is full of sand. At midday his wife would be frightened he might find the meat too tough again, and in the afternoon she would fuss and worry about the evening meal, for he was fastidious, and every day he had to have something different.

He wanted a woman he could make his own; he wanted to be a man.

Octavie and Ursule were ready to fulfil his wish. He only had to speak, to give a sign, and why didn't he take her tenderly in his arms, that would be enough. They were filled with longing for him, but they didn't admit it to each other, they talked about him as they would about a stranger, but it was only him they talked about.

Since that evening when he had let her go off alone, Ursule often doubted whether he felt anything more than mere friendship for her, but Octavie felt sure it was because of his shyness, and she set about breaking down this obstacle. He was the sort of man she wanted, docile and obedient. He was of the stuff she could mould into a model husband. He needed guidance. She could see that he was undecided about accepting the office of burgomaster and he would be only too glad of sound advice. She gave him the sound advice he needed.

There had to be a new burgomaster because it was scandalous the way things were with the one we have now. Father Claerebout thought he could be trusted because he had such a good name, but now it turns out that he is two-faced, with some he says one thing and with others he'll say just the opposite, so as to please everyone. Last summer they started a gymnastic club in the village, and he got himself made chairman. Then all the club went in the procession, and when they felt too warm they took their jackets off and carried them over their arms, and everyone watching was horrified. There they were in their tight pants and shirts with short sleeves, and down to here at the neck. When the burgomaster was told about it he didn't dare do anything, and nobody could tell Father Claerebout because he was carrying the Holy Sacrament. Oh, that's just one example, mijnheer André, and there's a hundred more. Then his son is always running after girls, and what a lot of nasty gossip that causes, mijnheer André. Oh well, it's the way they're brought up. She'd make sure, if she had any children, that they were brought up to be respectable.

So there'll have to be a new burgomaster, and if anyone should take his place, mijnheer André, it's you. It's only right, considering your position, and you have no axe to grind, and you do so much good in the parish. The whole village wants you to be burgomaster, they all think so highly of you. And then your name: d'Hertenfeldt!

She rattled on like an alarm clock running down, and it pleased her to see how he always nodded like a puppet and listened and agreed. This was a man for her, a man who had to be led. She was convinced that he was grateful to her for removing all his doubts. What did mijnheer André think himself?

Mijnheer André fidgeted with his red, freckled hands, and conceded that, at first, he had had a lot of objections, but, when you consider everything, then...

She had triumphed, and in his thoughts he gilded the cage he was being driven into. Perhaps this was the price that had to be paid for Ursule. Once he put fruit on the table for them, pears, oranges, and melon. In the countryside almost no one eats melon; it hasn't enough taste to it. But he liked melon, and he pressed Ursule to try just a slice. After a long hesitation she would rather not; she'd take an orange. He said of course she must do as she wanted and eat what she liked. I only want you to be happy.

He was startled himself at his rashness, and for a few seconds the sisters were dazed with astonishment. He thought they understood what he meant, that they knew now it was only for them that he had agreed to be burgomaster, that he would marry Ursule if it would make her happy. He waited for an answer that would be just as vague, but just as unmistakably clear, and Octavie made it clear that he had said nothing unusual. So that Ursule wouldn't go imagining things, for Ursule was getting paler and more delicate with the years, and Octavie was putting on weight.

Father Claerebout wasn't vague. He came with the glad tidings that everything was arranged as he had expected. The owner of the Koevoet would head the list. He said nothing more about thinking it over, the Little Lordie will be burgomaster, Amen.

The Little Lordie made one last effort to save the illusion of his independence. Though his name was already printed in large letters by the village printer, he strode off decisively to ask the advice of the Van den Heuvels. He knew what Octavie thought, now he looked timidly inquiring at Ursule. And juffrouw Ursule, what do you think? A surprised, happy blush, but no reply. Her man mustn't do what she wanted, he mustn't ask her advice. She would follow him and love him, she would lie in his arms and give him kisses, clinging and affectionate as a purring cat. Of course, there was no honour too great for her man, burgomaster and more than that. But André didn't seem so interested in the honour of public office; he let everything depend on her. Oh, André, all she wanted was for him to be happy.

There was a silence.

'What should I do, juffrouw Ursule?'

'I don't know what you would like to do yourself,' she said.

So he had to be burgomaster without being able to convince her that it was for her alone that he did it. If she had just said yes, he would have gathered all his courage and answered: *Bon*, he was doing it because she said he should. Then came the darkest day of his life, the installation ceremony. The only ray of light was a shy glance, when, seated in the coach that brought up the rear, he rode by her house. She bent down to a small boy, who approached the coach with carefully rehearsed solemnity, and handed him a heavy bouquet.

At half-past eight farmer Van den Heuvel got up from the banquet table. The dinner was far from finished: there was a long list of delicacies on the menu that still had to be served, and the burgomaster still had to respond to the toasts. Thuur tugged at his father's coat, but Father wasn't to be restrained. As it happened, Father had a little weakness, he was addicted to chewing-tobacco. It was only a small, very respectable wad that no one would ever notice, and there were only very few who knew about this little weakness of his. But small as it was, he couldn't go without it. Year in and year out Octavie and Ursule had nagged and nagged at him over that little wad of tobacco, for girls who have been to school at a convent in Wavre had the right not to be disgraced by a father who chewed tobacco. But he resolutely kept his supply of plug from the Yzeren Leen in Malines on the second step of the

196

stairway to the cellar, and every weekday after the midday meal, and on Sunday after Mass, he slipped away and cut off a flake that he poked carefully into his mouth. He would ask Octavie gruffly if it got in her way.

But that day he had stepped into the alderman's coach after Mass to ride in the parade in front of the burgomaster's carriage, and after that he had to take his place at the banquet table and he hadn't had his chew. It was all fine food, but farmer Van den Heuvel stood up and said: 'You go on eating; I'm off.'

His walk was none too steady. Outside, the wine went to his head, he whistled softly. The Lord, who didn't begrudge this honest man his simple pleasure, was with him, and had inspired his two daughters with the happy idea of spending the afternoon with Elza. Farmer Van den Heuvel stepped up to the cellar door, but as he bent over, his hand clutched at a dark emptiness. He fell head-first down the stone steps. They found him there two hours later when Thuur brought his sisters home. Because the cellar door stood open, Octavie screamed there must be thieves, and Father was upstairs. But Father was lying in the cellar, struck down by the Great Thief who needs no door to enter by.

For three days the farmer was unconscious. When the Little Lordie came to ask how he was on the morning of the fourth day, Ursule opened the door and sank weakly back against the wall. Instead of holding her tight, he leapt into the room to fetch a chair for her, but by the time he had done that, she had recovered. She gave him a hand he could hold as long as he wished, but he pressed that hand for just a fleeting moment of silent sympathy; that was as long as he dared.

15

It was something altogether different that the Major discovered when he came home unexpectedly. He found his eldest son with his wife wherever he looked, in the fields, in the garden, on every sofa. The first time he had made a noisy scene, which, according to all the rules, should have ended in revolver shots. The second time he stamped and shouted, and the third time he waited till they had combed their hair and escaped out of sight. He took the view that, after all, 'Il faut être philosophe dans la vie.' With his car, he was soon in Brussels where he could console himself.

The oddly-assorted family he had put together with soldierly simplicity when he returned home disintegrated just as quickly. It was like one of those sets of wooden blocks that can be combined in all sorts of patterns, three men and an army wife who was trying to recapture, wherever and however she could, the unforgettable feverish passion of her all-too-short first marriage. He had started by making a couple, himself and Mouche, but a further combination of son and stepmother was no more improbable, and then why shouldn't Jacques take his turn as well? That still didn't exhaust all the possibilities. Why not a combination of Mouche, Willy, and Jacques, with the Major himself as an occasional stand-by for the insatiable widow? She had no motive of malice against anyone; she was only driven blindly, by the dark force of instinct, to seek a renewal of a happiness that was gone and could never be renewed.

But Jacques had other preoccupations. He had met a girl who was also a law student and who was, besides, a staunch Flemish nationalist, and to judge by his face and by the care he took with his clothes, it was not a passing fancy. Willy thought that Jacques's sudden serious-mindedness was a reaction against his own waywardness, and he could, he said, see Jacques entering a monastery to do penance for him. Jacques couldn't take a joke any more. Once there was a banner hanging above the table: 'We demand justice for Flanders! We demand a Flemish university!' He ripped it down with his walking-stick, and a couple of glasses on the table went with it.

Willy was too far gone to change. He was caught in a whirlwind of passion that swept away all discretion. The hunger of that hot-blooded woman could not be stilled. No man could love her wildly or violently enough. If he wasn't berserk with folly, if she couldn't devise some insane mischief, it couldn't be the same love she had known with Marcel. Her embraces, her intrigues, her tantrums, it was all a fire that consumed their reason, yet left their lust unsated. At first she picked quarrels with the Major, and then goaded Willy into taunting his father to prove to her that he was ready to face death for her sake. She would say that this time the Major was going to shoot both of them, and she would ask him if he loved her enough to die together with her. But the Major wasn't so foolish, and then she made Willy fail in his exams. He had never been studious, and he was too thoughtless to realize he was making a havoc of his life.

Then the Major had a word to say. Willy had to finish his studies. He stamped and shouted, and once again she triumphed. Why should Willy, the man of the world, spend his best years poring over books like a schoolboy? He thought he was doing what he had decided to do himself when he applied to go to the Congo, and it was her idea. But she clung to him, sobbing and pleading. Didn't he gave any consideration for her? Couldn't they go on loving each other here? Didn't he see that they could have everything here that they wanted, and did he think she was going with him to that dreadful Congo? She couldn't stand it again. And Willy the cynic became the infatuated lover. She would go with him or they would die together. That was what she was waiting for. This delirium was her life. Yes, she would go with him. Oh, in the Congo she had known what love was, and there she would love again, so much more, so much more than the other time.

In the ordeal of mayoral office the Little Lordie found his only solace in the secret, unworthy thought that after the family was out of mourning, Ursule would have to find a husband. And with that thought went the fear that she might, in uncertainty and desperation, throw herself into Jacques's arms. Everything would have to wait until they were out of mourning, but, in any case, his fears were groundless, for Jacques had no time any more for flirting, the Major wasn't inclined to let his nephew see how his wife brazenly carried on under his very eyes with his own son, and for Willy and Mouche the surroundings were unimportant. So the family from Louvain stayed away.

Once Octavie said they were frightened at night, alone in that big house. He sent them a bell that had been brought from the attic in Brussels to the attic in the Koevoet. It was big enough for a church, and they could ring it if they ever needed help. But he sent a letter as well. Providing they had no objection, his gardener would come and sleep in the house—for the time being. For the time being, he wrote, timidly daring and hopeful. Surely they would understand. If they didn't respond, that would be a sign that they had rejected his advances. For him it was as if he had proposed, and now he only had to wait until they were out of mourning to have his wish fulfilled.

Octavie found that 'for the time being' rather odd. Why shouldn't Seppen sleep there always, from now on? He was old and his dozen or so children were all grown up. Octavie looked at Ursule, who didn't seem to have heard her question, and then Octavie had an explanation that sounded perfectly logical. He meant that he didn't want to force his gardener on them, that they could look for someone else if they thought that would be better. Mijnheer André was always so modest, so considerate, always frightened that even his kindness might give offence. Ursule realized that she had misinterpreted that 'for the time being'.

He doesn't really want to get married, she told herself. I thought it was just that he was too shy to ask me, but that's not what he's afraid of. He's afraid to think about marrying. He's frightened of women. Perhaps he has a vague affection for me, but it's no more than that. She often went with Octavie to call at the château, and almost every evening Seppen would bring something for them, fruit, flowers, a chicken, a goose, a bunch of asparagus, or liver sausage, for he was a connoisseur of liver sausage. Whenever he had Seppen slaughter a pig, he made the liver sausage himself from pure liver and according to the finest recipe. Then he would send them some with a letter giving them the assurance that it was wholesome and filled with the choicest ingredients. He embellished these letters with allusions they didn't understand and so never reacted to. Whenever Octavie took the initiative, Ursule saw that he shrank back in confusion, and it was more and more obvious to her that he didn't want Octavie but her, though his longing was no more than a platonic fondness. Then Octavie would be afraid that Ursule might win his heart, and she used more cunning than ever to throw a false light on all the obscure hints he gave. The old verger understood all those hints and signs far better than they did. He asked how long he would have to go on sleeping here, and he didn't know, he said, why they had to think so long about things like that. They blushed.

Father Claerebout, too, thought it had gone on long enough with those presents and those letters. Seppen liked his glass on Sundays, and he couldn't keep quiet, and soon the villagers would be singing songs about it, and the dignity of authority must be preserved. So Claerebout brought his canary, that wouldn't whistle, to the Koevoet, to put it in the aviary with birds that were good whistlers, and from canaries to women is not so far. A woman is like a songbird, for a woman fills a house with brightness and joy. In the Bible it is written: 'Woe to those who live alone.' It must be dreary sometimes here in the château. We have an ideal burgomaster, and the man who sacrifices his time and energy for the good of the village certainly deserves a full measure of happiness. Father Claerebout had heard what everyone was saying, and the whole village knew the burgomaster's choice, and yes, it was an excellent choice indeed. And the party concerned was certainly not unwilling. So before long we'll be able to hang out the flags on every house in the village.

The Little Lordie stuttered that if it only depended on him...

Father Claerebout answered: 'That's what both of you are thinking. It's only a matter of coming to the point.' 'I'll pass by going home,' Father Claerebout said, 'and discreetly pave the way, and you drop in tomorrow afternoon and do the rest. Before you know it, you'll be whispering in each other's ears, and then it's all settled.' He laughed, and strolled jauntily down the lane through the pools of sunlight under the beech tress. As long as he could arrange everything and manage everything as he wanted, he would never die, but something might have cracked in that rigid back of his if he had only known what a tragic farce he was contriving. And when that leaked out there would be ditties sung about it.

Even Father Claerebout could make a mistake. Octavie was alone at home when he came by, and he didn't know for sure whether she was the one his burgomaster wanted to marry. But for years he had been used to hearing Octavie speak for both herself and Ursule; everyone in the village knew that Ursule played second fiddle to her brawny sister. So never a doubt entered his head, because anyone could see that it wasn't an Ursule his burgomaster needed, but an Octavie who knew her own mind and knew how to manage a household. He didn't lose any time getting round to the subject that had brought him. From the Children of Mary she had picked out for the next procession, he veered on to more worldly affairs. Courting. And that there was such a lot of courting going on these days. And Octavie couldn't deny it, the whole village knew about it, and, from what he had heard, there would soon be a happy ending. Don't say he had been here, Octavie, but, of course, the burgomaster had often mentioned it to him, and now he had told him he would be coming to see her tomorrow to name the day.

So the next day Ursule had to go and visit Elza, although it was Octavie's turn, and so the Little Lordie found himself sitting opposite Octavie. He understood. He knew that Ursule didn't want him, and this pious harpy had plotted with that meddling priest. That day his cup of bitterness and humiliation was full. One of the sheep in the stall suffered for it. Three sheep turned their backs on him when he leaned against the wall and wept. He kicked each of them hard in the udder.

16

It was round that time that war broke out. Jacques and Willy joined the throng of volunteers, and the Little Lordie suddenly disappeared. By the time Father Claerebout and the Van den Heuvels heard he was gone, he had given his fowls, his sheep, and his horse to Seppen the verger, he had sent the parlour-maid back to her parents, he had hired a room for Marie in the Home of Rest, and made the necessary arrangements for his replacement as burgomaster. Never in all his life had he settled so many things so quickly as in those few days, and the rash folly his desperation drove him to acquired an aura of patriotic fervour. The bene-factor of the village became the hero of the village.

The hero wrote to Ursule from Namur. He had, dearest friend, decided to volunteer for the defence of our fatherland, and he begged her to forgive him his hasty departure. Soon he would be face to face with the enemy, and he cherished no illusions about the consequences for himself. So he was writing this letter as a letter of farewell. The sincere love that he had always felt for her would give him courage in the stress and strain of battle, and if it was to be his fate to die for his country, this love for her would strengthen him and confort him in his last moments. Meanwhile, he hoped that the war would come to a speedy end with a victory for our troops and that she and all who were dear to her would be spared. Farewell, dearest Ursule, sincerely and lovingly, André d'Hertenfeldt.

It was by the River Yser that he performed his first feat of arms after a hasty retreat from Namur. He fired twenty shots and fell with a wound in the rump. After the bullet was removed he lay in hospital without much pain, while his flesh healed and his heart exulted. This was a world turned upside down as he wanted it. Death and suffering, healthy young men maimed, groaning, bleeding, dying. In the evening the dying were carried out of the ward to breathe their last somewhere else. He used to lie awake waiting for this daily ritual. So they got you too, friend. What was it, rusty shrapnel in the lungs, a shot through your guts, both legs blown off, or can't you stop pissing blood? All the best, friend, curl up and croak. Shout for your mother, curse and pray, and what will your wife say, all alone in bed?

There was an unending stream of new candidates for the grave. He would lie watching them brought in, wondering what their wounds might be. He imagined the most agonizing and incurable mutilations, and wished these on them. The howling shrieks of pain that infuriated the others was music to his ears. He meditated cynically on the war. All these Flemish admirers of German culture were now suddenly filled with hate for everything German, and they shot at Germans as they would at wild beasts. Now that great vanguard of culture was marching through the land, destroying, plundering, tyrannizing. After nineteen centuries of pious preaching that all men are brothers in Christ, and pious exhortations not to hate an enemy, to bear wrongs and injustice meekly and patiently, and to turn the other cheek, it only needed the flash of the first rifle shot for all the brothers to exterminate each other like vermin, to repay wrong with wrong and extol hate as a patriotic duty and a Christian virtue.

When his wound throbbed he would sneer gloatingly at all this pageant of evil. This was the world he knew, a world without goodness, without love or honour. There was nothing but lies, viciousness, rottenness, depravity, and now it was all laid bare. Why was this hell let loose? Who got anything out of it? Did it serve any purpose? Was it for a noble ideal? It was kill and be killed, a senseless slaughter, and that pleased him. The one they put in the next bed started to roar with pain, filling the whole ward with his curses. His eyes rolled dementedly and if twenty nuns were praying together all their Hail Marys wouldn't have been as many as the lurid oaths he gasped and shouted. It maddened the others, and the nurses asked him to be quieter, but his only answer was to curse louder and harder. The sound of a footstep approaching his bed would start off a new crescendo. The louder it was the more the Little Lordie enjoyed it. If the cursing seemed to be dying down he would whisper ssst to keep it going. From near by the heavy guns were rumbling. Outside, lorries were tooting, horses stamping, and soldiers marching. Inside, the wounded lay in the heavy hospital stink writhing and groaning. For the Little Lordie it was the end of the world. He wanted to sink down into an oblivion of total destruction with a lullaby of curses screaming in his ears.

When the Germans had overrun half of Belgium they came up against Father Claerebout. Their arrival was heralded by scouting parties that came through the village, firing more shots than was necessary for they were never sure they wouldn't be ambushed.

Old Tistje, who was nearly stone-deaf, lived in a tumble-down house at the edge of the village. Tistje had seen that the call-up was just like in the seventies, but he never expected these German soldiers who burst in on him one afternoon with pistols in their hands. He was able to understand that they wanted water to drink. He filled a bucket for them from the well. To do that he had to put the bucket on a pole with a hook, and as the pole went up in the air then down into the well and up in the air again, the Germans suspiciously watched these signals that could be seen from far off. They thought he was pretending to be stupid, and they were so unconvinced of his deafness that one of them stood close behind him and fired his revolver. Tistje turned round slowly and calmly because he had heard something, and the Germans were certain then that Tistje was a sly yokel who had a marvellous measure of self-control. They helped themselves to bread spread thick with butter, then they left. But the revolver shot had warned a Belgian patrol, and the Belgian patrol opened fire from a ditch. The Germans ran to get back into the house, but Tistje had bolted the door. Now they saw how he had tricked them, and while Tistje, who didn't hear the bullets whistling, stood at the window angrily waving his arms as a sign that they had had something to eat and they had to go away, they shot him down.

For Father Claerebout that was a black mark against the Germans. To come into a stranger's house and eat and drink, and then shoot him, that was something he would never allow in his village, war or no war. More than half of his flock had fled, the ones who stayed weren't the best sort, and then all these troops, Belgians and Germans, coming and going, it was as if a spectre of lawlessness and disorder was haunting the parish.

When the Germans finally occupied the village, and there wasn't a living Belgian to be seen, he strolled calmly, with his hands behind his back, around the church and the presbytery. He couldn't go round the whole village watching over every house, but he would stand guard here.

They wanted to go into the church. Quiet, Father Claerebout ordered. He was prepared to let one officer and a few soldiers go with him to search the church from top to bottom to see if there was anyone hiding there or whether there might be a look-out post in the belfry. But not all of them together. Tomorrow something would be missing or broken and no one would have done it. Calmly and quietly. But the armies were not under Father Claerebout's command, and the end of this conflict of authority was that the spiritual authority was taken for a couple of hours' march, hands bound behind his back, and then locked up as a prisoner in the town hall in the next parish.

Now it was a question of finding another figure of authority for the village. The problem was solved when they broke open the door of one of the cellars at the Schrans. Thuur, Elza, the baby, Octavie, Ursule, and a maid were lined up in front of the soldiers and two high-ranking officers, and Thuur was declared responsible for whatever might happen in the village. Once the sight of a young girl passing by had awakened in Thuur an unsuspected strength and a determination he didn't know he had, and now the curt orders of a German officer did the same. He was to represent the parish council, and he and his family were hostages, just in case anything happened, anything at all—*verstehen Sie?* They wanted accommodation for the Oberst, a house, *ein ganzes Haus, und kommen Sie mit.*

As long as they live, the Van den Heuvels will burst out laughing every time they think of the tragic look on Thuur's face as he turned round, kissed his wife, kissed his child, kissed his sisters, never saying a word, and walked off between two tall, broad German officers, taller and broader than they were. He soon realized he wasn't going to be executed. He saw soldiers handing up wine and bread and meat from the cellars to their comrades above. And there was the riffraff of the village, too, out to get a share of the loot, making friends with them and showing where to break in. Doors were battered open, windows smashed. Thick smoke was belching out of the chimneys. Thuur pointed and said: '*Nein*, not that.' He showed them barns and houses where soldiers could be billeted without causing too much friction, and the officers nodded with growing satisfaction. *Sehr gut!* He fetched Seppen, who had the keys, and took them to the Koevoet, and he put his sisters' house at their disposal. '*Danke schon*,' they said.

Thuur Van den Heuvel faced them and declared, with his finger pointed to his chest, that he would see that order was preserved, and, pointing at the Oberst, Thuur said that he must do the same. There were enough common words in their two languages for them to understand each other. The Oberst gave a friendly laugh, and because farmers always seal an agreement with a handshake, he made it clear that it was a bargain by giving Thuur Van den Heuvel his hand. They went back with him to the Schrans to show the ladies that they were returning him safe and sound. Then they took their leave. They stood stiffly facing the women and kissed their hands. A shudder ran from Ursule Van den Heuvel's fingers along her arm and up and down her spine.

The Oberst asked her if she was frightened. No. He could feel it, he said, *an dieses kleine Händchen. Ach, es tat ihm Leid.* But the Fräulein needn't be frightened. Her brother would see to keeping order, and, for his part, he would do everything he could to help. Nothing would happen. War is dangerous, but, even so, we don't all have to die, *liebes Fräulein.*

Here, for years and years, the d'Hertenfeldts had kept order, and after them we had Father Claerebout. We would never have believed it would be thanks to a Thuur van den Heuvel that we were safe and our houses and our barns were spared. But there it was, our Claerebout wasn't there, and the village still survived, and fairly well, too. It was soon known far and wide that here not a single house had a broken tile, while everywhere else there was burning and shooting. The Little Lordie heard this from a smuggled letter that reached the hospital. The burgomaster they had now was a certain Van den Heuvel who was hand in glove with the enemy. He'd given them the house where his two sisters lived, and they cooked, and more than that, too, for the officers. Father Claerebout had been found murdered in a ditch after he had been to the Van den Heuvels and caught the two whores sitting on the officers' knees. Every night there were orgies with wine and champagne, with those two sluts shouting and singing for all the village to hear. Now we know what they are, those two prudes. There's nothing said because as long as it goes on like that we're left alone, and no one wants to follow Father Claerebout. But when the war is over, Jan, my boy, then we'll see who'll sing and shout.

17

The Little Lordie was only too ready to be sent back to the front line, not because he wanted to die, but because he was indifferent to everything. Pleasure in the misery and suffering of others didn't mean anything to him any more. Sometimes his trenchmates would confide their sorrows to him, they took his quietness and reserve for a source of strength that could comfort them. He let them talk, he glanced at their photos. Isn't she pretty? Yes. Isn't that a fine baby? Yes. One of them had found out that his wife was unfaithful, and he was going to make sure he got killed. The Little Lordie said nothing. Later, the cuckold wanted to stay alive so, after the war, he could shoot both his wife and her lover, only for that. The Little Lordie still said nothing. There was a wild-eyed one who talked to him a whole night long about women, a mono-logue of obscenity. A painter, who had taken to writing poetry, let him see his verses. A farmer's son, who used to get a smuggled letter now and then, told him that everything was going on as usual at the arm. Tomorrow or the day after the heifer would be calving, this year they would have five truck-loads of potatoes to sell, they were getting sixty litres of milk a day, just count up how much that's bringing in. There was a student who thought he could have interesting conversations with him, but the Little Lordie said nothing.

Once they were all silent under the pounding of a heavy bom-bardment all through the day. The shells burst, one after the other, in the trenches on either side of them, but in the evening some of them recovered their speech enough to moan. The farmer's son crouched, with his teeth chattering, next to the Little Lordie, and the poet mumbled something every time his back twitched after an explosion. When that had gone on for an eternity of a night, and it seemed that the morning would never come, after twenty-four hours of hell, the Little Lordie suddenly couldn't understand what he was waiting for or why he stayed there cowering in the dark. He stood up, he wasn't timid any more, and he just walked straight ahead. Then a burst of shrapnel caught him full in the face and he fell. In the morning, the stretcher-bearers hesitated because he didn't seem to be worth the trouble of picking up.

It was around that time that Father Claerebout finished his tour of Germany. The regiment that had marched him off and locked him up in a village a few hours farther on left the next day without telling him, and the regiment that followed didn't know what he had done, but they could see he was dangerous. They questioned him and, because he was a priest and must have done something, they asked who he had been sending signals to from the church tower, and he answered that he wasn't going to talk to them, he wanted to be taken to that Oberst with the grey moustache and the scar on his left cheek. He didn't know who they were, but he had a bone to pick with that fellow. They barked at him that they would shoot him if he didn't shut his mouth. He crossed his arms and said, Shoot then, and did they think that was how to win a war. But if they were going to shoot him they had to reckon with God, too, and he stood there as if God would make the bullets bounce right in their faces.

That was the sort of defiance spies and other scum put up when they knew they were caught. So they were certain he had done much more than send signals, but to find an excuse to let him go they asked him how old he was, and when he told them they stared. The Oberst felt a twinge of pity, but to keep up appearances he snapped at him that he had better get off home and not start meddling with the *Krieg*. To be treated like an old dodderer was, for Father Claerebout, a greater indignity than all the threats about shooting him. He snapped back at the Oberst—he would show them they would have their hands full with an old dodderer —what had they done to his church, who was going to pay for all the damage. He shook his fist and warned them that injustice wouldn't win a war, and he lost any sympathy the Oberst might have had for him by asking if his Protestant faith taught him it was right to persecute a Catholic priest. The Oberst wondered if it was indeed a Catholic priest he was talking to, a man of God, meek and humble. *Aber das ist ja egal*, he was going to send him off to Germany where he could study the Protestant faith.

In Germany Father Claerebout only had to wait for the intervention of the German bishops. On his way back he was the guest of quite a few German priests who couldn't do enough to give him pleasant memories of his stay in Germany, but it didn't help. Four score years he had lived, and he had held his own against bishops and curates and so many other enemies. But to be thwarted and humiliated, far from his church and the parish he had ruled for so long, that was too hard a blow to bear.

Then to come back to the village and hear that everything had been saved by the shrewdness of that Thuur Van den Heuvel, a schemer no one trusted. Then to meet the Van den Heuvel sisters and ask: How are things here?

They stared at him as if they had seen a ghost, they burst into tears, they thought he had been killed. He nodded coldly. Nothing had happened to him except that they had wanted to intern him, but he had taught them better, and here he was, back again. That was all, it was nothing unusual. But how is everything here? We're lucky with the military authorities we've got. Everywhere else there's been a lot of trouble, but we've no reason to complain. The Hauptmann is refined and charming, and he comes from a very distinguished family, he has a coat-of-arms on all his things. One of them drinks a lot, but everyone says he is the best to deal with. Of course, they're Germans, but still we can't deny the truth, and it could have turned out far worse. Things had been stolen here and there, but our own folk had done a bit of thieving, too, in the beginning.

That was too much for Father Claerebout. In the first place, there were no good Germans, and, in the second place, there were no thieves in his parish. He looked at the sisters with those eyes that saw through every folly and pretence, and he said: 'Indeed?'

Disconcerted, they began another chorus of anxiety over his health, but as far as he was concerned the conversation was finished. He was taking a walk. Good-bye. Octavie never forgave him that.

The first to notice that he wasn't the same was his old house-keeper, Cato. There was more than one flagon missing from his cellar, and that had made her tremble when he suddenly appeared in the kitchen and said: 'Good morning, Cato.' Every time the curate had gone visiting the sick, he had taken a bottle of wine in his pocket. Now that he's in heaven the good Father won't mind, he had said. But the good Father wasn't in heaven, and he did mind. The good Father didn't believe a word of those visits to the sick. That was one of those saints who never drank, and the moment I'm not here he's at my wine. After thirty-six years Cato could read his thoughts, and she knew what he was thinking now. She insisted that the curate was such a good, virtuous man. Claerebout only said: 'Yes, yes.' But when he saw the curate he said nothing at all, and Cato, who for thirty-six years had heard the thundering wrath that fell on the heads of his curates, knew that Claerebout was crushed and broken.

Soon others noticed it, too. He would have nothing to do with the Hauptmann and his crew, and whoever wanted to play the burgomaster here had to acknowledge the Hauptmann. He had no dealings with Thuur Van den Heuvel because Thuur Van den Heuvel was burgomaster and acknowledged the Hauptmann. He avoided the Van den Heuvel sisters because they truckled to the new masters, and if there was anything more to it, that wasn't his concern. If they weren't old enough and wise enough now to know right from wrong there was nothing he could do about it.

And he found that all his flock were like strangers. They had all changed. No one showed any respect for him any more. There were new masters now and new laws. Being without a pass, singing the 'Brabançonne', and smuggling were the sins now, but stealing, cheating, and informing seemed to be permitted.

There is a true story of how a fire once broke out in a room full of friends, and the friends fought with each other and trampled on each other to get through the door. And when they were outside they weren't friends any more. There had been fire here too, and the fear of it still lingered. Everyone was trying to save himself and grab what he could, scruples and loyalties were forgotten. When Father Claerebout crossed the street he felt that his prestige and his authority had been taken from him. If they were in trouble the villagers ran to Thuur Van den Heuvel, who could always put in a good word for them, and it was the Hauptmann they were afraid of now.

Father Claerebout was tired after his German tour, the weariness ached in his bones and lay heavy in his veins. He lived out in a few months the fifteen years he could still have counted on, but no one knew. Those lips that had once confided their grief were a thin line in a drawn, set face. The curate said that Father Claerebout just couldn't keep up with the times, he felt out of place, and he was just pining away. But what sort of worldly prattle was that from a saint? For the Lord had learnt through the countless years to bear with his priests and to reckon justly with each of them. None did He let pass unbowed through the portals of heaven, and He had needed the German cohorts to chasten Claerebout, to tone him down a little. But He had said: 'Carefully, not too rough, it is Claerebout.' And now He spared the old crusader the final indignity of being nursed like a sick child. He even let him wait at the dinner table until Cato and the curate had both gone off to their rooms and they didn't see what an effort it was for him to get up out of his chair. He let him climb the stairs all alone and stretch out on his bed, and He expected no thanks from Claerebout. 'Lord,' Claerebout whispered, when he saw that this was the end, 'into Thy hands I commend my spirit.'

A saint wouldn't lie like that, with a sharp, beaked nose, but this was a warrior.

18

Every family here had always had its cross to bear, but now there were the sorrows of war as well. The verger had had no news of his two sons, though their mother was always saying they must be able to write because they had been to school. Just a few words would have been enough: Mother, I'm still alive, and so is Frans. There was never a sound now from the tailor's window, where he used to sing as he worked, not since September when he had heard his son had been killed. They'd had news, but what was better, that or none at all? The baker's wife knew her son was safe in Harderwijk, in Holland, where he would get enough to eat. Gunner Slooter's wife knew that her husband in Soltau couldn't see what she was up to with his own brother, and Thuur Van den Heuvel kept in his pocket an official telegram addressed to a mother of eight children. He took the two eldest daughters into his house as maids. He lied to her for months, until in the end, she screamed: 'I know he's dead and you've got the paper in your pocket!'

In those two years Major Van den Heuvel had lost his two sons, Jacques just a year after Willy, both in December. Now Mouche wanted to go and live in town, but in the towns hunger was stalking, and here the enormous rhododendron bushes had to be cut down, the Major was planting tobacco, and a hired handyman was planting potatoes. If only there were a bit more ground for a patch of wheat. Then the trees, too, would fetch quite a bit. There was no one any more now to creep behind the rhododendrons with Mouche, and even if there had been, there were no rhododendrons any more. There wasn't cover for a cat to hide in, and at night the Major would often keep watch for potato thieves, and he would come back late to bed, shivering and old. *Et pas un seul mot d'André.*

Had the God André didn't believe in struck him in the face with a burst of shrapnel as if to say: 'Have you had enough now?' The doctors looked at him and hesitated, just like the stretcher-bearers, who wanted to leave him lying—but what was the war but a colossal laboratory turning out stuff for experiments? The one in the bed next to the Little Lordie would start groaning every now and then from the pain in his two legs that he had left behind in Ramskapelle, but he had fits of desperate trust in the medical skill that fitted golden ribs and screwed on legs with golden joints. If they found someone else with the top half shot away, could they bring him the legs? Maybe they could make them grow on to his stumps. He had five children, friend.

Friend was just the same as he was at the front. Then he never spoke, now he couldn't, but it was the same silence. He was covered with bandages and plaster up to his eyes, and where his mouth had been there was a metal spout. He lay there without moving, without thinking.

The first time he could think was when he was allowed to get up. He stood in front of the little mirror over the wash-basin where the nurses were always washing their hands. He came so close that the choking sigh he gasped through the metal spout cast a mist over the glass, and then he thought: A chimpanzee. Under the bandages his red hair was grey. But the tears were the same as before.

The second time he could think was when the bandages and plaster were cut away. He went straight up to the mirror, and a hoarse, dull cry came out of his throat. His face screwed up as he wept, and the gruesome, patched-up lips opened over the jaw-bones of rubber topped with false teeth. The tears flowed down his cheeks, over this hideous disfigurement, and what he thought this time was: A revolver.

He could think, and that was something, but it didn't go any farther.

The first thing he did do was leave the hospital when they said he could. They didn't send him back to the front, though he was whole enough to be shot to pieces once again, but he had had his share. He travelled at night. He stayed a few days in a hotel on the Riviera, where he kept out of sight, until he had hired a cottage away from the noise of the city and the beach, and engaged an old woman to do the cleaning and the cooking. She learnt the language he spoke, a language of vowels. EE was *oui*, and oh was *non*. Ahi was *tartine*, ahé was *café*. Ohoo was *bonjour*, ehee was *merci*, and he had one word that served for everything: ah. *Monsieur, la table est servie. Monsieur, j'ai arrangé ça comme ça.* Then he expressed his approval and his appreciation with ah. Before, he had been always satisfied with an inner, secret rebelliousness that had embittered him. Now he knew that nothing remained for him but to be satisfied with his sorry lot, and his ah was sincere. There was no resentment any more, because he had no right to anything. Never may this monster covet a woman.

The months passed.

Slowly, he lost the feeling of surprise that he had found peace and contentment here, and that he was no longer bitter. He wondered how he could ever have wanted to put an end to his life, and his heart filled with tenderness. It was a joy for him to watch the children playing and the young couples strolling by arm in arm, and he grew attached to an old man who came every afternoon to sit on a bench and read his paper. He made his old Lucie happy with a magnificent present on her birthday. The cottage was a haven for him, the silence soothing and friendly, and the glory of summer, with the blaze of flowers, a ceaseless delight. Within him formed the words he couldn't say: the goodness of it all.

A tiny bud blossomed on the long branch of a climbing rose. The branch bent with every breeze, and the rosebud swung right up to the window to nod a cheery greeting. Ohoo, the Little Lordie gurgled, *bonjour*. As it grew bigger it weighed the branch down, and now the rose bloomed the whole day through in front of the window-pane. The Little Lordie found himself holding silent, tender conversations with the rose. In his thoughts he spoke to it as if it were a little girl dressed up in her Sunday clothes: Oh, aren't you pretty today!

Then he started reading newspapers. He sent postcard after postcard for trial subscriptions. He had set a maximum of twelve subscriptions, and his days were taken up with calculating which papers he would drop for new ones.

One afternoon the twelve newspapers weren't enough. He went to the kitchen, patted old Lucie on the shoulder, and his language of gurgles was too limited to convey all that he wanted to say. He asked her in writing if she would, from now on, in the afternoons and in the evenings, when she had finished working, come and sit with him in the miniature smoking-room, a round annex built on to the dining-room. She was sixty-five, and her husband and her three daughters had died of consumption. She didn't like to be alone with her memories. She knew when to speak and when to stay silent. She could talk of the past with a southern garrulousness, and his ah, ee and oh were more than enough for her. Now and then she would doze off, and when she woke she would take up her darning and talk again. 'Je vous aime,' she said, 'je vous aime beaucoup.' She wished she could have had a son of her own, who would have been just like him. They were so good and so kind, monsieur, all her daughters, *des anges*. Her husband, too, monsieur mustn't ever think that she looked after him and the house just because of the money or because she was sorry for him. No, now she had something to live for. *Le bon Dieu* had sent him here. Ee, he said, oui.

Slowly he began to live again. The past faded, not as the horror of a nightmare vanishes, but as a vague memory blurs to a hazy nothingness. Once old Lucie said he should grow a beard and a moustache to cover the scars. He was strangely moved to hear her speak of his hideous mask of a face as if it were nothing unusual, just as a mother might have told her daughter to rub cream over a birthmark. She looked at him as she spoke, and it surprised him that he didn't hate her for that, and it surprised him that he neither blushed with shame nor broke out in a sweat. A thankfulness heavy as lead surged through him, his head leaned drowsily against the back of the chair, and he yearned, as in a dream: Look at me, see what a monster I am, and love me even more than you do.

She sat there in front of him. 'I wonder,' she said, 'if the hair will grow on the scars.' He could have told her the answer, he knew exactly how many little tufts he still needed his razor for, but he was too listless to make the sounds. Her face was close to his, a thin, wrinkled old women's face that could hardly have been pretty even when she was young, and she saw that the plan to cover that hideousness with hair would never work. Her finger went lightly over the patches that were red as raw flesh. *Non, ça n'ira pas.* He knew now how many reasons there were to long for a woman, for it is good to be near a woman. Her tough had transformed those gruesome scars, he was no longer a monster.

That evening he called her by her name. Uhi, he said, and blinked happily at her. He still had his two eyes. Puzzled, she regarded him over the pages of *Le Courrier du Midi*. Since she didn't understand his winking he tried to smile, and the gash that was his mouth split open. Through the months she had learnt to understand his language of sounds and signs, but never yet had her kind and gentle monsieur laughed or cried. She thought his affectionate, inviting smile was the grimace of tears, and at once she understood his sorrow. Only that afternoon she had spoken to him like a mother about his scars, she had looked at them and touched them to make him realize that his disfigurement didn't mean anything to her, and to give him the courage perhaps to go out for a walk in the daylight. But she could see she had gone too quickly. He must have stood in front of the mirror and all his misery had welled up again. She thought that, as he wept, he was opening that travesty of a mouth as if he were saying: Look what they did to me, you didn't know how repulsive I am, but look at me now, and shudder.

She was sick with remorse. She went over to him, her eyes were filled with tears, she pressed his head against her cheek. 'Mon fils,' she whispered. His arms gripped her, his hands twisted restlessly. She held him confortingly, and suddenly she realized that it was more than misery when he clutched at her withered breasts. She wept a mother's tears that flowed over an old woman's sad smile. He tore her clothes open, and what his frenzied hands uncovered was not a woman, but an old dry carcass, with the ribs sticking out gauntly, and flat, sunken breasts that three consumptives had suckled at and four consumptives had wept on. Now, a lonely outcast, whose soul was still not yet purged of impurity, pressed his mutilated mouth of rubber and red splotches against that shrivelled flesh. Then he began to sob, she smiled and called him by his name, happy at the forlorn bliss she could still bestow. She took his head gently in her hands and kissed him on the forehead. 'Et maintenant tu seras sage. C'est un péché ce que tu as fait, sais-tu, mais le bon Dieu comprend cela.'

She sat in front of him again. 'Va dormir maintenant.' He went and he was not ashamed. He walked with sure, steady steps.

She never spoke about that evening, but she never avoided the memory either. She talked now more intimately, and it was because of that evening. She told him once how her eldest daughter had broken off a love affair after her young man had tried to go too far with her. It was always a problem, she said, and she was sure that it was more curiosity than anything else. With girls as well as boys. She thought that most of the girls who got into trouble were led astray by their curiosity. *Mon Dieu*, once they know what it's all about, they say: Is that all it is? Then she talked about the burdens and sorrows of marriage, *la vie n'est que misère*.

It was a wondrous luxury and a relief that he could discuss these things with a woman. He didn't notice how tactfully she accustomed him to the loneliness to which he was doomed. He lived in a tranquillity he had never known. Every day the newspapers were repeating that the war would be over within two months. The Germans were exhausted and had suffered such heavy losses that it seemed doubtful whether the massive offensive the allied armies were preparing would be necessary. The final collapse could be expected any day. Then the Little Lordie thought of Ursule and the Koevoet, but without any longing.

And Ursule didn't think about him because he was dead. After that declaration of his love it was impossible that he could still be alive and not write another word. The two sons of Seppen the verger, though neither of them could write, had managed to send news that they were alive and well with the artillery. Sooner or later everyone heard something from the front. It was only the dead who never wrote. In that letter from Namur there was nothing about coming back. He must have had a premonition, right from the beginning, that he would be killed, and premonitions are never wrong. No, the ones who didn't write were dead, and the ones who weren't reported killed were missing, and missing meant more than dead, it meant blown to pieces, unrecognizable fragments. That was what had happened to her André. Her castle in the air slowly toppled. She would live out the rest of her life in this emptiness, she would be like Auntie Trees in Cobbezele, ugly and mean and heartless and sour.

Then, in July, 1918, the friendly Hauptmann, whose family belonged to the nobility, paid a visit. He had always been so sympathetic about the fräulein's betrothed, and he had even had inquiries made in Brussels. He had read André's letter and he had discussed all the possibilities that might explain why she had heard nothing more. He came back after a year at the front and a year and a half in hospital. He came to the Schrans to see Thuur Van den Heuvel, he kissed Octavie and Ursule as if they were his own sisters, and the younger of the two girls Thuur had taken into service saw it through the gauze curtains over a glass door. She was wheeling the pram up and down in the next room to get number four to sleep. She slipped out of the house and ran off to tell her mother. The mother went and told three neighbours, and they told others, and next day everyone knew.

He asked Ursule about André, and when he saw she had given up all hope, he didn't make any further inquiries. It was war, and war claimed its toll. She couldn't tell in what way exactly he had changed, the change was total and beyond all definition. He had surprised her and Octavie with his kiss. Octavie couldn't forgive him and didn't want to see him again. But she did. It had happened so spontaneously that he was perhaps surprised at himself, but, in any case, he would never have done that before. There was something disturbing in the way he had kissed her hand, but even so she didn't avoid him. The war would not last much longer. Then he would disappear, go away for ever, but here her life would start again, without hope.

At times she wanted to be kissed by him once again, but only the evening before he was leaving, and as a farewell, not to him but to the world. After that there would be no one in the village who would look at her or speak to her, and no one she would want to see or speak to, and she would live in loneliness and grow old.

He didn't wait until the evening before he was leaving, only until the days were a little shorter, the evenings darker. After a lingering kiss, he whispered that he longed for nothing more than to have a woman he loved and a house far away from everyone and never see another living soul. He had lost all his illusions.

She had no urge to make these declarations as he did. She understood only too well that this love of theirs could never come to anything serious. She realized, too, that it was unforgivable to take up with the enemy. She knew she was being watched and talked about. But she wanted a little tenderness before it was too late, and nothing could keep her from tasting this last chance. Once he said he had no illusions either about the love between them. Every day could be the last for him, and it was better to be honest with her. She had lost the man she loved, he had lost everything, and when they felt an affection for one another it was the affection of companions in sorrow who were trying to comfort each other. Did she see it that way too? *Ja.*

Her simplicity and gentleness fascinated him. At the front, in the hospital, and back home he had seen the disintegration and the threatening collapse of the ideals he had been brought up to revere. The experience had destroyed in him every hope and every belief. He had talked with intellectuals until his head spun, he had pondered a thousand times by himself until his thoughts were engulfed in the dark contemplation of suicide. This simple girl understood him because she was suffering too, she understood him without words, with a kiss.

He scrupulously avoided raising any false hopes. He loved her, *sehr, sehr viel*, but he wouldn't write to her after he left. He would certainly think of her often, but he would never make a cult of the memory. Did she feel that way too? *Ja.*

Their last tryst in the dark was one night a month before the evening of his departure. He wasn't sure now whether they weren't doing wrong. It was quite possible, after all, that he had killed the man she loved, and he would only have been doing his duty. But this secret love of theirs would be wrong because they were from different countries, and because they had both forgotten their sorrow in a kiss. After he had gone he would always say to himself whenever he thought of her: *Ursule war nur gut*, but would she think: *Der grosse Willy war schlecht zu mir?* She said: *Nein.*

It was then that the widow with eight children came by and said: 'Good evening, juffrouw Ursule.' In those times no one, not even a man, risked going by that lonely pathway after dark, but this woman knew from her daughter what went on there three evenings in the week, and in her heart there was bitterness enough for her to risk anything.

And what the two sons of Seppen the verger, and the twenty-one others of the eighty-four we saw march off—and maybe some more as well back from Harderwijk or Zeist or Soltau—what they had in their hearts when they got up out of the mud after four years and plodded homewards with their eyes fixed on the tower of the village church, they themselves didn't know. They hardly looked at their mothers, wives, and sweethearts. Where are the Germans' whores, they yelled, and the moneylenders, they're the ones we've got to settle with. And they did. There weren't many. But the widow with the eight children knew them all, and she led the way, to the Van den Heuvels first of all. The beginning is always the best.

They dragged Octavie and Ursule out into the street, while another group went off to look for that boot-licking burgomaster, and him they dragged off to a cellar in the town hall. They shaved Octavie's hair off and chased her home with kicks and abuse. They shaved Ursule's head, and then they started undressing her. When she stood in her chemise and they hesitated to go on with it, she grabbed at a soldier's revolver to shoot herself. The soldier caught her breasts and squeezed them. She fell in a faint, and what a pleasure it was for them to lift her up and carry her to the porch, then bang on the door and shout out that Madame Hauptmann was back. After that they calmed down a little. They shaved the heads of the other four they had to see to, but it didn't come to stripping them and chasing them through the streets.

Door, the miller, had hidden his daughter behind a stack of flour bags. Three of them knocked him down and he lay dazed and bleeding where he fell, on a heap of white flour, between his whirling machines. He could have fallen on the pulley belt and been crushed to death, but a bloody head was nothing; that could happen at any village fair.

For the Little Lordie nothing changed except that now he could order newspapers from Brussels, and after hours and hours of indecision he finished up going over the maximum of twelve. He brought the figure up to fifteen. That was the start of his restlessness. The news from Brussels and the villages he knew was more and more important for him, and, at first, he tried to put these thoughts out of his mind because he didn't want to leave Lucie, but it was Lucie who said why didn't he just go and have a look at the places he remembered. Just go and have a look, her words soothed his conscience. He could just go and have a look round, sell the Koevoet, and come back. If she went with him. She would go with him. He was standing at the window again, over there was the Schrans, there was the villa with the windows closed and shuttered, but here there was no Little Lordie any more. And once again he didn't have the courage for that five minutes' walk, but for other reasons this time, and now Lucie was here.

'I'll go and tell them,' Lucie said, 'and I'll warn them.' He would see how well she could take care of everything.

So she went to the Van den Heuvel sisters, and there was no putting her off. She didn't notice their shaven heads under their dark-blue woollen caps, and naturally they said nothing about it. They tried to find an excuse, but it isn't so easy to invent a reason for not visiting someone who has come back from the war after four years. When they heard that he was horribly disfigured and could hardly speak they were more dismayed and more ashamed than ever. They hadn't dared to show themselves outside the house again, but they went into the next room, while Lucie sat waiting, and assured each other that it was better to see him and tell their side of the story before someone else told him a lot of lies, and so they went with Lucie, as pale as corpses, and shaking so much that they could hardly walk.

In those days, you remember, it still wasn't safe for the war-time whores to let themselves be seen. If they couldn't go and live with relatives in one of the big towns, where they would pass un-noticed, they had to stay inside or they were pelted with stones. This time it began with the shouts of the schoolchildren, and in a moment or so the whole village was there with Seppen's two boys in the lead. They didn't stop at shouting: Hey, you dirty sluts! They threw lumps of earth and stones. The Little Lordie heard them coming. The three women rushed past him in the passage, and, in the same daze of folly that led him right into a bursting shell, he went out on the steps and stood in front of the crowd in a cloud of turf and lumps of half-burned coal. 'Oioi,' he called out, 'what is all this?' For a few seconds there was a silence. He saw women turning away with their hands over their eyes, the children gaped with fright, but Seppen's two had seen worse than that. Wawa, these two yelled, and the others wawaed in chorus after them. 'Oauowiao,' the Little Lordie said, stupefied, what are you shouting that for? They had all heard now how that gargoyle talked. It must be a rich foreigner, with some filthy disease on his face, who had bought up the château for a song now that the Little Lordie was dead, and he could pay those dirty bitches a lot of money to get into bed with him. He couldn't find anyone else, the swine, and neither would they. In case they thought we were going to let them off lightly there were Seppen's two up the steps in a bound beside him. You rotten foreign rat, by Jesus, you filthy Spaniard, if you don't understand that, you stinking scabby corpse! They didn't want to get their hands dirty, but...

He called out: 'I'm mijnheer d'Hertenfeldt,' but they didn't understand his ay ay i ehehe. The crowd roared eheh and then the two of them—and their father, Seppen, had been his handyman and still rode round on his horse—the two of them grabbed him by the throat. Hehehe, that's what they did with hehehes, you stink like a rotten fungus. And now they were going to go and wash their hands. Get inside, funny face.

When the Little Lordie staggered into the hall, red and purple from the throttling, Octavie and Ursule saw his face properly for the first time. They forgot Lucie's warnings, the lumps of turf, the stones, the jeering and the shaven heads. Octavie let out a shriek of horror, and Ursule gasped and fell in a faint.

Heavens above, we all thought that Seppen was going to commit a murder in his old age. No one saw how it started, in the old shed where they did the threshing, though there was hardly room to swing a flail, but when we heard Seppen shouting we all came running. First, two bangs on the wall, and before we were there, the eldest, Mus, the one who had grabbed the Little Lordie first, was off through the door and old Seppen after him with his flail above his head, enough to kill a bull. Mus streaked down the road to the Van Benedens' gate. That way you can get into the orchard, jump over the ditch, and then you're in the wheat-field, and Seppen was too old to jump over the ditch. Now, the Van Benedens' gate is never shut any day of the week for more than five minutes, but that day it must have been just those five minutes. Mus couldn't get it open, he tried to jump aside, but Seppen was right behind him, and Mus lay there on the ground.

We'll never forget Seppen's face as long as we live, and he was so mad with rage that we heard him grunt: 'If he's dead, he's dead.' We carried Mus inside. He certainly wasn't dead, but his mother was taking it badly. All through the war without a scratch and then coming home and being battered to death by his own father, she howled. And she never wanted to set eyes on his father again, never. Go and fetch the gendarmes. We sent three men off on bicycles to get the three doctors, we could do without the gendarmes. Then we went to look for Seppen, we were worried about him. Maybe you don't know Seppen. He isn't more than five-foot-six tall, but in Claerebout's time he was a match for anyone. Claerebout would call out in the middle of a sermon: 'Seppen, can't you see they're talking over there behind the third pillar?' They could be a full head taller than him, but if they dared to grin or shrug as if they thought he wouldn't try to lay a hand on them, then Seppen took hold of them and the next second they were in a heap outside. We found Seppen in his shed, back at the threshing.

One of us pushed the door open, and peeped inside. 'Shut the door again,' Seppen growled, 'or, by Jesus, there'll be another one flat on his back!'

When we saw the postman we found out what must have happened. The postman had a form from the Ministry for the two veterans. He brought it round and he said: 'Seppen, did you know? That scabby face in the château, that's the Little Lordie; he's come back again.' 'What?' Seppen said. 'Yes,' the postman said, 'they've got his address at the post office for the newspaper subscriptions. That always takes a few days, and now we've got all the news-papers to be delivered to him.'

Then it suddenly dawned on the honest Seppen that the bene-factor who had done so much for him had almost been strangled by his own son. After it was all over he could see that Mus didn't know who it was either, but the blow was struck, and both of them, father and son, could count themselves lucky.

Later, Lucie used to wonder to herself whether it hadn't started with that first day, maybe that's what the cause of it was. She had always been like that, first with her husband, and then with the daughters, the one after the other. She would wrap them up in blankets so carefully, but as soon as they started coughing she would remember the time they'd left the window open too long, it can get cold all of a sudden. Or when they were out walking and turned a corner, what a chilly wind there was.

But this was something else that she wasn't familiar with, a sickness that left her monsieur healthy, but changed him alto-gether.

They had agreed that he would just come and have a look round, but if she hinted at going back, he said *qu'on verrait*, and avoided her. That was the first thing she didn't understand about him. Here their ways parted. The helpless creature she had patiently taught to live again had learnt so well that she couldn't keep up with him any more. He had nothing to stay here for, she said. The château was ever so much bigger than the cottage back there, and it wasn't as comfortable, and it was much more expensive to keep up. And what a dreary countryside it was here! She could never get over her amazement that every foot of ground was ploughed and planted. They did nothing but work here. And didn't Monsieur remember that little rose at the window where he always sat in his chair? If they went back now there would be roses all round the window. She never asked him why the two sisters stayed on in the château as if they belonged, and she was quite ready to believe in their innocence, but, even so, their eagerness to be helpful disturbed the quiet existence she had shaped for him back in the little cottage. But worst of all were the people here, a dour lot who spoke a sort of crude German, and she would never ever forgive them for the way they had welcomed her monsieur.

One evening she sat crying softly. Octavie and Ursule had gone to bed early as they always did, because they felt they weren't wanted and would be intruding in a companionship they couldn't share. Outside the wind was howling. She felt cold, but she wanted to wait until he got up from his chair, and so, far away from the four graves of her family, she was sad and homesick. It was a real old woman's dream: she saw her own grave. Monsieur had put a little cross on it, but a farmer came riding by with his plough and when his horse stopped at the cross, and wouldn't move, he started to curse in German and to yell at the beast. He pulled the cross out of the ground, threw it away, and went on ploughing, and afterwards he would plant potatoes on her grave.

The Little Lordie saw she was crying, and, just as she had held his head in her hands that evening, he took her head in his hands, and stroked her hair. She wasn't thinking of herself, she said, she would stay with him as long as she lived, but she was unhappy because of him. It wasn't good for him here, so cold and bleak, and then the way they had treated him that first day, he deserved better than all this. He hadn't forgotten, had he, how happy he was back there, that was all it was... she didn't care about herself.

But he stayed, and the first thing he did was to make Seppen his gardener again. He went himself with Octavie and Ursule, and Octavie did the talking for him. He walked through the village with that hideous false face, and with the two Germans' whores by his side, to do a favour to the father of the man who had nearly strangled him. There are near-saints, and there are kind-hearted simpletons, but this was more than simpleminded goodness; it was something that wouldn't even happen in a book. Afterwards, Lucie was sure that she had noticed it then already, when he went to see Seppen, that she had said to herself then: There's something wrong with him.

How could anyone do such a thing? As they were walking back to the château, Octavie asked him if he thought it had made a good impression on Mus. She knew that Mus; his father was honest and hardworking, but he was just the opposite, that Mus, a good-for-nothing. The Little Lordie had to admit to himself that he hadn't paid any attention to Mus. This time Lucie didn't hide her disapproval: *Vous êtes trop bon, monsieur*, but she spoke a language he didn't understand any more. He didn't act with any awareness of the sublime goodness of what he did, nor did he seek in that goodness any pleasure of self-satisfaction. He had reached the ultimate limit of suffering where all resentment, all thought of self, was banished, a martyrdom of suffering that absolves and purifies, until there is nothing left but goodness.

Then there was that afternoon when Thuur Van den Heuvel came to fetch his sisters. All through the war years he had waited for the armistice when he would be acclaimed as the saviour of the village, and they had indeed led him round in a procession, but only to take him to jail, for the first night in a cellar under the parish hall. He had crushed three rats with his boots, and his heart had cankered with bitterness. But the court admitted his innocence, and when he came back home there was still all that talk about Ursule. He was livid when Elza told him that for weeks now she and Octavie had been living at the Koevoet. Another scandal, he said to himself. This as well, when he wanted his name cleared, and Ursule's, too. His sisters didn't dare to live in their own house any more, they said, and they couldn't stay with him and not help with the farm work, and they weren't going to do farm work any more. That was their attitude. His attitude was that staying at the château was a proof of their guilt. When that didn't have any effect, he lied that the whole village was talking about strange goings-on at the Koevoet. He glared at them across the room. It was an insult the Little Lordie surely couldn't overlook, surely out of self-respect he would have to ask Thuur to leave. That was what Octavie expected when he got up, but he only got up to go and bring a bottle of wine from the cellar. He filled the glasses and handed Thuur a cigar. As calm as could be. They looked at each other and at him, they drank, they forgot their quarrel and sat without saying a word.

In his mutilated, hideous face, the grey eyes that had always been so dull and shifty began to glow with a gentle, unobtrusive goodness. He would walk round the pens and the stalls but now it was to stroke the turkey and the sheep, or to feed them. Once he went to visit the Schrans and there was no one in the sitting-room but a snotty-nosed five-year-old with a big dog. The dog made the child bold. He pointed with all his fingers and called out: 'Ya, ya, you got a pig's snout. Sick him, Blackie!' But the dog did nothing, and the boy got a piece of chocolate.

Every afternoon and evening he played cards with Ursule. Octavie couldn't sit still for so long, and she preferred to help old Lucie. If the door-bell rang it was a caller who came to ask a favour, not always money, for there was little poverty in the village now, bur farmers wanting to buy land, or raise a loan, and others wanting to sell something. The Little Lordie never refused a request. Octavie would warn him that this one didn't deserve it. Another was a liar and didn't need it. This one didn't go to church, and that one had an illegitimate child somewhere. But the Little Lordie neither judged nor censured, he gave, and went back to his game of cards. He walked with a firm and steady step, his hands were calm, and he didn't sweat any more. Sometimes Ursule thought to herself: Maybe I could get used to it. Then she would glance at that blotched and mangled face, and she knew it was impossible. And their thoughts were on their cards, with a smile at each other now and then. Both had known the depths of anguish and now they could say all they needed to say in the gentle, passionless language of their eyes. They heard Octavie and Lucie conferring each evening over the next day's work, each jealously defending her plan with the argument that it would be easier for him. Lucie insisted that monsieur couldn't chew carrots, and Octavie repeated that she cooked them so soft that he could. If the Little Lordie had to make the decision, then Ursule spoke for him and let them both have their way. He would thank her with his eyes.

And so the great benefactor or our village lingered on for three years more in our midst after he had, as a true hero, given his life for our beloved fatherland.

It was Ursule who noticed it first, even before Lucie, when he paired a queen with a king. She pointed out the mistake, but two minutes later he did it again with an ace. When she mentioned it to the others it had gone so far that he couldn't follow the game any more, and then they discovered that they had, all three of them, noticed it already. Since he almost never spoke, his mind might have been weakening long before they realized anything. But the doctors they called in admitted that, even if they had been warned sooner, they couldn't have helped. He would die painlessly and peacefully. They called it atrophy of the brain, but it would have been nearer the truth to say that a ripened fruit was ready to fall.

In his jumbled mind the one truth he clung to, but never expressed, became clearer: the weak and the afflicted must help each other with kindness. He was more cheerful and brighter than ever, he walked through the house humming softly. He passed his last days writing *Sincères condoléances* on visiting cards and sending

233

these cards to all the addresses in the death notices in his fifteen newspapers. The three women let him send them off because it was a gesture that would be appreciated. They wondered if he knew what he was doing, but still, it was the sort of thing he would do. *Ça, c'est tout a fait lui*.

He died as the doctors had said he would, slowly and painlessly, on a Sunday evening, just as Louis Van Acolijens went by singing, probably drunk as usual. The three women saw him move in the bed as if he felt restless. Lucie and Ursule carefully arranged the cushions behind him. That must have eased him a little, for outside Louis was singing 'Mie Katoen, kom morgen noen, we zullen een pintje drinken', and the Little Lordie listened, beating time faintly with his head and his finger, five or six times, no more, he was too tired.

BIBLIOTHECA NEERLANDICA

A Library of Classics of Dutch and Flemish Literature